I0773080

Also by Fae

SPOOKY BOYS SERIES

Bite Me! (You Know I Like It)

Possess Me! (I Want You To)

Hunt Me! (I Crave the Chase)

There's a Monster in the Woods

PNR/OMEGAVERSE

The Devil Takes

CHRISTMAS DADDIES

Let Your Hearts be Light

You Can Count on Me

If Only in Our Dreams

ALIEN ROMANCE

I'm Not Your Pet!

CONTEMPORARY

Cloudy with a Chance of Bad Decisions

King of Hollywood

BOOK 3.5

Spooky BOYS

FAE QUIN

King of Hollywood

SPOOKY BOYS #3.5

Cover Art and Interior Artwork by Fae Loves Art

WWW.FAELOVESART.COM

Typography and Interior Formatting by We Got You Covered Book Design

WWW.WEGOTYOUCOVEREDBOOKDESIGN.COM

Editing by Angela O'Connell

ORIGINALLY PUBLISHED AS PART OF THE
TALES FROM THE TAROT COLLABORATION

Dedicated to my husband.
The other half of my monstrous duet.

Life: it goes on.
unable are the loved to die;
for love is immortality.
living is joy enough

Author's Note

HELLO EVERYONE! THANK YOU so much for picking up this copy of *King of Hollywood*! This was such an incredibly fun project to embark on. I don't think I've ever laughed harder when writing a book in my entire life. I hope you love reading Felix and Marshall's story as much as I loved writing it. While this book deals with some dark elements, it is overall a humorous read. You can find a full list of the content on my website. Stay safe, my loves. Happy reading!

Chapter One

IT WAS a nice night for murder. The worried pitter-patter of Felix Finley's feet was annoying, but not annoying enough to dampen my mood. Cicadas chirped. Not a single rock slipped into my loafers. It was pleasantly chill beneath the thick foliage of the forest. And the body I currently had slung over my shoulder was lighter than expected, despite being dead weight—literally. Ha.

If one of my coworkers had asked me if I was doing something fun over the weekend I never would've expected to tell them *yes*. And I *was*—having fun, I mean. Because I was spending my few off-hours helping my very troubled, very odd, very *pretty* neighbor dispose of the body of the man he'd "accidentally" killed.

I say "accidentally" (in quotations) not because I think behind his bumbling facade that he's actually an evil mastermind, but because as the only serial killer that lived in our cul-de-sac, I figured I was kind of an expert.

I'd always been a practical person. Logical to a fault. Stubborn, maybe, if you ask my sisters. I rarely opened up. Rarely got excited. Rarely had fun—because fun (according to most) tended to be a complicated, awkward thing that involved too many people.

Which is why this was quite monumental.

"Are you sure we won't get caught?" the small blond fretted. I ignored his worries, determined to waste as little energy as possible on him, as I had much more efficient uses for it at the moment. "Marshall?"

"Finley," I injected as much ire into my voice as possible. "It is quite difficult to carry on while you are yapping at me." It wasn't, not really, but he didn't need to know that. The scent of the garbage bags Felix had used to cover the body clogged my nose, but I managed to ignore it, my mood too chipper for even plastic to ruin.

We were going through the back of the property, as I didn't think it was a good idea for the general population of our small mountain town to recognize how often I visited the local crematory.

Once a year to be exact. On my sister's birthday.

"Yes, yes. Sorry. My apologies." Finally, silence. At least, there *was* silence—for a solid…ninety seconds? But who's counting? "It's just—" *Lord, give me patience.* "Well…I've never done this before."

"I can tell." It was difficult not to scoff. I wasn't sure I managed. Though Felix didn't seem to notice.

"You're unfazed," he added, hopping along beside me, having to work twice as hard to keep pace. I blamed his shrimpy legs, as they were a quarter of the length of mine. Oddly enough, he reminded me of the chihuahua we'd had growing up. It'd chased us around on its tiny little legs, constantly getting in our business, nosy bastard. Only, Felix was more muscular than a chihuahua, and somehow yappier too. "But of course you are! I mean, you're *you*, Marshall. You're never fazed. It's like your super power."

His voice quaked, and he was so distracted that he nearly ran head first into a low hanging branch. Shifting the body on my shoulder, I lifted the branch just in time. Felix strode right through where it had been, completely unaware that he'd almost gotten brained.

Amazing. Truly. I'd never met a more oblivious person.

Don't mistake me for a good Samaritan.

I didn't help him out of a misplaced sense of chivalry.

I simply didn't think Felix had any brain cells to lose. I was only protecting my peace, as I was the one that had to suffer through living across the street from him. It wasn't that I liked Felix or anything, or that—despite his penchant for leaving packages out on his doorstep *all day long*, his unkempt lawn, and his apparent allergy to sunlight—he was my favorite person in all of Beach Town.

I didn't pick favorites. (Why would I, when everyone sucked?)

I didn't like people. (What was there to like?)

I didn't help people. (A waste of time, if you ask anyone with sense.)

Except for…today. *Now*. This specific, very bloody situation. I still hadn't figured out how exactly *Felix Finley* of all people had managed to murder a man. But I figured once the body was taken care of, there'd be plenty of time to question him.

The prospect made me almost giddy.

Would he talk in circles? Would he lie? Would he fake innocence?

I couldn't wait.

And yet, somehow, Felix was still fucking talking.

"Like last year!" he chirped, as though I'd given him any sort of indication that I wanted him to continue his inane chatter. "When Barry hosted his annual Summer Bash in his backyard and told everyone to dress up in Hawaiian shirts." *Did he always talk this much? Or was he nervous? I* suppose dead bodies could do that to some people. "Only, he changed his mind last minute about the theme—when you were out of town. He left a note on the door, but you must not have seen it—because when you got back, you showed up to the party in a rather spectacular shade of pink."

"Yes, I remember."

"With flamingos."

As if I could forget the flamingos.

God, that party had been an absolute nightmare. It was every year. But last year had been particularly grievous. There were fairy lights, of all things. Fruit punch. And they'd been playing music from dated musicals on loud, tinny speakers. The warped voices made me feel like an ice pick was being driven through my ear canals.

I hated having to fit in here almost as much as I hated the chaos of amusement parks, or the general disgustingness of public bathrooms. There wasn't enough booze in the world for me to tolerate Barry, and that was a simple fact. I had never been more tempted in all my life to blow my cover entirely than I had been at that damn party.

It hadn't taken more than a glance to realize that I was off-theme. Like dominos falling into place. I'd found Barry, on instinct, two seconds from twisting his vapid little head right around just so I could enjoy the *pop* sound it made.

It had been a while since something had upset me enough to be tempted to throw caution to the wind. If there was one thing I hated more than shitty speakers it was being off-theme.

"Everyone else was dressed in their Sunday best, on account of the new theme being 'Night on the Town.'"

Not everyone.

I'd been tempted to head home to lick my wounds in private, but I hadn't wanted the sharks to taste blood in the water. Before I'd had a chance to contemplate options aside from murder and escape—I saw *him.*

There was one person who hadn't followed the herd. One person who'd stood by me in solidarity. One person who'd shown up to the party—despite rarely leaving his house in all the years we'd lived across the street from each other—dressed in orange with patterned board shorts, and an awful crocheted lei around his neck.

"Everyone except you," I hated that my tone softened, but it did.

"Except me," Felix echoed.

We were getting close to the break in the trees that would lead to the back of the crematory. Allen would be waiting for us at the door like he always was, and our conversation would finally, blissfully be over. I wouldn't have to think about *Guys and Dolls,* flamingos, and crochet hopefully ever again.

"So…" Felix started up again, and I lamented my life. "We're neighbors."

I prayed to God for strength. "Yes."

"We've been neighbors for a while."

"Ten years."

"We've never really talked." Felix sounded…nervous? At least, I thought he sounded nervous. I'd never been all that good at reading people.

"I don't talk to most people if I can help it."

"That's fair," he laughed, and to my surprise, didn't look offended. Not at all. Not even a little. Huh.

I thought the conversation would end there, but it did not.

"I like your vest," Felix said, sounding oddly demure. I glanced down at my favorite sweater vest—the tan argyle one that matched every one of my button-downs. I dressed in pastels, despite hating them. Because people were less likely to be afraid of a man dressed in baby blue. The double layer of fabric—both shirt and vest—also served to help cover up some of my muscle mass. Which I much preferred as I knew my rather in-your-face body size could come across as intimidating. It wasn't like I was trying to attract attention. The opposite really.

"Thank you."

"Do you work out?" Felix stared at my arms and I flushed a little, embarrassed that he'd noticed.

"Yes."

"That's…*handy.*" He stared at them some more, his eyes glazing over as he watched my biceps flex where I carried the corpse. He licked his lips. "Very handy."

"It can be, yes." I frowned down at him.

"You're quite big," Felix blurted, then immediately looked like he regretted the words. "Apologies, that was rude. I shouldn't comment on your size."

"You wouldn't be the first." I was six foot five. Most people couldn't help but point it out.

"Then I am even more sorry for bringing it up," Felix said, proving once again why he was far more palatable than most of our other neighbors. "I'm not…used to talking to people. It's been a while since I had a real conversation."

I highly doubted that, seeing as I was currently carrying the evidence of one of his nighttime visitors. Of which he had a decent amount. Like clockwork, every few weeks if he wasn't assaulting my eyes with an ugly package on his front porch, he'd disturb my peace with the arrival of a visitor. It was like he couldn't help himself. A sex maniac.

Not that I was judging—because I wasn't.

Okay. Maybe I was. A bit.

But it was only because I didn't understand it. I hated being touched by people. Hated *talking* to them. Hated strangers. Hated sticky, sweaty, messy things. The idea of willingly inviting someone I didn't know into my bed was abhorrent. What if their shampoo stank? They'd ruin my carefully cultivated ecosystem.

Oh god.

No thank you.

I assumed Felix's barrage of questions was due to his nerves, so I didn't fault him for them. Even though they were annoying. And so was he.

"You have very nice biceps," Felix complimented me, obviously trying to move on but unable to help himself. He then promptly almost ran into another tree branch. Without thinking, I lifted that one too. This time, against all odds, he *noticed* what I'd done. Felix flashed me a grateful, embarrassed smile. "Thank you. Almost walked right into that one."

I grunted in response.

Felix had peculiar teeth. They were one of his more recognizable traits. Dark eyebrows. Dark expressive eyes—though right now they looked oddly…red. Pale hair that was obviously dyed. Pointy teeth. They were slightly crooked, and it was…charming. *Maybe.* At least, I'd think so if I was a lesser man. A man that was even remotely interested in other people's teeth, or crooked grins, or crinkly little scrunched-up freckle-covered noses.

But I wasn't.

I wasn't.

My heart did a weird thing in my chest that immediately filled me with anxiety as we finally broke through the tree line and began walking across the manicured lawn. Luckily, the crematory was located at the edge of town. There was very little traffic even during daylight. At night, it was a ghost town. The woods blocked us from view of the single winding road as we crept across the night-dark grass, fireflies flitting around our feet.

"Are you sure we won't get caught?" Felix asked again, that sweet pointy smile anxious. I readjusted the body on my shoulder so I would have something to do other than reach out and tuck the stray lock of unkempt blond hair away from his face.

He had his usual ridiculous bucket hat on. Wide-brimmed and black. There was no sun to block, so I didn't understand his need for it. If he was trying to be inconspicuous, he was failing.

"Yes, *Finley*, we're fine. It's fine." Sucking in a fortifying breath, I exuded as much confidence as I could muster. Because we were fine. Of course we were. I would take care of everything.

Comfort was not something I was very adept at offering, but I tried now, because he very obviously needed it. "Now be quiet, please?" Felix nodded. "I'd leave you out here but I don't trust you not to confess to the first person you see."

It was after midnight, no one was out, but I wasn't quite ready to admit I didn't want him apart from me just yet.

"I don't do well alone," Felix was quaking a little. Minute shivers trembled through his petite but muscular frame. For such a small man, he sure had broad shoulders. This wasn't the first time I'd noticed, but it was the first time I allowed myself to *acknowledge* that I was noticing.

Swallowing the lump in my throat, my voice still far softer than I was comfortable with, I agreed, "Good thing I'm not leaving you alone then."

Felix's smile returned. His eyes were bright as we reached the back door and Allen pushed it open for us. He was a grizzled man, in his sixties probably. In the ten years I'd known him, he hadn't seemed to age a day. His salt-and-pepper-colored beard twinkled from the light that spilled onto the lawn.

"He joinin' *The Club*?" Allen asked, gaze flickering over tiny Felix and his ridiculously big hat. At some point, when I'd been distracted by Allen opening the door, Felix had popped on a pair of *Gucci* sunglasses.

He was not very covert.

I wasn't certain we wanted him in *The Club*, after all. We didn't really have a choice though.

"I suppose," I gritted my teeth.

"Well, alright then." Allen eyed the body, then me, then Felix, his eyebrows shooting up. If I'd been less distracted by the body on my shoulder, I probably would've noticed the look Allen and Felix exchanged. But I did not. And as we stepped inside the sanctuary of my favorite building in town, I didn't allow myself to think of Felix Finley's lovely little smile.

Not once.

Not at all.

Not even a little.

Chapter Two

UNFORTUNATELY, BECAUSE—fuck my life—by the time we finished dealing with the body it was too late at night to properly interrogate Felix. So, instead of gathering all the juicy murder details, I drove him home with explicit instructions to shower and clean under his nails.

He was wearing one of the backup shirts I kept in my trunk, as we'd taken the opportunity at the crematory to burn our clothing. I'd been nothing but level-headed. I'd known what to do every step of the way. Shown no remorse. And yet, Felix still looked at me like I was an angel and not a man who had killed enough people he knew how to properly clean up afterward.

"You're amazing, you know that?" Felix said, his stupid sunglasses pocketed once again. Without thinking, I reached out and yanked his damn hat off his head. His floppy blond waves fell free as he stared at me, confused.

"I hate this hat." I shook it at him, trying to emphasize my ire. "We should have burned it."

Felix laughed, then sobered. "But I wasn't wearing that when I—"

"I. Don't. Care." I wagged the hat at him again. "You asked me for help. I'm helping you. The hat has got to go."

"Is it…contaminated?"

"Sure."

Felix nodded, staring at the hat with an adorable frown like it had personally betrayed him. "I suppose I could buy a new one?"

If he bought a new one I'd burn that one too. I didn't tell him that. As that was on a need to know basis. He certainly looked better without his face half obscured in shadow. Even drowning in my clothes, I much preferred him this way.

The moonlight that streamed through the window cast his pale skin in an ethereal glow. All his silly, pretty features clearly on display. The curve of his square jaw. The flicker of muscle when he clenched it. The swoop of his nose—regal almost—and the way his dark lashes were long enough that when they blinked they nearly kissed the beauty mark below his eye.

Felix Finley had always looked oddly…familiar.

Especially now, with his hat and sunglasses gone. From the moment I'd met him, I'd had this odd feeling that I'd seen him before. Perhaps in passing on a street, or in a dream I could no longer remember. That feeling was only amplified now that he sat beside me and I could see him clearly.

I locked those thoughts away as I cleared my throat, waiting pointedly for him to get the hint and get the fuck out of my car.

"Oh, sorry." Felix shoved the door open, sliding out with surprising grace that he immediately ruined the effect of, because his dopey smile appeared again as he ducked down to say goodbye. He looked like an overeager puppy dog, far too excited at the prospect of spending more time together. "You'll come over—"

"Later, yes. Try not to touch anything or…*god—spread* anything. Please."

"No spreading the crime sce—"

"Uh—" I cut him off, glancing around to make sure the street was still dead. Realistically it was four in the morning. No one was awake, aside from us. Not in our sleepy mountain town. "Watch your mouth, Finley."

"Felix." Felix's cheeks were splotchy red as he bit his lip.

"Whatever."

Finley-Felix-Whatever grinned at me, his eyes crinkling at the corners.

He was an odd man. He spoke in a dated sort of way, and despite being an idiot—came across as far older than he looked.

Sometimes, it even seemed as though he was from a different time period entirely, all "gosh's" and "neat"s, and vintage clothing. Often his accent was almost transatlantic, which I could only attribute to perhaps an upbringing reared entirely in front of black and white television.

I could relate, as my mother had been a movie buff before she died.

"I can have your shirt dry cleaned," Felix offered in that same lilting tone he always used, while simultaneously waving one of the aforementioned shirt's drooping sleeves at me.

I hated how cute he looked, swathed in Armani.

"Mmm." It was neither agreement or disagreement. The only dry cleaner I trusted was my own—as he was a member of *The Club*—but I wasn't about to shoot Felix while he was already down. "Goodnight, Finley."

Felix made an annoyed sound in response to the use of his last name, but his smile didn't waver. "Goodnight, Marshall."

Despite telling him to be quiet, I couldn't help but add in my severest tone possible, "Try not to kill anyone else, please?"

"Aye aye, Captain."

And with that, he was off, practically skipping up the steps to his front door.

I pulled away, parking inside my own garage across the street, though I didn't head inside.

Instead, I watched the lights in Felix's downstairs windows flick off one by one. Watched as the ones upstairs turned on, and the silhouette of his body peeped through the glass as he climbed upward.

Despite the hiccups, the hat, and the fact I hadn't sated my curiosity, today had been a good day.

The chirp of crickets was peaceful. It reminded me of my youth. Of nights spent on the farm with my window open, listening to the breeze.

I wasn't ready to go inside, not yet.

Despite the fact that the narrow house across the street was an eyesore at best. It was tall, comprised of three stories with dark wood paneling and drooping vines that dripped like ink down its walls. At night the house almost seemed to *loom*. It tipped to the side in an illusion that made it look like something out of a storybook for goth children. Very Poe, Felix's house was. Tim Burton-esque.

In the daylight, the chipped indigo paint was almost cheerful, but at night it gave the home a quite severe presence. It looked aged and worn. Ill maintained. Like the owner who'd had it before Felix hadn't known how to take care of a home at all.

The yard—which was more of a jungle than a yard at this point—only further solidified that assumption.

I wondered if he'd inherited the home.

It was odd that a man like Felix lived in a home like that. He was soft sweaters, rainbow yarn, and floppy hats. He should be in a home covered in flowers, with honeysuckle and brick. This house was more suited for Dracula than a man who wore his heart on his sleeve etched in unpracticed, loopy embroidery.

I wasn't naive. I knew Felix Finley had his secrets. We all did. Me especially. This town was full of them. *The Club* was a prime example of that. A town like Beach Town—small, quiet, off the beaten path with no beach in sight—should not have housed such an eclectic mix of murderers, but it did.

It was one of the reasons I loved it.

Like all of my colleagues, I was intelligent enough to hunt in the city an hour or so north.

Don't shit where you eat, and all that.

Which was why it was *uncomfortable* to think that Felix had so clearly not gotten the memo. He'd killed inside his home, in a town small enough that missing citizens would go noticed. I could only hope the man he'd been with had been a one night stand like the others—and that he'd traveled here, as I had no idea how else Felix planned on getting away with it.

I was tempted to warn him—to give him some…friendly advice. But I still wasn't certain if this was a one-off, or if he—like me—had a taste for things of a more bloody nature.

I wasn't about to blow my cover. Not to a man that wore pastel unironically.

So yes, I wasn't naive. Felix Finley could keep his secrets for now, just as I would keep mine.

I would wait, I would observe, and I would try to forget that sunny, pointy little smile—at least until later, after work, when I'd help him clean up the mess he'd made.

That smile certainly wouldn't follow me to bed.

No.

That would be inappropriate.

Later that day, at six thirty p.m. exactly, I arrived at Felix's door. I'd managed a few hours of sleep, but otherwise had been too excited to rest. Felix didn't answer when I knocked the first time, or the second, or the third. Irritated, I rang the doorbell, only for the front door to creak open, a beam of light flooding the dark hallway. I'd had to traverse his mess of a yard to get to the steps, and I was in no mood to be trifled with—even though the prospect of cleaning up after a murder was quite exciting.

"Finley?" I frowned, glancing left and right before finally spotting him, half concealed by the door itself. He was wearing pajamas. As though he'd still been sleeping. I stared at him as the soft melodic curl of his voice met my ears.

"Sorry," he croaked. "Just woke up."

I supposed it had been a late night. I'd always operated fine with barely any sleep, so I couldn't actually understand. But still.

Felix didn't move into the light. In fact, he didn't move at all. He stayed half hidden, his sleep-heavy lashes blinking as he stared at me. "You can come in," he offered, clearly waiting for something.

I supposed it wasn't that odd that he was hiding behind the door— even though it was. If he hadn't been Felix Finley—social recluse—but a normal person, he would've greeted me and ushered me in rather than skulking about in the shadows. But he *wasn't* a normal person. So therefore, lurking was to be expected.

I shrugged off my unease, entered the house, and moved out of the way so he could shut us inside. Immediately the scent of dust hit my nose and I nearly sneezed.

"Would you mind closing that for me, please?" Felix cocked his head toward the shade that covered the stained glass that lined the side of his door. "I forgot when I got home last night."

How very polite.

I squinted at him, but did as I was told, pulling the shade into place. For a moment we were fully enveloped in darkness. When Felix reached for the light switch and flipped it on, the long cluttered hallway was illuminated.

Ah. So *that's* where the dust was coming from.

Everything.

I itched to march across the street, grab my bucket of cleaning supplies, and return to fix the issue. Though I knew that I may end up doing just that—depending on the state of the murder scene. So I bit back the urge for now.

The carpet was worn and old. The pattern dated and out of fashion, as was everything else. Portraits lined the hallway, depicting scenery from all over the world—some of which reminded me of movies I'd watched with my mother as a child.

Hundreds of letters were framed and mounted in glass. They took up the entire back wall beside the long, winding staircase that led upward, ending in shadow. There was an antique air to everything, though luckily—for both me and my nose—the scent that usually accompanied old houses and old people was missing—apart from the dust.

I'd always had to pinch my nose when visiting my grandmother's home. Only when she wasn't looking, of course. My mother had gotten quite offended the first time she'd caught me doing it—and I hadn't repeated that mistake ever again.

I *hated* disappointing her.

Even though Grandma smelled like mothballs, Mentos, and dried-up flowers. And it almost physically pained me not to say something about it. I still managed to keep my mouth shut.

It only took me a moment to take everything in, before my focus moved back to Felix. Back to his nearly red eyes, and the dark circles beneath them. Back to his broad shoulders, and the way the silk of his navy pajamas hugged the curve of muscle.

He had a movie star's body.

One that was far too pretty to belong to a man who hid himself away.

He should be flaunting it, not…whatever it was he was doing.

The only reason I didn't show off my own physique was because I maintained my body not for aesthetics—though that helped—but because muscle was kind of a requirement when one's hobby produced corpses.

"Thank you for your help," Felix said, voice shaky and soft, slow—like he was still half-asleep. He sounded almost drunk. My hackles rose.

"You haven't been drinking have you?" I asked, disapprovingly.

"No, why?" Felix frowned up at me, an adorable little wrinkle between his dark brows.

"You're acting odd."

"Oh," Felix laughed, his shoulders relaxing as the tension bled away. "It always takes me a while to get my brain to fully wake."

"I see."

That made him vulnerable.

His guard was down. He was breathing evenly. His eyes were warm, if not a little nervous. There was tension in his frame but it was a normal amount of tension. Equivalent to what I would feel if *I* had let a stranger into my home for the first time.

Could he not sense that I was a predator?

Maybe not.

Most prey did not greet their hunters at the door.

Not that I was hunting Felix at the moment—believe me, I *wasn't*. If I was, he would not be looking at me like *that*. Whatever the hell *that* face meant. If he was *Bambi* then I was the hunter with a gun. He should not be staring at me like he wanted me to run him over—with his guard down entirely.

Felix clearly had no self-preservation skills. He was very lucky I'd decided to take him under my metaphorical wing—and that I protected men like him, rather than eating them.

Though perhaps he'd like that?

He certainly *looked* like he wanted to be eaten.

Maybe he was lying, and he really was drunk. I had no other explanation for the blatant hunger in his eyes, or the way his gaze kept dropping to my throat. His Adam's apple bobbed, his pink tongue flickering out to wet his lower, very chapped lip.

I'd always disliked alcohol. It had a tendency to alter a person's behavior to the point they were often barely recognizable. It could turn even the kindest man into a monster. (I should know, I was one.)

It could cause mistakes that never should have been made—like that time my mother had started covertly drinking the wine she'd bought for the Christmas roast and nearly burnt our house down.

Regrets were not something I nurtured, unlike some of my sisters, and half the people I'd gone to college with—which was why I not only didn't participate in alcohol consumption, but abhorred it entirely.

I hated it almost as much as I hated bullies.

And that was saying something.

"How are you today?" Felix asked politely, his eyes a luminous red in the light.

Did he wear colored contacts? Why?

He had such impeccable manners. My mother would've been proud.

"Fine."

Quick, say something clever.

"Your house is a mess." Shit.

Felix laughed, his eyes crinkling. "It is," he shrugged, then glanced around. "I'm…working on it." His lips tipped upward and I—once again—tried not to find his smile pretty.

He was a lot more interesting than I'd thought he'd be.

"I have bleach," I offered, and Felix snorted.

"Duly noted."

This was odd. Uncomfortable. Standing here in his hallway. *Talking*. I'd never been inside his house, despite being his neighbor for nearly ten years. We didn't speak often, or really at all. Only in passing, when he was sitting on his porch in the dark with a reading lamp on his head and I was returning from a late shift working overtime.

Oh, and that one memorable time he'd been out walking his cats.

On leashes.

In the middle of the night.

Felix had excitedly waved at me, despite the fact it was nearly two in the morning, and the only reason I was out late was because there'd been a damn Christmas party at work and I'd felt obligated to go. My boss, Harold, was a decent enough man. I didn't hate him. And he'd asked me to stay after everyone else had left, so I had. Even though he was dressed like Santa and smelled like rum. He'd just gone through a messy divorce and I supposed he'd been lonely.

I hadn't waved back at Felix.

Now I wished I had.

Seeing him out at night like that hadn't struck me as odd then, mostly because I very rarely spared thoughts for Felix Finley—but now…

Now I wondered why he'd been out on the road that late.

It was Christmas Eve.

Why was he…alone?

Now that I thought about it…aside from his paramours, I hadn't ever seen anyone visit Felix. On occasion, Barry would go over there to bother him, sure. But he did that to everyone, me included. I couldn't recall ever seeing the same guest return. Nor had I ever seen family or friends arrive to visit him. Not even on Christmas Day, when I left to visit my sisters.

How long had he sat quiet in this mausoleum of a home? Surrounded by things and not people, alone in the dark.

Even at Barry's party—the party that we do not speak of—Felix and I had barely shared a sentence or two.

Felix's awkward, "Hi, Marshall, nice shirt" had seemed sufficient.

Besides, the lack of conversation hadn't actually mattered, if I was being honest. Because Felix had shown his true colors that day, and though they'd been painfully *orange*, ever since he'd stood beside me when no one else had—I…well, perhaps I'd decided that even though I didn't *like* him—because I didn't like *anyone*—that Felix was the kind of man who needed looking after.

He was confident in a way most people never were. Like now. The way he was looking at me, the way he'd invited me into his home without care. That was something I never would've done. My home was my safe space. Everything was exactly where it should be. It didn't smell like other people, and they didn't track their dirt, their pet's fur, or their problems inside it.

Felix moved like he knew exactly what his body looked like when he did so—all effortless grace, like a dancer. He spoke fluidly, the cadence of his voice like spun gold.

Felix was confident.

But he was *brittle* too.

I may not have been good with people, but I'd always made a habit of observing. Especially those that were vulnerable, as that was an integral part of my yearly murder ritual. Felix looked exactly like the kind of man I'd try to defend.

Somehow…he'd managed to wheedle his way to the side of my heart that was reserved for people I would not kill, even under duress. There weren't many people there, so the fact that someone who was practically a stranger had managed to climb over what I'd thought was an impenetrable wall, was…alarming, to say the least.

And that was before I'd caught him with a dead body of his own.

Felix somehow managed to get more and more interesting with every day that passed.

Maybe *that* was why I'd bolted across the street to help when I'd seen him attempting to get the corpse inside his garage. He'd looked *frightened*, and *panicked*. Even from as far away as my kitchen window I'd been able to see that he was shaking as he lugged the corpse through his jungle of a yard. When he'd paused, glancing both ways down the street to make sure no one was watching, my fate had been sealed.

Because he was an amateur.

An amateur who *needed* me. Because he'd been kind to me when I needed an ally. Because my mother had raised me to be the kind of man who recognized a good person when I saw them. The kind of man who helped those that needed it, even if I'd never been good with people.

Felix had been lucky I was the only neighbor close enough to see his amateur attempt at disposing of the body. We lived in a cul-de-sac, but thankfully, at the end of it. Separated from our other neighbors by a tiny little park meant for toddlers and dogs—and other creatures without fully developed frontal lobes.

He was *lucky* he hadn't been caught, despite the distance between our homes and theirs. We certainly weren't alone, after all. And our neighbors may be what society deemed "nice" (questionable—I'm looking at you, Barry the bitch). But even nice neighbors would certainly notice a small, floppy-hatted young man yeeting dead bodies across their lawns.

"Are you okay?" Felix asked, because I'd been silent too long, probably.

I hated that. Getting stuck in my own head. It didn't happen often anymore. Apparently Felix brought out my weaknesses as much as he benefited from my strengths—literally.

"Yes," I replied curtly, focusing on the present. Focusing on the tilt of his jaw, the light in his eyes, and the fact that he looked surprisingly well-rested for a man that had just graduated with a degree in manslaughter. "Where am I needed?"

"Oh, right." Felix blinked, still groggy. "Um." He bit his lip. I tried not to stare, and failed. His lips were chapped. They looked painful. *I can fix that.* Without thinking, I pulled a chapstick out of my front pocket. Popping the cap off, I slid into Felix's space without a second thought. When I grabbed his face, my palm nearly enveloped it entirely.

He's so small.

It wasn't the first time I'd had that thought.

It certainly wouldn't be the last.

As he was…quite small.

Almost offensively so.

Felix's size was not new, but the little thrill that curled in my belly when I looked at him was.

"Hold still," I commanded.

His skin was buttery soft beneath the pads of my fingers. The prickle of stubble rubbed the base of my palm as I forced his head back to a more helpful angle. His eyes were wide, his lashes fluttering. I could count them, I was so close. Sliding my other thumb across the tip of the cherry chapstick, I then brought it to his lips, gently swiping across them to spread it evenly.

All the while, Felix stared at me.

He's always staring at me.

So very quiet. Far more quiet than I'd ever seen him. His usual useless chatter was notably missing. He was so still, I wasn't certain he was even breathing at all.

The softness of his cool, petal-pink lower lip kissed my fingertip as I pulled that hand away. Heat curled in my belly, uncomfortable and unfamiliar as I tried to forget the peek I'd gotten of those pearly, sharp little teeth. Sucking in a fortifying breath, I recapped the chapstick, and ignored the fact that my skin was *tingling* where I still gripped his fragile face.

It would be so easy to crush him. To twist his neck. To be done with him entirely.

I don't want that.

"*Gosh,*" Felix said, his voice low and rough, breath brushing my palm.

Gosh, indeed.

His pupils had expanded. His cheeks were flushed. I could feel his gaze heavy as a caress. I could feel the way he was looking at me, like he wasn't quite sure what to make of me. Like he didn't understand, but he *wanted* to.

Felix's eyes said, *please.*

They said, *I'm scared.*

They said, *touch me.*

I cleared my throat, released his face, and took a half-step back. If I'd been slightly less affected, maybe I would've realized Felix still hadn't breathed. Not once. But…I was—*affected,* I mean. Unfairly so. Irritated with myself, I ignored him entirely, and focused on the hallway behind us.

"Where do you need me?" I kept my tone curt, so as not to invite questions.

"In the bedroom," his voice was low and scratchy.

In the—

"*Excuse me?*" I stared at the tiny little gremlin man, and his completely inappropriate suggestion. Felix stared back—equally…confused?

Huh.

Oh.

Had he not meant?—Oh.

I watched in real time as what he'd said finally dawned on him. Immediately, he stumbled back a step, his arms waving frantically.

"No, no. I didn't mean like *that*. I mean—not that I wouldn't, because… look at you. I just meant—well." He sucked in a panicked breath. "That the—I mean. I…the guy…the one—"

"Breathe, Finley."

Felix sucked in a breath gratefully, like he actually had forgotten until I'd reminded him. "I just…I mean, I *killed* him—by accident—in the bedroom." Felix blinked, voice quaking. "Don't look at me like that. It wasn't what you think—I mean—it's hard to explain." Felix said the word "*killed*", like he expected to get his mouth washed out with soap afterward. I couldn't help but feel charmed—maybe a little.

Especially because he looked so miserable.

I kind of wanted to push—to see how easy it would be to break him— but that would be rude.

"Show me to your room. You can explain as we walk."

How had someone so small and *soft* killed someone?

It didn't make sense.

I supposed I was about to find out.

Chapter Three

FELIX FINLEY was a silk-patterned-pajama-wearing enigma, that was for sure.

He made me feel *giddy* in a way very few things in my life ever had. Maybe it was the fact he was a murderer—right across the street from me!—or maybe it was his smile. Either way, my good mood had followed me all day.

Even now, as I watched him like a hawk, I couldn't turn off the buzz of excitement that vibrated beneath my skin.

Felix relaxed fractionally.

It was a small change, but I was adept at reading body language so I noticed anyway. It was a skill that was necessary for a man as socially challenged as I was. I had many strengths, but *this* was not one that came naturally. I had been forced to learn through trial and error and it had taken me many years to recognize the reactions that I did not instinctively understand.

I'd had a lot of mishaps in my youth.

Mishaps I was reluctant to repeat.

Obviously grateful for the reprieve I'd offered, Felix led the way down the hallway toward the staircase that sat at the end. When he stepped beneath the overhead light, I could make out his pajamas a little more clearly, amused to find that the silk was covered in a myriad of different constellations.

Does he like stars?

It seemed a very specific choice to make. I'd never worn patterned pajamas. At least—not without being forced.

I shuddered when I remembered the horrific matching plaid monstrosities that our parents put us in for Christmas pictures throughout my childhood. That was one thing I was glad had ended when my mother died. And people thought *I* was sadistic. I, at least, had never forced children to wear matching pajamas. When I'd told Winnie that, she'd cried—and I'd never brought it up again.

Felix led me up the stairs, hopping one graceful step at a time—no longer bumbling when he wasn't self-conscious of what he was doing. "Do we have to talk about how I killed him?" he fretted, voice hushed. "Can you just…believe me when I say it was an accident?"

I grunted noncommittally as I followed after him, trying not to judge him for the dust that lined the ancient wood.

I'd ask him whatever I damn well wanted.

As if he could read my mind, Felix pleaded, "Marshall, please?"

He whirled around at the top of the first landing, effectively cutting me off from the rest of the cluttered house. This floor was somehow worse than the one below it. *Was that a gramophone?*

Felix's hands were on his hips, frustration evident in his eyes as he leveled me with a pleading look. "Please, just…drop it?"

"You want me to drop the fact that you killed someone?" I asked in disbelief.

"Yes."

"Even though I spent all night helping you dispose of the body?"

"Yes."

"And I am here, to help you make sure there is no evidence left behind?"

"Yes."

It was a ridiculous request. And one I would've never in a million years expected. Which was why…*huh.*

Which was why I was going to respect it.

Clutter and cobwebs be damned.

"Fine." Life was monotonous. There were very few things that brought me joy. And though I loved Beach Town and the members of *The Club*, I had no true friends here. I kept my coworkers at arm's length. I fraternized with the neighbors, if only to keep up appearances. The only proper social time I had was when my elder sister Winnifred (Winnie) came to visit once a month.

It wasn't like my social schedule was all that packed.

So really…was it such a bad thing to let this continue? If I didn't get answers now, the curiosity would eat at me. Which meant I may possibly get weeks, maybe even months more of entertainment out of this whole situation. I could visit Felix. Poke at him. Prod him. Enjoy the way he dodged my questions until the day he inevitably didn't and I lost interest.

I'd find out eventually, so what was the harm in making him think he'd won?

"Really?" Felix perked up, his concerned expression melting away as he beamed down at me. Ah. There was the idiot that had waved at me while walking his cats at night.

"Really," I confirmed, amused.

"Wow! Okay. *Gosh*, I did not expect that to be so easy. Thank you, Marshall."

"You're welcome." I cleared my throat, arching a brow pointedly toward the rest of the stairs that he was still blocking.

"Right, *right*. Bedroom. Murder. Clean up." Felix offered me a jaunty salute, before turning himself right back around and marching up the steps. This time he moved quickly, and I realized belatedly, that he'd been practically dragging his feet before.

Like he'd been nervous and now he was *excited*.

"It's a lovely house, isn't it?" Felix asked when we neared the third floor.

Lovely was not the word I'd use. "It's large," I said, trying to be nice.

"It is!" Felix laughed and the sound was a little brittle. "Maybe too large for one person."

"Maybe."

"I got a good deal on it when I moved in," he added, then seemed to regret his words immediately, because they offered the opportunity for me to question him.

"When was that?" I asked. He looked like he hadn't aged a day since I'd moved in across the street from him, so I knew he had to be older than he looked.

"Ah, you know. A while ago." Felix waved me off vaguely, his shoulders hunched up tight again.

"Why Beach Town?" I asked, curious as to why he was acting so guilty.

"It's quiet?" He sounded like he was asking me, not telling me. Which was confusing.

I knew why *I'd* moved here. There'd been an odd little shopkeep who had suggested it to me when I'd been passing through. I didn't understand why anyone else would. Especially a man like Felix.

"It is," I agreed, figuring I'd leave it at that, as we'd finally reached the top floor. I was surprised to find that his bedroom was on the third floor. The reasoning behind that was quickly revealed as Felix pushed the antique door open.

The first thing I noticed was the surprising lack of clutter.

The *next* thing I noticed was the frankly *massive* telescope that took up a quarter of the room. How the hell could he see anything through the— *oh*. The ceiling was fully made of glass—aside from the blackout blinds that currently covered it—*Well, that answered that.*

Beside the star-hunting monstrosity there was a desk covered in haphazard papers, as well as a utility cart full of a myriad of different colors of yarn. Across the room lay a bed, a trail of crocheted wisteria drooping from the ceiling above it. The bed was far larger than a man of Felix's size needed, and decked out in a plethora of pillows and lovely navy blue comforters.

He clearly spent a lot of time up here, which made sense.

But it still surprised me.

So far, this was the only part of the house that wasn't crowded with objects and covered in dust. The telescope especially looked well-loved.

There was personality dripping from every inch of the room. Along with the lavender-colored wisteria, looping vines made entirely of yarn decorated the cracks and crevices, draping over the four poster bed like it'd come straight from a swamp. *How many hours had that taken him?* I had a feeling I didn't want to know.

Most interesting of all, however, was the cat tree that lined a back wall, and the regal beast that sat atop it, her green eyes disapproving.

"You have cats."

"I do," Felix declared proudly, hands on his hips. "That one's Dolly. She thinks she's the boss of the house. She's also the fattest, as she steals Tiffany's food." Felix cackled, very obviously delighted by her. He was *clearly* unhinged. "Watch out though. You're not a pipsqueak like I am— if you walk by her tree too close she'll probably try to swipe at that pretty silver hair of yours."

He thinks my hair is pretty.

"It's not silver," I scoffed, arching a brow. I only had a smattering of gray in the front, so his statement was entirely inaccurate. Not that I cared all that much about what color my hair was, or how others perceived it.

"Blond then," he smiled. "*With* silver."

I couldn't argue with that so I shoved the thought aside, instead focusing on the feline so that I could avoid it. Distracted now, I side-stepped toward the giant telescope that took up the other side of the room. "You like stars." It was obvious. No man who didn't like the stars had a telescope like this.

I didn't get all that close before Felix reacted. His shoulder brushed against mine as he crossed the room, before stopping at the base of the large telescope. He laid a hand on it, the copper shining between his fingertips. The lovely veins on the top of his hand flickered as he tipped his chin up toward the covered ceiling and hummed.

This was the first time I'd truly seen him still.

No fidgeting.

No noise.

"I *love* stars," he countered, voice reverent.

"Why?" Curiosity once again got the better of me.

"They're steady." Felix murmured, voice reverent. "*Constant.*" His lashes kissed his cheeks as he sighed. When his eyes opened, they stared unseeingly at the covered ceiling—as though he had memorized the stars that lay hidden behind the fabric.

My throat was dry as I admired the slope of his nose, the swoop of his chin, the span of his long, pale throat. There was a peculiar smattering of freckles at the base of it where his collarbone flirted with the fabric. I'd never noticed them before, but I certainly did now.

"Until they explode," I added helpfully. Felix laughed, and I shivered, enamored with the way his body came to life. Quaking, like a statue resurrected.

"Until they explode," Felix agreed, twisting to look at me. There were mysteries swirling in the depths of those lovely eyes. His nostrils flared, and he sucked in a greedy breath.

His attention felt heady as he stared at me.

For the first time in his presence, I felt hunted.

I licked my lips, my heart thumping unsteadily in my chest.

"The last supernova was discovered on February twenty-fourth in 1987," Felix told me, somehow holding my entire attention. I could feel the weight of his gaze tingling all over my skin, making the hair on the back of my neck stand up, and my stomach jerk. "You were probably a child. I doubt you remember."

"I don't."

"It was bright enough you didn't need a telescope to see it."

"Oh." I blinked, then cocked my head, confused. "You talk as though you were there."

"I was."

"But you…" I stared at him in disbelief, gaze dragging over his very young, very lovely face. There was no way he was a day over thirty. Right?

"I'm older than I look."

At a loss for words, and far too overwhelmed by Felix and his nonsense, I twisted to observe the rest of the room. I was here for murder. Not stars. Not pretty throats, or odd men who claimed to be older than they were.

Clearing my throat, I forced Felix's bullshit out of my head. "Where did the murder take place?"

"Oh! Yes. My apologies. Right over here." He gestured toward the bed. There was a jerkiness to his movements that I made a note to revisit, as I approached the bed with a frown. All his earlier grace disappeared, and he was a bumbling idiot again.

I did my best to ignore him, though that was difficult as I fumbled around in my satchel for what I needed. I'd brought my tools with me, a black light for one, and as I raised it to inspect the fabric I was surprised to find…*nothing*.

At all.

Huh.

"I thought you said there was blood."

"Oh," Felix's voice wavered. "I mean—there *was*."

"But there's none here."

"I uh…" he sidled closer, staring at where the light illuminated a whole lot of nothing. "I guess there's not?"

"Did you clean it already?" Annoyed, I huffed at him. I had *specifically* told him not to touch anything. But…I supposed if he had, he'd done a pretty damn good job.

And if he hadn't…Well, *that* didn't make sense. He'd said there was blood, so how could there be none? Admittedly, I hadn't really gotten a good look at the body as I'd been preoccupied with getting it into the car. It'd been bagged up in garbage sacks, so there hadn't been a solid opportunity to gawk.

Now I wished I had.

Especially because now that I was thinking about it, I wasn't certain how to *accidentally* kill someone at all.

Every time *I'd* murdered someone it had been quite intentional.

He truly was an enigma.

Fascinating.

"One moment." I took several minutes to make sure that I was correct, that there wasn't anything to cover up at all. When I finished, I turned my attention back to the small-gremlin-man only to realize he was also staring at the spot I'd been inspecting.

There was a haunted expression on his face. I'd looked at him before that moment, yes. But I hadn't *really* paid attention. And now that I was, it became readily apparent how tired the poor thing actually appeared. There were papery bruises beneath his eyes. And his lips—despite the chapstick I'd applied—looked bitten raw.

"Are you…" without thinking, words spilled free, "alright?"

Felix blinked. He blinked again. He blinked a third time.

And then he did something horrible.

Something *terrible*.

The worst possible thing he ever could've done.

He began to cry.

"Oh." I didn't know what to do. Tears spilled down his cheeks, an awful, *shuddery* little noise escaping him. He ducked his chin down and away—like he was trying to hide—like he was ashamed of the emotion he was currently experiencing.

"I'm—okay," Felix hiccuped out, somehow. "Really. I'm just happy you're here. I didn't know what to do." More tears spilled free. "I apologize. This…" Felix waved at himself, encompassing the wetness probably. "Is not like me. It's been a trying day."

He'd said he was fine, so he was.

But he was also still crying.

Unsure what to do, I reached out, and gently patted his shoulder. He felt even more solid than he looked. A delicious span of muscle filled my palm as I gave him a gentle rub. "It would…be okay if you weren't. I am often not fine, and I survive every time."

There. That was a good thing to say, wasn't it?

"Thank you," Felix sniffled, pressing into my touch as greedily as a cat tipping toward a puddle of sun.

"If you don't normally cry, why do it now?" I frowned. Even I could connect the obvious dots here. It didn't take a genius to infer that a normal person might be at least somewhat disturbed after they'd committed murder. I assumed so, anyway. "Is it because of the man you killed?"

"*I feel bad,*" Felix stared up at me, a frankly pitiful look on his face. He tried to duck his head away again—still ashamed—but I latched onto his cheeks and yanked him back into place.

Once again, he reminded me of the dog we'd had growing up. Dogs liked to be petted, apparently so did Felixes. "I didn't mean to do it," his voice shook, vibrating my fingers. "He didn't *deserve* that."

"I believe you," I hadn't before, but I did now. I'd grown up with a truck full of sisters, therefore nothing frightened me more than a person who cried. I hated this. It made me uncomfortable.

But it also made me…*well*…

It made me see Felix as human.

I supposed I hadn't ever seen him that way before.

He intrigued me in a way nothing but death ever had. The fact that I recognized him, but couldn't place his face bothered me. I'd always had a spectacular memory. I could admit, my curiosity was most definitely piqued—especially after Felix had convinced me to leave his secret alone.

"Would you cry if he *had* deserved it?" I asked, because I couldn't help myself. Something itched beneath my skin. Something primal and needy. A beast, blinking awake. "Would you feel bad?"

Felix thought for a moment. A dark expression crossed his face, like he was remembering something, or someone. Someone he wished he'd killed.

Then he shook his head, lips pressed into a thin, serious line. "No…I… don't suppose I would."

I wasn't sure he would've confessed that to anyone else, as it was akin to approving of murder. But his walls were down, and by helping him, I'd whittled my way inside his heart.

My blood began to sing.

I looked at Felix in a new light then. Tears and all. A man who felt bad—not because he'd killed someone, but because he didn't feel they'd deserved it. A man after my own heart.

"I think I must be a bad person." Felix sniffed. "I feel bad, but I also feel worse that I involved you. What if you get in trouble because of me?"

"The only way I'll get in trouble is if you implicate me." I said it to be soothing, but Felix was not soothed.

"I would *never*," his voice shook with vehemence, his tiny body quaking. I pulled him in by the grip on his face, unsure why I did it—only that I wanted the shaking to stop.

He was so little, his solid frame oddly chilly as I curled my bulk around him. Awkwardly, but earnestly, I gave his back a gentle pat.

"I would never, ever do that to you," Felix trembled.

"Thank you." *Pat, pat.* "I appreciate that."

"You're a good guy, Marshall." Felix sniffed, getting his awful sadness juice all over my nice work suit.

I felt…*bad.*

Huh.

I felt bad.

Because this entire time I'd only been thinking about how entertaining this would be. Not once had it ever occurred to me that Felix might be devastated. That he might feel frightened—or alone.

He needs me.

Yes.

He did.

Curling tighter around him, I *squeezed.* His tears seeped cold and wet onto my shirt, his little body quaking. I inhaled the sugary lemony scent of his shampoo for the first time—and immediately melted. *God, his hair was soft.* I couldn't help but rub my face in it as I held him.

He smells so good.

I'd never held someone before.

Not like this.

Not to comfort them.

"Thank you," Felix said, curling his fingers in my shirt and further ruining it, this time with wrinkles. "I'm so s-sorry I dragged you into this. I just didn't know what to do. I've never—I mean. It was an *accident*. I got overzealous."

"It's fine." Pat, pat, pat.

I sniffed his hair some more, still nuzzling the silky soft strands.

One thing became certain as I benefited from our embrace, and Felix continued to leak all over me.

And that was the fact that Felix was wrong. I wasn't a "good guy." I wasn't even good-guy-adjacent. If he knew just how *often* I'd killed, he'd surely feel less guilty about involving me. He wouldn't feel like he was corrupting me.

But I didn't tell him.

I didn't tell him, because I was a no good, selfish, very bad man.

Because he felt *right* inside my arms.

And if I told him I was a monster, I didn't think he'd ever let me hold him again.

Chapter Four

I DIDN'T SEE Felix again for an entire month, despite actively hunting for glimpses of him. That didn't mean I didn't think about him though. Often, I'd catch myself spacing out at work as my thoughts spun away from numbers and back to Felix's tiny but solid form.

He'd felt so wonderful in my arms. Like we were two gears in a tractor's transmission, perfectly sized to fit. His skin wasn't hot and sticky—something that had bothered me about past lovers. Instead, it was cool and soft. And it hadn't been overwhelming in the least when we'd pressed together.

He was small enough that he didn't set off the *threat* radar I constantly had going in my head. And he'd smelled…*lovely*, honestly. Lemony and fresh, like the soap I favored in the kitchen sink.

The only other person I'd ever thought I liked the smell of was my dentist.

Which you can imagine, at the ripe age of thirty-eight, meant that there were quite a few awful smelling people I'd had the unfortunate experience of meeting.

It wasn't till my sister, Winnie, came over for her monthly visit that I let myself acknowledge how disappointed I was by the lack of Felix in my life. Before, I would've rejoiced. No Felix meant no awkward, stilted conversations. No random tears. It meant no socializing in general.

But it also meant no hugging. No murder. And no pointy little smiles.

No telescopes.

No crochet.

No cats—

I could admit…I was maybe a bit obsessed. It had grown on me. A seed at first, that had blossomed, and swelled—expanding far larger than I'd ever expected it could.

I still didn't like him.

I didn't like people.

But that didn't mean I didn't want to see him more.

"He never leaves his house?" Winnie asked, frowning at me. We'd bought a pizza. More accurately, *she'd* bought a pizza. She'd been over for two days now and had told me in no uncertain terms that if I tried to feed her plain chicken breast one more time she'd shove it so far up my asshole I'd start to cluck.

Therefore pizza.

"No," I sighed, crossing my ankles and shifting in my seat. "Not during the day."

"Not at all?"

"That's usually what never means, yes."

"Asshole." Without even breathing, she continued. "Does he have that thing…you know…the…" she frowned while she thought, taking another bite of pizza and chewing with her mouth open as her brow remained knit. I stared at her aghast. "Shit, what's that called?"

"The word you're looking for is agoraphobia. Now please shut your mouth. Mother didn't raise you in the barn, did she?"

"I mean, kinda?"

We'd grown up on a farm till we were in our teens, so I supposed that was fair. Therefore a new tactic needed to be implemented.

"Are you a pig, Winnie?"

"Oink, oink." She threw the pizza at me, and I narrowly dodged having cheese grease ruin my cashmere sweater. I glared at her. Then I plucked the slice from where it had thud, squashed on the wall behind my shoulder.

As slowly, and pointedly as possible, I rose from my seat, and gracefully crossed the kitchen. With the pizza slice pinched between my pointer and thumb, I stepped on the lever that opened the garbage can lid, and deposited the offending piece of food in the trash where it now belonged.

Immediately, I decided to terrorize her right back.

"Are you done with this?" I asked, gesturing at the still-mostly-full pizza box.

"No." Winnie frowned at me, then made a horrified face as I made to grab the box so I could toss it in revenge. She slammed both hands onto it, gently tugging it away from me, her eyes wide. "Okay, *okay*. Fine. I'm sorry. I won't chuck shit at you again. Leave my pizza alone, you cold-hearted, chicken-breast-eating bastard."

I wasn't actually going to throw it away.

She knew that, I knew that.

We'd grown up where food was plentiful, but that didn't mean we hadn't struggled. Neither of us were the kind of people who were wasteful. But still, the threat was enough to cow her.

Ha.

Cow.

Because of the farm. And pigs.

"So. Boy toy." Winnie waved her new slice of pizza at me as I took my seat and sighed, head tipping back.

"Lord, give me patience."

"Is he agora-whatever?"

"No. He leaves his house." I frowned, thinking about Christmas Eve again and how alone he must've felt walking the quiet sidewalks of our little suburban neighborhood while parents filled their children's stockings indoors. Standing on the outside looking in. A voyeur. "Occasionally. At night," I added, cheeks a little flushed.

To be honest, I'd done a lot of research about this recently as I had wondered the same thing. Felix was wiggling around inside my head, and he wasn't even trying to. At least…I didn't think he was.

Maybe he was an evil mastermind after all.

An evil mastermind that crocheted.

How very formidable.

"Seeee and now you're smiling!" Winnie accused around another mouthful of pizza. I didn't scold her this time, too distracted by her very incorrect accusation to pay attention. I slapped a hand over my mouth, blushing bright red when she began to cackle. "Thinking about your little honey bee, huh?"

"He's not my anything."

"Isn't he?" Winnie blinked, arching a brow. She looked like me. Though she was a few years older, we shared the same tall, solid build. The same honey-gold hair. The same dark eyes. The same smattering of gray around our temples.

That was, however, where the similarities ended. Winnie and I could not be more different. She was loud where I was quiet. Brash where I was polite. She wore t-shirts she hacked the sleeves off of, and jorts in the summer. She liked pizza, hookup apps, and women with big breasts and colorful hair.

I liked…none of those things.

The only short thing I owned was my temper.

"Is he allergic to the sun?" Winnie joked, only it made sense—and therefore made a poor joke.

"I…think so? It's odd. I really don't think I've seen him outside during daylight."

"Haven't you lived across from each other for like ten years?"

"Yes."

"Huh." Winnie tapped her lip, head cocking to the side. "Maybe he's a vampire."

"Fuck off." I flipped her off and she cackled, clearly entertained.

"I want to meet him."

"No."

"If he pretty much never leaves the house that means he's home now, right?" She nodded to herself. "And the sun just went down—"

"Winnie, *no.*" I could see where this was going. I did not like it. I did not like it one bit.

My panic did not dissuade her—because she was obviously evil. She rose from her seat, pizza slice in hand, and headed toward the front door, my protests be damned.

Immediately, I skidded after her. *Stupid* fucking socks, making me slide—

"Winnie—" I tried a third time as I thunked into the wall. I was as uncoordinated as I'd been as a teen now that she was teasing. My pleas fell on deaf ears. It only took her two seconds to slide her flip-flops on. I—unfortunately—was forced to watch as she skidded out the front door while I attempted to tie my shoes.

Fuck, fuck.

Fuck loafers.

Christ.

"Winnie, no!" I yelled after her as the front door shut. Horrified, I finished tying my laces as quickly as possible, all the while cursing Italian leather. Then I shoved out the door after her, and sprinted across the street, my heart pounding.

She's going to humiliate me.

Oh fuck, oh fuck.

She's going to tell him about the smiling.

The smiling that totally did not happen—but also definitely did.

I caught up just in time—Winnie's fist raised to knock, her cheeks full of the remaining bites of pizza.

"Don't do this—" I grabbed her wrist, pleading with her. As per usual, she ignored me and did as she liked.

Using her free arm, she rapped on the door, eyes dancing with mischief as I released her with a panicked groan. It was dark out—which more than likely meant that Felix would answer.

Please don't answer.

Please don't answer.

Please answer.

Please answer.

Even my mind was a traitorous bitch.

The door swung open, and my heart did a horrifying little flip-flop as Felix came into view. He was dressed how he usually was, a lovely soft sweater, crisp trousers. A ridiculously large hat—that I wanted to throw into a fire—and his sunglasses.

Winnie frowned, then looked down, obviously surprised she had to crane her neck quite so far. She was a giant like I was—like all of us were.

"Hi." Her smile was practically feral. Unhinged.

Why, oh why, could I not have been born an only child?

It wasn't fair.

"Hello?" Felix tipped his chin back, that lovely jaw peeking out from beneath the shadows as he glanced at her, then me, then her again. He cocked his head to the side.

This could not get any worse.

"My name is Winnie Warden."

"Hi, Winnie," Felix looked shell-shocked. "I'm Felix."

"Hi, Felix. My brother would like to ask you out."

Oh. My god.

It got worse.

"No, I would not," I countered from just behind her, then floundered, because for the first time in my life I was actually aware of how awful that sounded. "Not that I wouldn't ever—I just—"

Oh Christ.

Where was a black hole when you needed one?

Smite me down, God?

Pretty please?

"You want to ask me out?" Felix's voice was quiet, surprised—like he'd never been asked out before. "But..." he glanced at me, then her, then me again—this was a pattern I was sure was going to continue to repeat. I liked it, maybe a little too much. It was like he was looking to me for guidance. "Why?"

I could understand his confusion. The last time I'd seen him he'd cried all over me. We'd cleaned up a murder together. If I'd been a normal person we probably would've never spoken again.

But I wasn't a normal person.

And I'd spent a month daydreaming about him—and maybe, probably—watching him through the peephole on my front door.

What had started as simple curiosity, wanting to know why he killed—and how—had morphed into something...*deeper*. Something I wasn't sure I was ready to acknowledge the depth of just yet.

"Because," I countered succinctly. I'm not sure when, but this had turned into a ship I was ready to go down with. *Quick Marshall, say something sexy.* "You have nice teeth."

"Because I have nice teeth?" Felix's brows shot up.

"And you are...*interesting*," I added, flushed.

There, that was better.

"Oh." Felix looked pleased with himself as he peered at me through his lashes. The lovely pointy little teeth I'd just complimented flashed as he bit back a grin.

I was the youngest of four siblings—all sisters—no one had ever looked to me for guidance like *that* in all my life. I was the one that got picked on, made over, and forced to do the shittiest jobs. No one treated me like I was...*important*.

Like I was in charge.

"But I…" Felix was clearly not sold.

My chest puffed up, shoulders squared.

Winnie be damned, I would turn this around.

"But you?" I countered, arching a brow.

"I sleep during the day."

"I'll stay up late."

"You…will?" Felix looked at me, clearly surprised, though I wasn't sure why.

"We can stay in."

"We can?" Once again, Felix looked surprised.

Did I look like the kind of man that enjoyed socializing in the wild? I hoped not. A night in with Felix honestly sounded…nice. "And this would be a…?"

"A date," Winnie interjected from beside me, not even trying to contain her glee.

"A date?" Felix looked to me for confirmation again. He sucked in a breath, chewing on his lip, those lovely—oh so lovely—pointy teeth flashing. "I don't know."

My heart thudded unsteadily, I reached out, grabbed Winnie, and shoved her out of the way so that I was the one primarily in the doorway.

"Why not?" I asked. It was a valid question.

I'd never asked someone on a date before. I'd never *wanted* to. My palms were sweaty and I realized with a sickening lurch, just how badly I wanted Felix to say yes.

"Why not?" Felix had clearly not been expecting the question.

"Yes."

"I…" Felix frowned, his dark eyes searching mine. Today they were nearly black. It was odd. I could've sworn the last time I'd seen them they'd been a far lighter color. He seemed at war with himself. His gaze flicked to my throat again. He swallowed. It felt like a century had passed before he finally nodded, conceding, "Okay."

I blinked, surprised he'd folded so quickly.

Flattered though.

Apparently whatever hang-ups Felix had did not compare to his desire to date me.

"Next week?" Felix offered, chewing on his lip. He wouldn't stop staring at me through his lashes. It was distracting. And god, that fucking lip. He was going to tear it up again if he kept that up. I made a mental note to buy him some chapstick.

"Why not tomorrow?" I was free. There was no need to wait.

"I…uh…have plans that I need to…um. *Yes.*" Felix was clearly lying, but I had no idea why. Either way, I'd gotten a date so I wasn't about to question it. Felix's nostrils flared, and his gaze snapped to my throat. He licked his lips, forcing his eyes back up, though he didn't look like he wanted to.

"Friday? Next week," I countered.

"Friday." Felix agreed, sucking in a fortifying breath. A happy little smile spread across his face. "*Friday*," he repeated, more excited this time. "Nine?"

It was a late starting time, but I wasn't all that surprised. I hadn't been lying when I told Winnie that I'd never seen him go out during the daylight. Nor had I been lying when I told him I didn't mind staying up late. "Nine is great."

"Swell!" Felix beamed up at me, his smile positively sunny. For a man that was allergic to daylight, he sure looked like the sun. My cheeks hurt, and I was suddenly quite certain I was smiling too.

"I won't end up like your last date, will I?" I joked quietly, under my breath.

Felix's eyes widened, a startled laugh escaping him.

It'd been a gamble, bringing it up.

But I figured…sharing a secret like this only gave me a better chance with him. We had something no one else did. A pact of silence. I licked my lips, suddenly desperate to smell the lemony shampoo he used or feel his fluffy hair against my lips. The damn hat was in the way though. I was lucky enough that he'd tipped the sunglasses far enough I could see his gaze.

"No hat," I plucked the brim.

"No hat?" Felix snorted out a laugh. "You *really* hate them."

"I really do."

"Okay," he agreed. "No hat."

"Friday. Nine. I'll come over." I figured he'd be more comfortable in his own space, though I did eventually want to invite him over to my place. Mine was quite a bit less chaotic. I had no cats. No telescope either.

"Okay," Felix beamed at me, flashing me his teeth again. God fucking dammit.

"Goodnight, Finley."

"Goodnight, Marshall."

When I turned around, Winnie was grinning at me, her hands on her sturdy hips. She looked far too pleased with herself. But I was in too good of a mood to do anything other than roll my eyes at her and knock our shoulders together as we headed back across the street.

"Seeeeee?" Winnie said as we reentered my modest home. It wasn't nearly as tall or as foreboding as Felix's was. White paneling, a picket fence, a perfectly manicured lawn. We could not have been more opposite if we tried. "And *this* is why you should always listen to me."

"Whatever," I rolled my eyes. Leaning down, I carefully untied my loafers one by one, before kicking them off. Winnie's flip-flops hit the wall by my head, and I twisted to glare at her. Only, my glare was lost as she wandered back toward the kitchen, a spring in her step.

"I demand details," she called around the wall as I rolled my eyes. "A play by play."

"I'm not telling you shit."

"*Marsha*," Winnie gasped, head popping around the wall. She was closer than I'd realized. Her meaty fingers gripped the frame. "You can't deprive me of my fun."

"You'll find I can, *Winston*."

"But you wouldn't."

"I would."

Winnie frowned, seeming to process this. After deciding I wasn't bluffing at all, her smile softened, and her eyes grew warm. We often fought, our claws out like kittens in a roost. But she truly was my favorite person. She was the only person I was comfortable enough with to drop my guard.

"I'm happy for you, MarMar." The use of my favorite childhood nickname made me flush, and I shook my head, embarrassed but pleased.

"Nothing's even happened," I countered.

"Yeah, Marshall." Winnie's eyes were soft, gentle. "But it *could*."

It could.

I hadn't…well…

I hadn't thought of that.

It's true, I lived life with the reins twisted so tightly there was no room for error. But that also meant I never strayed from the path I set. There were no new sights, no new wonders. My world had become a bleak, unexciting place. This was…a new trail, a new terrain, new beginnings.

I might see something wonderful, if I stepped off the path.

Felix could *be* something wonderful.

His name *did* mean luck, after all.

Chapter Five

I HAD NEVER been an impatient person. Ever. With my kills, I often planned them out months, sometimes even years, in advance. I picked people by a code—a code which I followed to a tee. If they didn't meet the code, I left them alone. Which meant a lot of stalking, investigating, and hard work.

Murder was a full-time job, if you let it be.

However…I found myself impatient for my date Friday with Felix. I didn't understand why he'd wanted the date to be so far away. Winnie had teased me for the rest of the time she'd spent at my house, before heading off with explicit instructions that I was required to keep her updated at all times.

That was not happening.

The longer I had to wait, the more frantic my thoughts became.

Would Felix be as fun without murder involved? Would I enjoy talking to him? Would he enjoy talking to me? What if he didn't smell like I remembered? What if it was awkward? What if he cried again? What if it ended badly—and then we still had to live next to each other for the foreseeable future.

No, no.

I'd move.

Yes.

That's what I'd do.

If this date did not go well, I would move. I loved Beach Town—*kinda*—but I could settle somewhere else. Maybe there were other branches of *The Club*? I would miss Allen, if I was being honest. The crematory was incredibly convenient for my hobby but…

I could bite back the compulsion, couldn't I? If I had to.

I could choose not to kill for a while if I had to move.

I'd done it before, I could do it again.

Maybe I was comfortable here, with my systems, my patterns, and my people—but I could abandon them. I could.

No.

Fuck.

Once again I was worrying myself into circles. This didn't serve anyone, least of all me.

Winnie's voice in my head whispered, okay bitch, so we've thought about what could go wrong. But what about…if it goes right?

What if Felix had a penchant for death like I did? We could…well… We could kill together, couldn't we?

And outside of that, there were other things that might be nice, right? Felix certainly didn't have landscaping skills, but he was an excellent crafter. It would make Christmas easy, wouldn't it? He could make presents for my siblings. They loved handmade stuff—which meant they always scoffed at my gifts, as I was not the kind of man who created anything but mayhem.

They'd love him, wouldn't they?

We'd have to work around the sun thing—but Winnie hadn't seemed all that fazed by it—and she was one of the judgiest people in my family. If Winnie could get behind it, everyone else could too.

Accommodating Felix in my life was as simple as investing in blackout curtains.

Yes.

And those blinds that Felix had.

We could work around anything with a little elbow grease and determination.

Oh! And on top of having a Christmas-gift-partner, I'd *finally* have someone to take with me to the company parties. I'd stop getting pitying looks—and Felix wouldn't wander the streets alone anymore. It was a win-win situation.

I'd always been single.

It wasn't that I was unattractive, truthfully I was quite aware of my good looks. They were the only thing I had going for me most days. What I *lacked* was a winning personality. It only took a solid thirty seconds for most people to realize that I was not the kind of man you wanted to spend extended periods of time with.

Which had never bothered me until now.

I didn't want Felix to think that about me.

He didn't seem to? If his reaction to my presence was any indication. He looked at me, not like there were screws loose, but like I was the screw he'd been missing. It was a nice look. Odd, but nice.

Things could go badly, yes.

But they could…*wow*.

They could go so so well.

I'd even put up with his cats if it meant he'd like me.

Being in a committed relationship didn't seem nearly as daunting as it had before.

Still…

Impatience won over. It was the Saturday before our date, and I was already over at Felix's house again, fist raised to knock. It was after dark, as I hadn't wanted to be rude—even though I was about to be very rude. The weeds were taunting me. There was only so much patience a man could possess when it came to proper lawn management.

Also maybe I missed him a little, and worried he'd been holed up alone for far too long. *What if he was crying again?* Don't mistake me for a kind-hearted person. I'm not. I was simply looking after my investment. Because that's what Felix was. An entertaining, cat wrangling, hat-wearing investment.

Knock, knock, knock.

When Felix opened the door, this time he pulled his hat off the second he saw me. Which kind of—maybe—*definitely* made me grin.

"Marshall?" He smiled shyly. "I thought our date was Friday?" His eyes looked darker than the last time I'd seen him. There was a smudge of dirt on his cheek like he'd been cleaning. When I glanced behind him, the hallway remained just as cluttered as it had been before. Perhaps he'd been working on the mess upstairs?

"It was. *Is.*" I sucked in a breath. "I just." I nearly lost my nerve. "Your lawn—"

"My lawn?"

It was overgrown. An eyesore. *Ugly.* With weeds that wagged toward the sky, scraggly and tall, and grass that broke up the sidewalk. All in all it was *awful. I could tell him this. Yes! What a good idea. Delicately.* I could tell him, and *that* would be why I came over. I could take care of his lawn—and have an excuse to be close to him every week.

I was. A. Genius.

I wouldn't even need an excuse!

Every Saturday like clockwork, I could manage his plants, and knock on his door after dark to see if he was as pretty as I remembered him to be.

I just needed to convince him.

Delicate, Marshall. *Polite.* This is the man you want to date. Be gentle.

"You have the ugliest lawn I've ever seen." The words were out before I could stop them. It was the truth, but I hadn't meant to say it quite so… bluntly.

Fix this, Marshall.

Fix it.

You need to fix it.

"It's awful. Truly horrendous." *No, no. No. No. Oh fuck.* "I mean—have you *ever* mowed it?"

Why wouldn't my mouth stop going?

Someone shoot me.

Please.

"It *is* quite ugly, isn't it?" Felix frowned, glancing out toward the raggedy foliage thoughtfully, like he was not offended at all—but instead contemplative. I'd complained before about this exact thing to the HOA, but I'd never complained directly to his face. Maybe I should have.

I hadn't expected *this* reaction.

Felix hummed, like he was *actually* listening to me.

Like my opinion mattered. Like he even agreed with me.

"It is." I wilted a little. "I…"

"You…?" Felix turned to look at me, dark eyes dancing. "Did you come all the way over here to tell me you hate my lawn?"

"Ah. Yes. *No.*" I had never felt like my skin was tighter than I did then, squirming a little despite being easily three times his size. I felt about an inch tall. "Can I…maybe…fix it?"

There. I'd done it.

Now he just had to agree and I'd have the perfect stalking opportunity every weekend.

We both had our strengths. His was creating what I assumed to be quality knick-knacks and mine was…lawn work? Yes. Lawn work. Stalking. And carrying dead bodies—but I was trying to expand on that, as it wasn't necessarily a marketable quality.

Couldn't put that on my goddamn resume.

Or my profile on a dating website.

Even if it *was* a very useful skill, depending on who you asked.

"You want to fix my lawn?" Felix cocked his head to the side, staring up at me with those lovely, dark eyes. "I mean…" He chewed on his lip. *C'mon, c'mon, c'mon, Felix.* "That would be nice, actually. Someone keeps complaining about me—and yard work is really difficult when I can't go out during daylight. It's always too late by the time I'm up to start mowing. I didn't want to be rude—I know you work early in the mornings."

When he laid out the facts like that it made me feel even worse that I was the one complaining about him. I supposed I'd never thought about it from his perspective. Every Saturday morning, like clockwork, I was out mowing and trimming my yard so it remained picture perfect. Felix *couldn't* do that. He was trapped indoors till the sun went down—and like he said—he couldn't very well start yard work at night.

There were several kinds of sun allergies. I'd researched them extensively, and while I didn't know what Felix possessed, I could only assume it was bad. Perhaps he had Solar Urticaria? And exposure to the sun caused hives.

Either way, working at night was not ideal.

It was loud, yes, but more importantly it was *dangerous*. There were a lot of blades involved—and the idea of Felix out in low visibility trying to trim his hedges because I'd complained was—no.

No.

"I'm going to take care of it from now on." Confidence felt good as I stared down at him, heart thudding. "Don't worry about it. No one is going to complain about you ever again."

Because I won't be, I thought but wisely didn't say.

Apparently I didn't need to drink alcohol to have annoying regrets.

"Will it wake you if I start tomorrow morning?" I asked, shifting to look at the lawn more critically. I'd need to get out my weed whacker, that was for sure. A lawn mower was not enough to tackle this beast. If my sister, Melissa, lived closer, I'd ask to borrow her riding lawn mower. She'd just gotten a John Deere 7345R, and had been bragging about how smooth a ride it was. It felt like I'd blinked and she'd popped forty kids out.

I could barely keep track of their names.

Okay, so that was a lie. I knew all their names. And had their birthdays memorized. And made sure to send money for them.

"I'm a deep sleeper," Felix grinned, leaning against the doorframe, watching me through his lashes. The little beauty mark beneath his eye mocked me. I'd never thought a mole was kissable before—but his certainly was. "It's never bothered me when you do your lawn in the morning."

Fuck, that hadn't even occurred to me.

Ooops.

"Okay," relieved, I twisted back to look at him. "Goodnight."

"Goodnight, Marshall." Felix laughed, his forehead still leaning against the frame as he watched me retreat. The only reason I could tell anything was amiss was because his hands were trembling. I wasn't certain *why*—maybe he was nervous around me after what we'd been through—but I'd just have to train him to trust me.

I had the capability of great violence, but I already knew that I could never raise a hand to Felix.

That wasn't who I was.

I hoped after our date, perhaps he wouldn't look so haggard—perhaps he'd feel *safer* knowing I was looking out for him.

"Have the police bothered you?" I asked, keeping my voice quiet. I probably shouldn't have brought that up—especially after we'd already said our goodbyes, but it was a thought that had been plaguing me. Felix had killed at his own home, after all. He'd brought his kill here—and that meant there was less room for error—not that there was ever much room for that, all things considered.

"No," Felix shook his head. There was an almost guilty look on his face. "I don't think they will, either."

"No?" I frowned, curious. "Why do you say that?"

"I just…yeah. I don't think they will."

Over-confident, but that was okay. I'd make sure he had an alibi if I needed to. I would take care of this. I made that vow to myself.

Because he was an investment—just like my car, or my stocks. And that meant he needed to be looked after.

"Have a good night," I said for a second time, still flushed. I hate to admit this but I was a *little* excited that I now had an excuse to spend more time on this side of the street. Sure Felix would be asleep—which meant there wouldn't be opportunity for chatting, or seeing his little grin while he dodged my questions.

But…being close to him was enough.

I inhaled, sighing when a waft of his lovely lemon shampoo tickled my senses.

Yes.

Yes.

That was why I was doing this.

Lemons. His smile. The mystery—the opportunity to be entertained.

Not because I liked him. Of course not. That would be silly.

It wasn't my fault he smelled good and had a nice smile. Those were just facts.

"You too," Felix smiled at me. His hands were still quaking as he slipped back inside his house and shut the door. It was odd, how fast he'd retreated—but I didn't mind. Perhaps he had something to do? That was fine.

If I'd been less oblivious, I maybe would've connected the dots. Would've realized that the reason Felix quaked was not because of fear or nerves, but because of me.

But I didn't.

Instead, I spent a half hour wandering his yard, making plans for the Sunday morning to get started. When I returned across the street to my own home, I was buzzing with excitement.

If only I'd known then, what was about to happen.

Maybe I could've prepared better.

Maybe.

Chapter Six

FELIX'S YARD was harder to fix than I'd expected. Yes, it looked awful—and I'd known that. But the *true* horror was hidden beneath the tall surface of the grass. There were ten-plus years of neglect to pick through—and I may be good at lawn management, but I wasn't Jesus.

It took me hours to get it chopped down to something manageable, and even then, I knew I'd have to split up the work into multiple weekends. Now that I'd taken on this task, I was quite giddy at the prospect of spending more time near Felix's home.

Maybe…if he murdered again, I'd witness it?

Besides.

I'd never minded a little hard work. In a way, working on Felix's jungle reminded me of when I'd been a kid and Dad had us working the farm. Typically, I'd been with the animals, and not with the crops, but the memory remained.

Dad and I were similar people. He had few words, a plan, and was adept at execution. We talked twice a year, on my birthday and on his. And that was how we liked it.

This was bringing up a lot of nostalgic feelings. Making me think about my family—about my sisters, and my mother. About relationships in general, and if I was fit to have one in the first place. I'd been told I was like a cactus, prickly and dry. But some people *enjoyed* cactuses. So that didn't necessarily mean I wasn't boyfriend material. Not that I *wanted* to be a boyfriend—I couldn't possibly shop for another person for Christmas. I didn't have it in me.

Or at least…I *hadn't*.

I'd never wanted one before Felix, so I'd never pursued it. And though I had a certain fascination with my neighbor, I wasn't sure I was even capable of being a loving, committed partner.

The only things I'd remained committed to for an extended period of time was my hobby and my friendship with Winnie.

Actually…huh.

Maybe that in itself answered my question.

I'd maintained a friendship with Winnie since childhood. Which meant I was capable of it, right?

Yes, she was my sister, but that didn't *mean* anything.

Plenty of people had horrible relationships with their siblings, and being blood-related to someone did not guarantee friendship.

Perhaps I had it in me after all?

Besides, *Winnie* liked me—and she was my oldest and closest friend.

At least…I *hoped* she did.

I texted her, suddenly worried.

Me: You like me.

Winnie: No I don't.

I glared at my phone, grumpily shoving it in my back pocket. I weed-whacked the back edge of Felix's lawn for another half an hour before checking my phone again. Surely, Winnie would've texted something a little more *flattering* by now. Maybe about how good a brother I was—and how important I was to her.

There was no such message waiting.

Just a simple emoji of a—*was that*—? I frowned, put the weed whacker down, and fished my reading glasses out of my chest pocket. With them perched in place on my nose, I was able to see the tiny emoji better.

I wished I hadn't bothered.

It was a little fist with the middle finger up.

Me: Fuck you.

Winnie: Love you too, baby bro.

It took me twenty minutes to flip through the emoji…*catalog*? Thing. The thing with all the emoji options on my phone. Eventually, I found what I was looking for. *Ha*! Take that.

I sent her a mirroring middle-finger icon.

A neighbor walked by on the sidewalk with her dog on a leash. She stared at me for a second, and I waved—not wanting to look *too* murder-y with my weed whacker in hand, and an evil grin on my face.

I missed whether or not she waved back because my phone buzzed.

Winnie had replied.

It was another middle-finger emoji.

Go-figure.

I replied back with two.

She sent three.

Stuck in a war I didn't want to be a part of, I nearly missed when a nondescript black van pulled into Felix's driveway. I saw it in my peripheral vision, however, and tugged my safety headphones off and around my neck, twisting to watch the new arrivals.

Who were these people?

And why the hell were they at Felix's house when he was asleep?

My hackles raised—but fell rather quickly when I realized these mystery men were actually the bearers of his package. Packages, more accurately—as he got the same giant box of what I could only assume was some sort of meat—at least once a month.

It was rather large, and quite heavy when I went to investigate after the men left.

Maybe it was nosy of me—but I could see the "refrigerate immediately" sticker, and as I had every intention of courting the box's owner, I was remiss to leave it behind. It was heavier than it looked as I hefted it across the street and into my garage. Luckily, I had enough room in my backup refrigerator to shove the box in whole, which I did.

Then I promptly forgot about it—

Because Winnie called me, and I had to spend the next half hour defending myself because I'd dared to try to wheedle a compliment out of her. I would not make that mistake again. She kept poking fun about

Felix and our date—and by the time I hung up, I was a mess in more than one way. Covered in grass bits and sweat, I abandoned Felix's lawn for the rest of the day and headed home to properly clean up.

It wasn't till Wednesday that I remembered the package I'd taken.

And by that point…well…

It was too late.

Only two days remained until our date. I was practically buzzing with anticipation. I could feel it itching beneath my skin as I planned out my outfit—then replanned it—then planned it again. I didn't know what Felix would wear. I'd seen him in practically every shade of the rainbow, and as we were staying in, there was no way to anticipate his choice.

I'd just tried on my favorite indigo-sweater-vest-white-shirt-combo, when I spotted yet *another* unfamiliar car pulling into Felix's driveway.

Which…reminded me of the package I'd accidentally stolen three days ago.

Oops.

Without thinking, or changing clothing, I bolted downstairs to my garage to retrieve the box. I'd drop it off—as Felix was likely to be up now. If I knocked on the door, he wouldn't even know I'd taken it. And I could possibly—maybe interrogate his guest a bit too. Find out why the hell they were bothering Felix this late, and perhaps scare them off—never to return again.

It was a perfect, fool-proof plan.

Because I knew the box was heavy, I opened the garage door before grabbing the package. As it rose with a creak, I couldn't resist a curious peek across the street to Felix's home. The stranger's car was still there, and a man was climbing out of it with a sunny grin and—

Flowers.

Flowers?

Why in the hell does he have flowers?

Package forgotten, I stared as the man made his way across the sidewalk I'd just fucking trimmed, and up the steps to Felix's home. Was this…a *date*? Why in the world was he at Felix's house?

My eyes narrowed as I watched the stranger knock on the front door.

For a split second, I imagined crossing the street—quiet and slow—stalking in close, and snapping his neck before Felix had even known he'd visited at all. But…that daydream quickly faded as reality snuck back in.

I couldn't just cross the street and *kill* the man for daring to buy Felix flowers.

I'd get caught.

Therefore I had no choice but to will my hurt away.

The crushing weight of rejection was obnoxious. I had better things to do than wallow—even though I felt half-tempted to do just that.

Perhaps it was…sex?

Somehow that thought didn't soothe me, even though I knew sex was not on the table for us—even on our Friday date.

Christ, what was wrong with me? It wasn't like Felix had promised me his undying fidelity. We hadn't even gone on a single date yet. And besides! I had a *code*, dammit. An innocent man with flowers did not meet it.

Still though, that didn't stop me from imagining it again.

And again.

And again.

Is he innocent if he's talking to what's ours? It was difficult to ignore the beast inside me, especially when he had a valid point. No matter how hard I tried to rationalize that there was nothing untoward going on—especially after the stranger was let into Felix's home—I couldn't stop the burning heat of *anger* that simmered beneath the surface of my skin.

Especially as the night grew darker and darker—the stars came out—and the man's car had not. Left. Felix's. *Driveway.*

I was so close to heading over there, caution be damned, and bodily separating them—that I was *forced* to resort to drastic measures.

I called Winnie.

"What do you want?" Winnie's voice was a welcome irritation. This feeling was at least more familiar than the riot of angry, all-encompassing bitterness that had been eating me alive for hours now.

"He has a *date* over." Wow. I *sounded* awful.

I didn't need to say Felix's name for her to know who I was talking about.

Winnie paused, to process. As she should. This was horrific. Awful. Horrible. The worst thing that had *ever* happened. Something rustled on the other end of the line that sounded a lot like her awful beast—Buddy. "Felix has a date over?" She repeated carefully.

"*Yes.*" God, why was she *repeating* it?

"Oh, honey." There was so much pity in that single phrase I nearly threw my phone against the wall.

"Do not '*Oh, honey*' me. This means nothing. We're not...dating. We haven't! Not even once. I barely asked him out." I was trying to convince myself, more than her, and I hated how obvious that was—and also how manic I sounded. "He can date whoever he wants to date, it doesn't mean our date won't happen—or that he won't find it special. Or that he'll compare me to the mystery man. Oh god, I need to get him flowers. I have to get him flowers! If I don't, I'll already be losing. I can't lose, Winnifred. I can't. I hate it. You know I hate it. I hate losing almost as much as I hate pickles. Do you think they're kissing? Oh god. No. No, no, no, no."

"Some people like to kiss."

"You *bitch*. How could you say that to me?"

"I'm just saying—" Winnie laughed, though her tone softened. "It's *okay*. There's no need to panic. It's not like he's over there getting married two days before your date. Maybe he planned this before you asked him?" She offered, obviously trying to make me feel better—and wisely ignoring my current downward spiral.

"*Maybe*," I chewed on my lip, pacing my kitchen because it had the best view across the street. The car was still there. "But *why*? Why must he date at all?"

"If he *didn't* date, he wouldn't have said yes to you." She was right and I hated her for it.

"But he was so reluctant—"

"…Yes…" Winnie sighed, "but he said yes, didn't he?"

"Then, is it just me he was reluctant with?"

"I don't know, Marshall."

My ego had never taken a hit quite like this.

"I…" Fuck. I sat down, chair scraping. The lights were on in Felix's teetering horror mansion of a home. "*I don't understand.*"

"I know you don't, buddy." Winnie's voice was uncharacteristically gentle. "You know what I think would help?"

"What?" *Why was the stranger's car still there?* Christ. It was eleven p.m.. That was far too late for visitors. If they were having sex I was going to—I don't know what. *Scream?* Burn the house down? Bodily separate them with a yardstick? Slice Felix's date's throat open—then move Felix across the country and lock him away where no one could ever ogle him ever again. Somewhere so far away even Amazon couldn't deliver more stupid hats to him.

"Why don't you ask him?" Winnie's voice somehow filtered through my murderous, kidnapping plans.

"Ask…him?" That…hadn't occurred to me.

"Or, you know, you could just kill the dude. Get rid of the competition." Winnie was joking. I *knew* she was joking—because she was not a member of *The Club*. Not the literal club, or any sort of metaphorical murder club thereof. But that didn't make her suggestion any less appealing.

I didn't need to talk to Felix.

Ha!

Talking.

Fuck that.

No thank you.

"Murder is preferable," I deadpanned. Winnie laughed, oblivious to just how serious I actually was. "I'll use a machete."

"You do that."

"I will." I wouldn't. It wasn't *safe*. But…that didn't mean I didn't *want* to. I wanted to hack him up into itty bitty lipless bits—so tiny he could never kiss anyone ever again.

"MarMar," Winnie's voice was annoyingly gentle again. Like I was a child and she was trying to *soothe* me. "You *do* know that not everyone jumps into a serious relationship, right? Like…before they even go on a date? There's a process. And that process isn't always monogamous at first."

"I know," I scoffed.

"Do you?" Winnie kept talking. Because she was a flip-flop-wearing *asshole.* "Because you're really upset about this, honey. And I know that you *really* like Felix—and I'm happy for you. God knows, I never expected *you* of all people to like someone this much—"

"—Hey."

"But you can't expect him to follow rules when you haven't even told him what they are." I hated that she was right. "So talk to him about it? Yeah. Ask him what's up."

"God, you piss me off." I was not asking Felix anything. That would be humiliating. And honestly? I didn't want to fucking know.

"Love you too." Winnie blew me a kiss, then promptly hung up.

If I'd known exactly what Felix was up to, perhaps I would've been less upset. Jury's out on that one. Luckily for me, it didn't take long to figure out *why* the stranger had stayed so late. Because by the time the clock struck midnight I received an unexpected visitor.

Relief, unlike anything I'd ever known flooded through me the second I spotted Felix's familiar floppy hat through the peephole in my door.

I hadn't even *seen* Felix cross the street, which was…odd, considering the fact that I'd been glaring at his house for several hours now. Either he was faster than he looked—or he could teleport.

Yanking the door open, I did my best to act casual—and not like I'd been planning murder for the last three hours.

Act normal, act normal, act normal.

"Good evening." *Boom.* Done. Perfect execution. Yay me.

"*I did it again,*" Felix said by way of greeting, his voice rough. There were new tear streaks streaming down his cheeks.

I hated him a little then, because the sight of his tears didn't make me balk like they should have—instead, I wanted to bundle him up in my arms again, and hiss at anyone that approached.

Felix came across as a proud man. Old school. The kind of man who rarely cried—and yet here he was, for a second time showing me the underside of his belly. The parts that were squishy and soft, and easily broken.

It was difficult for me to find sympathy for a person who was all soft sides—as I'd been raised on hard edges. But Felix wasn't all fluff and no substance. In fact, I got the feeling that when he was with anyone else—he acted quite different.

I knew walls intimately, as I had dozens of my own.

And yet…here Felix was with his down, looking to me—of all people—for guidance.

Felix's eyes were visibly lighter in color than they'd been the last time I'd seen him. Blood red. Was it a medical condition? I'd have to Google that later. Or perhaps he was wearing colored contacts for his date. The thought made me grit my teeth.

"You did *what* again?" I asked, less charitably.

Felix licked his lips, his gaze flicking guiltily over his shoulder toward his home where the stranger's car was still parked. "I did…*it*. Marshall."

He was clearly hoping I'd guess what kind of nonsense he was talking about without actually saying it aloud. I was not a mind reader, but I tried to guess anyway.

He'd done what?

Had sex?

"I'll kill him." Visions of slamming a hammer into the asshole's head assaulted my senses. For a brief, *terrifying* moment I saw red. "I'll kill him—I swear to God."

"You *can't*—" Felix stared up at me, lashes spiky and wet. God, he was delicious. It was *ridiculous*. He pissed me off. So much. So needy—like an animal in pain that needed putting down.

Broken, broken, *broken*.

He needs me.

I can't kill him.

He needs me.

I can't.

Not if Felix doesn't want me to.

It was a horrible, wretched thing to realize that I cared more about Felix than killing the man who had touched him.

The thought shook me to the core as I took a half-step forward and grasped his face in my palm. Felix's skin was spongy soft and slightly damp from his tears. With need simmering beneath the surface of my skin, I tipped his head up, only sated when I could admire how beautiful his turmoil was up close.

Prettier than hurricanes.

Prettier than morning dew.

Prettier than the brilliant crimson of freshly spilled blood.

"Why can't I?" I asked, voice soft, my fingers digging into his cheeks. "*Why* can't I, sweetheart?"

Don't say it's because you love him.

Don't say it, please.

You're mine, mine, mine.

Felix shivered, his tongue flicking out to wet his lips. His broad shoulders were hunched, like he was trying to make himself appear even smaller than he already was. Gone was the confidence he normally exuded. Like I was seeing—for the first time—the brittle, broken husk that hid beneath his person-suit.

And he was…*lovely*.

A pitiful, broken, tangled thing.

Felix's lips pinched into a guilty line.

Don't say you love him.

Don't—don't—

Oh.

And then it…hit me.

It hit me like a pile of bricks.

My cock jerked, butterflies fluttering around in my belly as my heart began to race. Heat coiled in my hips, at the same time I bit back a needy groan. Because I suddenly knew why Felix had said I couldn't kill his date.

And it wasn't because he cared for him.

My hand slid from his face, down to his throat, cupping him there to hold him in place.

"I can't kill him," I murmured, bending down close enough our noses brushed. My breath mingled with his, and something electric zinged between us. Greedy, greedy, greedy—I needed to hear him say it. Needed to hear him admit the awful, bloody truth as badly as I needed my next breath.

"Tell me *why* I can't kill him, Finley," I pleaded, nudging his cheek imploringly with my nose. Felix *groaned*. I could feel his Adam's apple bob beneath my palm when he swallowed. His lashes fluttered shut, as his strong, lovely hands moved to clutch the fabric at my waist. "*Tell me why*," my voice was deep and hoarse.

"*I…*"

"Tell. Me."

I'd never been more aroused by a person in all my life. This wicked, wretched little man—so beautiful, so perfect. My tiny little *accidental* killer.

"You can't kill him…" Felix whispered, the tension in his body melting away as he opened his eyes—blood red—gorgeous—ringed by a dark fringe of curly lashes. "Because I…"

"*Yes*, sweetheart?" My heart was pounding.

"Because I already did."

Chapter Seven

ALLEN ARCHED a brow at me as he pulled the door to the back of the crematory open. "Another one? So soon?" He cocked his head to the side, obviously judging me.

In *The Club* we had rules. Not that they were enforced or anything, because they weren't. Murder was not a sport that could be regulated. But that didn't mean we were free of judgment should any of us choose to act recklessly. No one wanted the local authorities sniffing around *The Club's* secrets.

Not even *I* knew all of them—as most of the time we talked in code.

Last week, the dry cleaner in our twisted little group had told us all he'd eliminated a rogue werewolf. We all knew that meant an uncouth hairy man—but the code made it fun all the same.

"It wasn't me," I said simply, adjusting the body over my shoulder as I shouldered my way through the door.

He eyed me critically, clearly amused. "You look very proud of that fact."

"Maybe I am." Felix was a fledgling killer, and not interested in another man, other than to murder him—so that was a win in my book.

Tonight was officially a good night, despite how rocky a start it'd had.

"Where's the boy toy?"

I scoffed, rolling my eyes at the ridiculous nickname. I didn't dignify it with a proper reply however, instead focusing on hefting Felix's kill where it needed to go. "He's in the car."

"You left him in the car?"

"You don't have to sound so *judgy* about it," I huffed, annoyed. "He was crying. He was hungry. I needed to dispose of a body, so I bought him a hamburger. What do you want from me?"

"He was crying…and you left him—"

"With a hamburger."

"With a *hamburger*," Allen repeated slowly like the food aspect of this was odder than the crying. I wasn't sure why he was speaking to me like I was a toddler—as I was probably the size of twenty of them.

"It's not as though I could carry him and the corpse at the same time," I huffed.

Unless…I could?

I squinted thoughtfully, imagining the logistics of *that*. Perhaps Felix could wrap his legs around my waist from the front and I could—No, *no*. Then he'd have a face full of trash-bag-covered body. That was not ideal for anyone involved.

"What do you want from me, Allen?" I huffed, dumping the body on the table and brushing my hands off. "Because *clearly* you have something to say."

"I'm just saying…" Allen continued to speak to me like I was stupid.

"That it's an odd way to comfort someone. To leave them…alone—in the woods—crying, with a *hamburger.*"

Why was Allen so concerned about Felix?

My eyes narrowed. Allen rolled his eyes. "I'm not after your man, Marshall—"

"He's not my—"

"I'm just trying to help you."

"I would've added cheese if I knew whether or not he's lactose intolerant."

"How thoughtful of you," Allen deadpanned.

Annoyed, I turned my attention away from the body to him. "He said it was fine." I wasn't about to tell Allen that I'd already given Felix a hug. A hug that lasted a full *thirty seconds.*

"Did he?"

"Yes."

"Well, if he said it was fine, then it's fine." Allen shrugged, staring at me—dead in the eyes—like he was trying to communicate something.

"You're telling me…" I squinted at him, trying to make sense of the look he was leveling at me. "That it's possible despite clearly telling me he was fine…he may…not be fine?"

"Ah." Allen nodded. "So you're not an idiot after all."

I threw my hands in the air. "Why in the world would he say he was fine if he wasn't?" This was not the first time Felix had told me he was "fine." Did I need to be worried? Had he been lying before too? No, no. I didn't think so.

"Because." Allen shrugged, then pinched the bridge of his nose. "Sometimes…people just do that."

"Well that's idiotic."

"Yeah," he laughed, "I guess it is."

"I suppose I should go back to him then?" I hummed, plucking at my clothing—Christ, I liked this shirt. Still, into the fire it would go. I pulled it off, following it with my pants and belt. "And leave you to deal with…" I grimaced, gesturing at the asshole I'd laid on the table. "*Him* on your own?"

"Sure," Allen folded his arms over his barrel chest, watching me with an annoying twinkle in his gaze, like he knew something I didn't. "So…you ask blondie out yet?"

"Why is everyone suddenly so interested in my love life?" I lamented as I shucked off my boxers and socks, then added them to my pile.

"Because you've never had one before," Allen told me, wandering around behind me like an annoying, bearded gnat. I headed toward the shower in the back. I hadn't used it the last time I'd been here—because it had felt rude to get naked while Felix was in the room—ah.

Oh.

Oh.

Perhaps I was more obvious than I'd realized.

Completely naked, with my hands on my hips, I stared unseeingly at the shower.

"I think…" I blinked, swiveling around. Allen shielded his eyes, purposefully looking away from my swinging dick. *Odd.* He had one of his own, why was he so frightened of mine? I shoved the thought aside, as I actually had less than zero interest in how Allen reacted to my cock. "I maybe…*perhaps*…*like* Felix."

"You think?"

"Maybe."

"Do you maybe, *perhaps*," he was mocking me, I could tell, "think you should hurry the fuck up then?"

"Ah." I blinked, frowning. "Right."

I had never showered faster in all my life.

When I returned to the car, Felix had not eaten his hamburger. Maybe he'd wanted cheese after all? Frowning, I slid into the driver seat, twisting to look at him. His expression was oddly blank, his cold food sitting in his lap, resting in a pile of plucked apart wrapper pieces.

Pluck, pluck, pluck went his fingers, decimating the paper even further.

He wasn't crying anymore.

I kind of missed it.

"You don't like hamburgers?" I offered in place of a greeting, Allen's voice still in my head. "My sister, Alberta, told me once that there's nothing that can't be healed by a cheeseburger."

"She did?" Felix didn't look at me, his voice hollow as he continued to pick.

"Was she right?" I asked, my heart pounding.

There had been one thing a cheeseburger couldn't fix. Death was resistant to all carbs. Alberta would know.

Felix twisted to look at me then, a soft smile on his lips. I'd been so certain he was devastated, sitting here alone, but the look on his face now was nothing of the sort. His eyes were warm, a deep sadness resonating inside them, but mirth twinkled there too.

I had the oddest feeling I'd never really looked at Felix Finley before.

My belly flipped.

"She was." Felix hadn't touched his burger, therefore he was *lying*. It just…took me a second to figure out why.

Felix lied, not because he was dishonest—but because he wanted me to feel like I had been useful. He lied because *somehow* he seemed to know that I had done my best to comfort him, lack of cheese and all. He lied… because he *cared* about me.

At least—I hoped he did?

I sucked in a breath.

"I looked at the stars on the way back," I told him, my voice as soft as his was. I didn't know how to flirt. So I wasn't sure that's what this was— only that it felt fluttery and soft, and my heart was racing.

The beast inside me wagged his tail.

"Did they explode?" Felix's lips quirked up.

"Not yet," I replied.

We were ridiculous. This was ridiculous. I couldn't stop smiling.

"*Pity*," he joked. At least, I thought he was joking. I'd never been very good at telling.

I couldn't contain my snort—probably more startled by the sound than Felix was. *When was the last time I laughed like this?* I couldn't for the life of me recall. My heart felt *fluttery*, the realization I'd come to when talking to Allen buzzing beneath my skin.

I like him.

It was a secret that had nothing to do with murder, and yet, was the most frightening thing I'd ever kept quiet.

I like him.

I'd had a lot of secrets throughout my life. And yet, I'd never been more tempted to spill them all than I was right then, sitting in the dark, with

Felix's eyes on mine, only the trees outside our windows for company.

If I laid all my cards on the table, perhaps it would give me a chance. A real one. Not one that I'd fostered and molded—manipulated into place. Not a card trick, an illusion. Not a game to win or lose or cheat.

Not entertainment.

Perhaps…if I told the truth…Felix might see me as a good bet.

I love stars, they're steady, constant.

Until they explode.

"Do you think they will?" Felix asked, his voice quiet, reverent. His eyes were on my lips. I had never been more tempted, in all my life, to kiss another person. To touch him. To see if he tasted as good as he smelled. "Explode, I mean."

"Maybe." My pulse raced as I stared at him. Stared at the mole beneath his eye. Stared at his lovely, red irises—there was *no way* those were real. Stared at where the roots of his hair were growing back in, ebony black, stark against his pale, alabaster skin.

We were opposites in so many ways.

He was shaky where I was solid.

But like a well-oiled engine, perhaps we worked because of those differences, and not despite them.

"Why'd you do it?" I asked him, my heart thumping.

"Kill him?" Felix frowned, expression pensive, those lovely pink lips flattening into a tight line. I wasn't surprised he'd jumped to that conclusion, as we had just traveled all the way across our sleepy town to dispose of a body.

"No." My hands were sweaty. I didn't think they'd ever *been* sweaty before. Not even when I'd been about to execute my first kill. Not when

I'd graduated high school and I'd searched the crowd for Dad—only to find out later he hadn't come because Mom had just died. Not when I crashed our truck into the cow field—and had to fess up before we lost the cattle through the gap in the fence. Not when we'd moved to the city and the world had been different, different, different. Not when I'd gone to the bar looking for Alberta that night—and found her, but quickly wished I hadn't.

"Why did you…" I tried again.

"Did I?" Felix tipped his head back, leaning against the headrest. His chin tilted to meet my gaze. He was half my size. Maybe less than that— and yet…he felt so very *large* tonight. As large as the stars he loved so much. Radiant, flickering—and as constant as he said they were.

"Why did you come to the party?" I licked my lips. My heart was *thumping* so loud I wouldn't be surprised if he could hear it—especially when his gaze snapped to my throat. "Why did you dress up to match me? You've never come to one of Barry's awful parties before. So why…then?"

It may not have seemed like a big deal, but it was to me.

I had a hard time fitting in, even when I got the memo about stupid block party themes. Struggling socially wasn't new. It was something I'd dealt with since I was a child. I was used to it, to the point that I'd spent many of my growing years researching meticulously how exactly to fit in—just because I was sick of sticking out like a sore thumb.

Every choice I made was carefully cultivated to make me appear more palatable. Every last detail. I knew the colors I needed to wear to be seen as trustworthy—pastels. What haircuts were in fashion. What clothing choices were respectable—flashy but not too flashy. Expensive, but not gaudy.

Years of research, of struggling, of masking who I was behind designer cologne and Italian loafers.

All in a desperate ploy to be likable.

To be disliked was to be observed.

That's what I'd told myself.

I told myself that I still acted on my childish urges to fit in, not because I cared, but so that I could go unnoticed. So that I could get away with murder.

But…that was a lie.

The truth was—I cared, not because of my bloody hobby, but because at age thirty-eight, I was so…damn *tired* of not fitting in. I hated people, yes. Hated them with a burning passion. They were fickle, rude, callous, and superficial.

But I was still human.

And humans, by nature, are pack animals. Humans crave social structure. Cooperation and collaboration. Social bonds. Communication. Friendship. Connections. To be…liked.

Which was *why* I'd bought the damn Hawaiian shirt in the first place. Despite hating Barry (the bastard) with a burning passion—and therefore more willing to hit him with my car than attend one of his ridiculous soirees.

I'd wanted to fit in.

And then he'd fucked me over.

Beach Town was small. It was very easy to become shunned without even knowing it. I mean—look at Felix. I didn't think I'd ever seen someone deliver him a casserole when he was sick, or offer to fix his flat tire.

Barry sent him invites to his parties once a year—but that was because Barry was an attention-whore who had a hard-on for sticking flyers on other people's doors.

Aside from that, Felix was very much alone.

I had always wondered if his exile was self-imposed, or if he'd done something before I moved in that turned him into the floppy-hatted social pariah he was. But if that was the case…why not just move? There were plenty of other creepy-goth-houses he could hoard his collectibles inside.

Not that I wanted him to move of course, because I did not.

I supposed…there were a lot of things about him that made me curious.

More things than didn't, if I was being honest.

When he'd shown up to that party last summer in his ridiculous orange shirt he'd changed me. I'd had my heart welded shut for as long as I could remember. Bolted, locked. Impenetrable. And yet…as Felix lingered beside the giant ten-tiered cake Barry had bought, and gave me a single, solitary, nod in solidarity—I could feel the bolts begin to slip loose.

My fascination with him had only grown after the conversation we'd shared all those weeks ago. When I'd shown him a glimpse of my monster, and he hadn't balked.

Would you cry if he had deserved it?

Would you feel bad?

No…I…don't suppose I would.

He'd awoken the beast inside me by offering it his belly, and I didn't know how to turn it off.

It was a miracle that I hadn't realized what was happening.

Not until tonight.

Not until Allen and his damn observations.

Not until I'd given Felix a comfort hamburger—and he'd told me it worked.

Felix was staring at me. I wasn't sure how much time had passed. Once again—I'd lost myself when I was beside him. Swallowing the lump in my throat, I continued to wait for the answer to my questions.

I could be patient.

Goddammit answer me, you tiny, beautiful bitch.

"Finley?" My heart continued to pound.

"I saw the new note on your door." Felix's voice was quiet when he spoke. He chose his words carefully. His head still leaned against the headrest. His face had remained tipped to look at me all this time. Apparently he could be patient too.

"I didn't know what you'd end up wearing to the party but on the off chance you hadn't seen Barry's costume adjustment, I…" Felix sucked in a breath, shaking his head to clear it. "I…know what it's like to be ridiculed. *Before*—" I imagined he meant his life before he'd moved here. "I…would often hear things. Empty observations about me—lies, speculation. People can be incredibly unkind, even the people that claim to love us."

His lips flattened, his eyes dark as he gazed out into the empty woods in front of us. Overhead the clouds opened up, pouring rain down upon us and blocking out our stars.

"I didn't want to leave you *alone*. It is the *worst* feeling in the world—" Felix added, his eyes a lifetime away. "To stand in a room of people and feel like an outsider." His lips tipped up into a sad little smile. "I've often wondered if I would've made some of the choices that I did—if I'd had someone who stood beside me. Perhaps I never needed the world to love me, but just one…single person. Maybe that would have been enough." There was sadness in his eyes. I'd noticed it before, but it was even more apparent now. "I am only one man, but I thought if I could save you that torment, I would."

Without thinking, I reached out, grasping his chin in my hand and forcing him to look at me. It was the second time I'd done that today, but I couldn't seem to help myself. "You talk as though your story ended in tragedy."

"I thought it had," Felix said, then his lips tipped up into a soft smile.

His eyes said, *until you.*

And my heart answered with a steady *thump, thump.*

His eyes bore into mine, making me feel shaky and young, and desperate.

"So, you left your tower to save me." It was a joke, but it didn't feel like one.

"I did." Felix laughed, and it was the prettiest thing I'd ever heard.

I wanted him to do it again.

So I did something I hardly ever did.

I joked. "My night in floral armor."

Felix snorted, eyes crinkling in amusement, his skin so very soft beneath my fingertips. Once again I marveled at how easy it would be to crush him—and how that very fact made me want to protect him instead.

"We were pariahs, all the same," I added, licking my lips. When he licked his own, mirroring me unintentionally—probably—I nearly groaned.

"But at least we were pariahs together," Felix murmured, his voice buzzing my fingertips.

I knew I should let him go, but I didn't.

"That is better, isn't it?"

"It is," Felix agreed. I jerked, surprised when I felt his chilly fingers curling in the hem of my shirt. A beat passed. A beautiful moment where suddenly the stars were close, and the forest was friendly. The cicadas continued to chirp. The rain that pattered on the windows was muffled through the glass.

Heat simmered between us.

"Allen says that cheeseburgers are not a proper way to comfort someone," I blurted because I didn't know what else to say.

I never want this moment to end.

"Does he?" Felix murmured back, his lips nearly brushing my palm. God, he looked delicious pressed against the leather seats of my Mercedes, like he belonged in luxury. Like a king. Regal.

"He says that you could've been lying when you said you were fine earlier." I swallowed the lump in my throat. "So…" I felt like a jerky, awkward teen again. "Were you?"

"Was I lying?"

"Yes."

I hadn't realized how much his answer meant to me till I watched his brow furrow—and his lips twist. "No, Marshall." Relieved, I couldn't stop my grin. "That would be idiotic." Felix laughed.

I wanted to *taste* that laugh.

Christ.

He was heavenly.

"That's what I said!" I chuckled, releasing him, my palm tingling where his lips had brushed it. I settled back into my seat, pulling us back out onto the road from where we'd been hidden in the trees. My thoughts were, however, not on the road. Not on the stars above. Not on the body I'd left behind with Allen.

No.

All I seemed able to think about was Felix's lips, and what they might feel like—not against my palm—but pressed to my own.

I carried that thought with me all the way home.

Chapter Eight

I THOUGHT I wouldn't see Felix again until our date. I was wrong. Very wrong. Because Thursday night, he came to my rescue once again, my tiny Prince Charming. Not that I necessarily needed rescuing, as I probably could've saved myself quite easily.

But still.

I was detailing my car while parked in the driveway, bent over the front seat, vacuuming my cup holders when the anti-Christ himself decided to appear. The sun was setting, dipping behind the trees—which was why I felt the pressure to finish up before night truly fell.

What if Felix murdered another guest tonight? Or! Wanted to visit me? I couldn't be busy if that happened.

"Marshall Warden," Barry (the ballsack) addressed me.

I'd recognize that voice anywhere. Because I hated it more than I hated picnics and pop music combined. And that was saying a lot. It was grating and simultaneously too high and too low—and Barry always sounded like he was trying to speak two octaves lower than his natural voice, because he hoped it would make him sexy.

It did not.

It made him sound like a buffoon.

"Barry." I didn't use his last name. I didn't know it. I'd made a point *not* to know it. Out of rebellion. And every time someone said it—I mentally plugged my ears and sang *La La La.* Not knowing Barry's last name gave me the opportunity to give him new and more accurate names every time I thought of him.

"Are you going to the carnival?" Barry asked, without so much as a "how do you do." My mother would've found him repugnant. I knew that for a goddamn fact.

"Maybe." I hated him at my back, almost as much as I hated him at my front. God, he was ruining *everything.* If he didn't hurry the fuck up I wasn't going to finish cleaning my car—and then I'd have to do it tomorrow and I couldn't do it tomorrow because I was going on a date with Felix—and—

"We're looking for volunteers for the dunk booth."

Oh lord no. *No, no, no.*

What had I done to deserve this torture?

Oh.

Right.

Fuck.

"Barry, with all due respect, I don't have a single article of clothing in my wardrobe that I am comfortable "dunking". I climbed back out of where I'd been bent inside my car, leveling him with my *friendliest—*

fakest grin. "Italian leather, you see." I kicked a leg out.

Go away, go away, go away.

"I'll let you borrow something from me," Barry grinned, not getting the hint whatsoever.

"No thank you."

He frowned, brow pinched, before his expression smoothed. Leaning in close—oh dear god, the man liked garlic—"But, *Marshall.*"

Oh dear god. No.

No.

He was about to say something terrible wasn't he?

He was going to bring out the C word.

The *blasted* C word.

"It's for *charity.*"

I was two seconds from smashing my head through my windshield so I could leave this conversation.

But then…I didn't have to.

"Hi, Barry." Felix's melodic voice popped up behind me. An adorable, exhausted-looking specter. I twisted to look at him, shocked to find him there at all. Glancing around, I realized the sun had set somewhere between Barry "swearing" at me, and accosting me in the first place.

Goddammit.

I wasn't going to finish cleaning my car after all.

That thought quickly fled, however, as my attention turned to Felix. I'm sure my surprise must've been written all over my face, because his lips twitched—like he was trying not to smile.

He looked *lovely* tonight. A soft cashmere sweater in a ridiculous shade of pink. Crisp black trousers. A pair of smart black dress shoes that completed the ensemble. He was gorgeous. Or—he would be—if he'd take off the damn hat and glasses.

My fingers twitched, aching to reach out and yank them off his head so I could see that pretty fucking face.

I must've spaced out staring at Felix, because I missed half the conversation he and Barry had been having. I only tuned back in when Felix turned to me, eyes dancing above the lip of his sunglasses.

"Is that okay?"

"I…what?" I blinked, confused. Felix laughed, eyes crinkling in the way I was growing quite fond of.

"Is it okay if I take your spot in the dunk booth?"

"I…what?" I repeated, brain broken.

"Barry said he already signed you up, because he'd been certain you'd say yes, seeing as it was for charity—and you occasionally work for a non-profit on the weekends." For a moment I was tempted to call bullshit. But then I remembered that I *had* actually told Barry that—one summer nearly five years ago when I'd been heading out to stalk my yearly kill and I'd needed an excuse to be gone for several weeks.

He hadn't bothered me ever since.

Oops.

Don't look at me like that.

I never claimed to be a good person.

Shame on you.

"Right…the non-profit," I agreed numbly. "But I…uh."

Uh, uh, idi-uh-t, I chided myself for stumbling over my words.

"The dunk booth is Friday," Felix was watching me, his tone gentle. "Tomorrow."

"But what about—" I glanced at him, then Barry, grimacing. I'd asked Felix out, but that didn't necessarily mean I wanted Barry to know about it. Not because I was ashamed—but because Barry was actually the worst. The fucking worst. And I didn't want him to know about anything that I did—especially stuff I cared about.

"Why don't you come with me?" Felix was still watching me, and he was acting so…so *sweet*. My chivalrous little gremlin man. His shoulders were squared, his arms tucked into his armpits. His pecs looked especially likable today with his arms crossed. I could see the supple curve of them through the clingy fabric of his oh-so-soft sweater. I kind of wanted to grab them to see how they felt as solid as they looked.

"Okay," I agreed, bitterly aware that we'd been cockblocked. Date-blocked? By Barry of all people. *What an asshole.*

Felix's Adam's apple bobbed, his attention turning from me back to Barry. "So. Is that fine?"

Already, he was leagues more confident than he'd been when we'd been together with Winnie. Like he was finally coming out of his shell.

I was seeing the true Felix, and he was just as gorgeous as his pitiful, needy monster had been.

Barry squinted at him, his permanent sunburn looking ruddier than normal as he scratched his head thoughtfully. He had Hair with a capital H. And by *that,* I meant—he was the kind of man who made his hair his entire personality, despite looking like a toe-thumb.

"You'll take the whole shift I signed him up for?" Barry was eyeing Felix warily, like he wasn't sure what to make of him. Almost like he was… scared of him.

Oh, god.

That made my dick twitch.

Or maybe—what made my dick react was the *look* Felix was giving him. Like he wanted to squash him beneath the heel of his lovely, vintage shoe. *God*, I'd pay good money to see that.

"Absolutely not," Felix's sunglasses slipped down his nose, his gaze threatening. I shivered, observing him with barely concealed lust. "I'll work the booth for an hour—out of courtesy to you and the charity you're working for. You'll have to fill the other three hours."

Barry had been planning on making me work *four* hours in the booth? Goddammit. I had never been more tempted to murder someone.

Don't shit where you eat, don't shit where you eat, don't shit where you eat.

"But—"

"No buts," Felix's gaze was positively chilly. "You didn't ask for Marshall's consent before signing him up. That was *incredibly* inconsiderate. This is your problem. *You* fix it. I think taking an hour shift—considering the fact that you were the one that was rude in this situation—is more than enough."

Barry's glare was not nearly as pretty as Felix's.

"Fine," Barry frowned as he stepped away from the hood of my car. Victory tasted like Felix's shampoo. Especially when I leaned down to surreptitiously sniff him as he twisted to glare at Barry all the way off the property.

My rabid little chihuahua man.

The awful squeak of Barry's flip-flops echoed through the otherwise peaceful night as he made his way back down the street, past the park, past the picture perfect houses, toward his evil lair at the end of the block.

I only watched him until he was out of ear shot, and then I turned on Felix, my hands finding his hips. Rubbing at the cashmere—even softer than it'd looked—I ducked my head low.

"My *hero*," I murmured, breath curling against the shell of Felix's ear. It ruffled his hair and I noted—with surprise—that he'd already bleached away the hint of roots I'd seen the night before.

"I ruined our date," Felix hummed back. We were pressed close enough together that I felt him shiver against me.

God, I wanted to make him do that again.

"You didn't," I promised, hands slipping further back of their own accord. They didn't even feel like my own hands. Especially when they greedily— shyly slid beneath the hem of his sweater to tease at his skin. Even here, it was chilly—chilly as the night air. "I promised we could stay in."

"I know," Felix responded, head tipping back as he looked at me. "But I can do this…for you." He sucked in a breath. "I *want* to do this for you.

"You do?"

"I do."

Now that Barry was gone, I had no qualms left. Not about this.

So I did the thing I'd been aching to do since the first night Felix had come to me for help.

I tore his hat off his head.

Then I threw it as far away from us as possible.

It fluttered to the ground at the other end of my driveway—traveling surprisingly far—but not far enough. It would *never* be far enough. "How many of these fucking things do you have?" I asked, horrified.

Felix was shaking. For a moment, I worried I'd offended him to tears. But when my gaze snapped to his face, my eyes wide with worry—I was assaulted with the prettiest fucking sight I'd ever, in all my life, seen.

Felix was *grinning*. Not a small, happy smile. Not shy. Not polite. Not contained. No. It was wide—and brilliant—brighter than a supernova.

His eyes crinkled, his nose scrunched. Dimples lined the sides of that lovely, expressive mouth—and I was…*oh.*

Oh, my knees were weak.

I leaned hard against my car, letting it take my weight because I was certain if I'd been standing on my own, I'd be on the ground already.

Felix was…so much more than I'd expected.

An accidental killer, a cat wrangler, a crocheting maniac.

A prince. A hero. A man who never wanted others to feel lonely, despite being alone himself.

I'd never contemplated Heaven. Even if it existed—I knew I'd never make it there.

But now I realized that if Heaven was real—

It looked like Felix's smile.

It sounded like his laughter.

And it smelled like lemon soap.

Chapter Nine

"MARSHALL…" MY BOSS'S voice was an unwelcome distraction. Annoyed, I pulled my headphones off, twisting to offer him what I hoped was a simpering grin—and not the glare I wanted to level him with. "Are you watching…" he read the caption of the video on my computer, his brow furrowed in confusion, "ten hours straight of cat sounds?"

"Yes." I stared at him, hands still on my headphones.

"Can I ask…why?"

I squinted at him, unsure why the hell he cared. "Because I hate them."

"You hate…cats. So you're listening to them for ten hours straight?"

Well if he put it like *that* it sounded rather idiotic.

"My boyfriend has two felines. I am simply acclimating myself to their horrible chatter, so that they will not startle me when I am at his home." That wouldn't happen today—fuck you Barry (the buffoon). But at some point in the near future, I would be inside Felix's home again. There would be hair.

There would be claws. There would be *sounds*. I was simply planning ahead.

And also, maybe, making myself feel better that our date tonight had been rearranged.

"You have a boyfriend?" My boss blinked at me, because apparently he wanted to bother me *all day.*

"Why do you look so surprised?" I squinted at him.

"I didn't know you were gay."

"I'm not." My hackles raised as I glared at him.

"Don't look at me like that. I don't care who you sleep with, Marshall. I just…" He cocked his head at me, folding his arms over his rotund belly. "I've worked with you for ten years. And I've never seen you go on a date with anyone. I didn't think you did that."

"If you *must* know, I am demisexual and demiromantic." Thank you, Google.

"I don't know what that means."

"It means, my sexuality is none of your business. Now leave me alone."

"Right," he laughed, eyes crinkling affectionately. Harold was a good boss. He had a tendency to ramble, yes, and he often smelled like Doritos, but he was always fair. Always kind. I didn't like people—but I supposed I didn't hate him. Not as much as I hated most everyone else. "I'll leave you to your cats."

Finally.

Before I could put my headphones back on to torture myself till the end of my shift—and my date with Felix—Winnie texted me. I lamented my life as I pulled my phone out of my pocket, frowning down at it.

Winnie: Don't forget to bring a condom.

A cond—oh. Oh no. We were *not* having sex tonight. We were going to a *carnival.* There would be caramel popcorn, cotton candy, dunk tanks—and screaming *children.* Can you imagine? Sex at a carnival? Too much noise. Popcorn in…crevices that should not be violated with confectionaries. The crowds, the people, the germs.

Absolutely not.

There would be no sex at the carnival.

I would rather die.

Perhaps afterward? But no. No, no. Not then either. There wasn't a lot I felt confident about lately. Seeing as I was now quite committed to someone, despite being sure I would never, *ever* feel this way about anyone. However, I *was* quite certain I wasn't ready for sex. Not without at least kissing first. *Right?* Wasn't there supposed to be some silly sports game that dictated how far you went on each date?

Something about goals.

First date meant first goal.

Not a hole-in-one.

Oh god.

Fuck.

I needed to do more research.

I was not ready for this.

What if Felix asked about the goals? I got the feeling he wouldn't know. I'd never even seen him with a phone out. The man was one of those weird people that barely benefited from modern technology. It was one thing I liked about him—at least…until now.

We could probably kiss—maybe. But if he asked to go further, I'd have to tell him about the dating rules. And if Felix asked me about the goals,

I was going to make a fool of myself.

Why had I not thought of this before?! I spent nearly four hours last night Googling sexualities and the gray-sexual spectrum. And yet, it hadn't even crossed my mind to look up sex itself. Jesus Christ.

Distracted now, I texted Winnie back.

Me: No.

Winnie: Marshall. Safe sex is good sex.

Me: No sex is good sex.

Me: At least…not tonight.

Me: I hate you.

Me: Why are you making me talk about this?

Winnie: I was promised details.

Me: I am horrified. You are horrifying. Horrifying, Winnifred.

Winnie: Look

Winnie: I don't want to know the nitty gritty.

Winnie: But I am concerned you don't know how to properly

date.

Me: Of course I do.

Winnie: …

Me: Did you just send me an ellipsis? Who does that?

Me: You know what…never mind. I don't even care. Don't bring up condoms again or I'm blocking you. I'm serious. I've done it before, and I'll do it again.

Winnie: Okay but joking aside Marshall

Winnie: Even if you're not planning on having sex tonight

Winnie: It's a good idea to bring condoms with you. Stuff happens and the last thing you want to be is unprepared. You're a planner. So plan ahead.

When I unblocked Winnie, I waited until long after I'd driven home from work. Unfortunately, I spent all the spare time I'd alloted in my tight *get-ready-schedule* panicking over what to wear while I wore nothing but socks and stood inside my walk-in closet.

Dinner had been chicken breast and rice, as per usual. And my shower had been molten hot. I scrubbed every last inch of my body till I squeaked. Then brushed my teeth three times just to be sure. Then, and only then, did I unblock my sister.

When my doorbell rang, I was annoyed at first, but only until I saw the gift awaiting me.

An apology gift.

Wrapped, practically luminescent, and perfect. The lovely, colorful box sat on my front stoop with a little bow on the top and a note that read: *Enjoy.*

Now *that* was more like it.

It felt too light to be anything cake-like. Perhaps it was one of the gourmet chocolate bars I liked? Humming to myself, I took my gift inside, shut the door, and pulled the ribbon free with one hand. With the other, I unblocked Winnie and called her. She picked up immediately.

"I take it you got my gift?"

"Yes." I tore through the wrapping paper, and then the tape, giddy. I'd always loved receiving gifts. Almost as much as I hated giving them. It was something my three sisters had always liked to use against me.

"Are you opening it?" Winnie asked on the other end of the line.

"Yes, of course I'm opening it." The tape was stubborn and hard to pull apart, but I managed—tugging at the cardboard with a grumpy, excited hiss—only for the box to tear open violently, spilling everywhere and—

Oh god.

Oh *god.*

"Winnifred Nadeen Warden." I stared in horror at the hundreds of colorful little packages that now covered my usually impeccably clean front walkway like porn confetti. "*Did you send me a gift wrapped box entirely full of condoms?*" Shell-shocked, I didn't even know what to say.

"Fuck you" did not suffice.

Winnie's cackling was so *loud* I was tempted to mute her so I could make it stop. But…my wits were not about me, so I didn't do that. No. Instead, I continued to stand there, staring at the rainbow of condoms like if I waited long enough—if I prayed *hard* enough—they'd disappear.

"Videochat me," Winnie commanded between wheezing guffaws. "Oh god. I wanna see your face *so bad right now.*"

"You are a bad person," I decided, standing in the halo of condoms, my eyes wide. "You are a horrible, bad, no good, awful person."

"I know, I know—" Winnie cackled. "I'm sorry—"

"You're not sorry."

"No." She laughed again. "You're right. I'm not." More cackling. "No glove no love, Marshall!"

I hung up on her then. But it took me a long, painful minute to decide how best to manage the mess that now littered my floor. I didn't want to run late—but my mind was too frazzled right now for me to feel comfortable leaving this…here.

If the date went badly and I came home to a landslide of condoms I would probably combust. So, with an unhappy groan I struggled to my knees—damn you, aging, you dirty bastard—and began to collect the rectangles one by one. All the while, I cursed Winnifred.

"Condom sending, motherfucking shit ass." I shoved handfuls into the box, righteously indignant. If this creased my pants I was going to have an aneurism.

"Goddammit."

By the time I was done, I was running five minutes off schedule—and *panicking* again. Felix was supposed to meet me at the carnival, as he'd be inside the dunk booth when I arrived. Which meant, he was probably already on his way.

I was going to watch him *drive*, dammit. I'd put that into my schedule and everything! It wasn't fair. Because of Winnie and her damn prank I had missed out on some valuable stalking time.

She wasn't getting a Christmas present for five years.

No.

Ten.

Fifteen.

Yes.

That seemed fair.

Because of her I had no idea what car Felix drove.

It. Was. A. *Travesty.*

Oh!

And for her birthday all I'd get her was a gift card to Marshall's. *Take that, you latex-sleeve-gifting-hussy.* Grinning evilly, the perfect revenge in mind, I pocketed a handful of the condoms—just in case (because Winnie was right, I was a planner)—and headed out the front door.

I dodged the pothole at the end of the cul-de-sac, grateful when I passed Barry's awful yellow house and realized his car was still there. I hoped that would mean I wouldn't have any run-ins with him on my date with Felix today—as he'd already ruined enough of our plans.

The sun had sunk below the horizon—the lavender sky peeping between tree trunks and white picket fences as I headed toward the fairgrounds right behind Main Street.

Beach Town was small but cluttered. We had every shop we needed, and then some. The streets were lined with cheery street lamps. And ivy dripped down houses and the lovely mom-and-pop shops that lined the streets.

As I drove, I passed by the building where *The Club* often met. Allen was outside, and he waved at me as I passed. For a moment I worried I'd missed a meeting—but I hadn't gotten the group text about it, so I was certain he must be there on other important business.

Beach Town was exactly the kind of town you wouldn't expect to be filled with serial killers. It was picture perfect from the outside, all sunny smiles, shiny buildings, and community.

I'd done my best to fit in here—as was the purpose of a chameleon.

And I thought I'd done a rather good job.

I didn't hate my work. I didn't hate my boss. I hated my neighbors—but they really only bothered me during the summer. Everyone knew me as Marshall the grump, and I was *fine* with that. I understood them and their need to gossip. I understood how the world worked here, and the social hierarchy inside it—all suburban moms who jogged in the morning, and PTA dads.

What I didn't understand was Felix.

Why he'd moved here when he so clearly didn't fit in.

He was not trying to fly under the radar like I was—unless of course… he was.

More confusing than Felix's decision to live in bum-fuck-nowhere, was the fact that he was so determined to *help* me.

Perhaps he felt he owed me? After I'd helped him.

Or maybe he…liked me.

That thought made me giddy.

Either way, I was just genuinely excited to spend time with him. Which was not a feeling I had ever felt about someone else before.

I didn't understand, but…I supposed I didn't have to.

At the end of the day, why he did what he did was none of my business unless he wanted to share it with me. Until then, I was going to brave the crowds, and do my best to woo him off his pretty—because every part of him was obviously pretty—feet.

Maybe if we went on enough dates he'd be willing to share some of his secrets with me?

A man could dream.

It took me quite some time to find the dunk booth. Not because it was very well hidden or because Beach Town's annual summer carnival was very big (it wasn't), but because I had stepped on a piece of gum on my way through the front gate.

I tried to ignore it for a while, determined to find Felix before he valiantly braved icy water for me—but with every step I took, I could imagine the gum sinking deeper and deeper into the grooves at the bottom of my loafers. I barely managed a few yards before I gave up and bolted back to my car where I kept my wet wipes in the trunk.

When I returned back through the gates of the carnival, ashamed, the teller who had sold me my ticket was *laughing* at me.

I growled at her, and she balked. Her laughter stopped entirely as I marched my way past the ticket selling booth and headed deeper into the crowd. *Served her right.* The fair was so loud. It had too many people. Too many sounds. Too many smells. Too many lights.

Why had I agreed to this?

Because he's doing it for you, my mind helpfully supplied.

Because he saved you.

Because cotton candy, Marshall.

Perhaps…Felix deserved a little loyalty in return. My small inner bitch reminded me that I'd disposed of two bodies for him—and maybe that was enough loyalty, but I quickly squashed that voice down.

The truth was…I *liked* Felix. I had come to terms with liking Felix. I wanted to spend more time with him, and if—my head swiveled, watching a gaggle of teens perform what looked like an odd, jerky mating dance in front of a selfie stick—dealing with *idiots* was the price I had to pay, I would do it.

Grudgingly.

But I'd do it.

When I found the dunk booth I was more than a little shocked to see just how many people had gathered around it. There were at least fifty. Which may not seem like that many—but when your town has a population of five hundred, that's a pretty decent chunk.

Ten percent of the entire population was crowded around the small see-through glass booth that currently housed Felix Finley, a tiny, masculine madman. They were loud, and smelly. Colorful. Distracting.

Fifty whole entire people.

Fifty.

And yet…my eyes were Felix's and Felix's alone.

He looked lovely up there. Which I know is a ridiculous thing to say about someone when they're dressed in a baggy t-shirt with a charity logo that says "Dunk for Fun-k" on it—but it was true. He *was* lovely. So incredibly lovely, even with his damn hat and sunglasses on.

He looked like a douchebag wearing sunglasses at night, but somehow that only made him lovelier.

The stars hung in the sky overhead. They were half blocked by the glittering lights of the ferris wheel that climbed toward heaven, framing him through the glass. It lit his pale hair gold, casting refracting, flickering lights on the icy water that sat at the bottom of the small booth. Above the water, with his short legs dangling, Felix sat on what looked to be a repurposed diving board. Said diving board was connected to a mechanism that ran along the outside of the booth where a rather large—too large, if you asked me—target sat mockingly.

There was a line of people already waiting ten or so feet away from the target. The first in line already had his hands inside the large basket that housed the balls that would be thrown at the target—to inevitably send Felix falling into the icy water below.

I'd appreciated his sacrifice before, of course I had.

But I clearly hadn't appreciated it enough.

Because as I stood there—tall enough I didn't have to crane my neck to see despite being at the back of the crowd—and stared at him sitting prim and proper on his little rickety red diving board, I was struck with an overwhelming rush of *relief.*

The idea of this had been hellish.

The execution was worse.

The fact he'd spared me from it was—*god.*

My heart was racing, my palms slick with nervous sweat. One of my hands gripped tightly to the bouquet of flowers that I'd brought Felix—because I refused to be shown up by a dead man. The thorns from the roses pricked my palm, not hard enough to draw blood—but certainly hard enough that they centered me in the present.

My head was in the stars.

My heart was in that tank with Felix.

The black trousers he wore clung to his muscular, supple thighs like a second skin. He was wearing sneakers that looked far too big for him, and I could only assume they were loaned to him by the booth itself so that he wouldn't have to ruin his own shoes. I hoped there wasn't something dangerous inside the water when he fell—like rusty nails at the bottom—or unfinished edges.

If he got hurt I wasn't sure what I'd do.

Send a very strongly worded email to the city council maybe?

Or cut Barry's head off with a hacksaw.

Both.

Both were good.

When Felix saw me his face lit up. I was so attuned to him now that I could see it, even with his horribly, shoddy disguise in place. A smile flitted across his lips, rapidly growing by the minute—like the clouds that had obstructed it from view were clearing.

He raised a hand just as the first kid in line raised his own. The ball went sailing as Felix waved, the lovely span of his fingers delectable, even from a distance. Behind him, a cheer went up as a roller coaster's passengers took a dive, the rattle of the tracks echoing through the crowded space. I raised my hand in return, high enough he could see—despite the fact I felt like an idiot doing so.

Felix had waved at me once before, that night last winter. I'd ignored him then. And I'd come to regret that choice. Now there was no ignoring him. I waved back, more enthusiastically than I'd waved to anyone before.

I looked like an idiot.

Just as idiotic as the teens I'd run into on my way here.

But I didn't regret the enthusiasm. How could I, when Felix's eyes widened with delight? *Thud, thump.* The first ball missed the target, falling to the grass beneath it.

My heart lurched, and all too soon our little, precious moment was over. A chime rang over the crowd, the *thunk* of a second ball hitting the target square-on, causing a riot of chatter to explode around me. There was a creaking sound, a snap, and suddenly Felix was in the water.

When he popped back out, I wasn't certain what I expected.

But once again, it wasn't what I received.

Apparently, I wasn't very good at predicting things today, because rather than looking contrite, irritated, or ready to murder—as I would—Felix looked…*god*—he looked *happy.*

Brighter than the stars that flickered in the sky above. His smile was riveting, all wide angles and sharp edges—pointy, crooked teeth glistening. When he stood, water cascaded down his lithe form. The t-shirt he wore left absolutely nothing to the imagination. It stuck to his nipples, creasing at his shoulders and chest, highlighting the swell of his pecs and the curve of his supple biceps.

His trousers were no better. They clung to the curve of his cock, wrinkling around it, and making its presence rather obvious. When he pulled the hem of the shirt up—flashing the crowd his flat, pale belly, I nearly shoved my way through them to cover him up.

But I was far too riveted.

There was a dark trail of delicious that led from the hem of his pants upward toward his belly button, and it taunted me as Felix wrung water out of his borrowed shirt, then let it drop back into place. Water droplets tickled down his sculpted forearms into the small pool he stood in.

The water came all the way to his knees, practically drowning him.

Somehow, Felix had lost the hat and the sunglasses.

They floated and sunk, respectively, as he tipped his head back and *laughed.*

I'd never truly believed in God, despite living in a home that went to church every Sunday. My mother had sworn by his grace, and all my life I'd prayed, despite never truly feeling any faith myself.

But in that moment, I *believed.*

Because Felix Finley was so damn beautiful, only a god could've made him.

His eyes found mine, and my stomach squirmed as that *gorgeous* grin was directed my way. There was something familiar about his smile. Like I'd seen it before. Like this wasn't the first time it had caught my attention—but that thought quickly passed.

When Felix's eyes met mine the crowd melted away like they'd never been there at all. It was just us, just the stars, just the long, lovely line of his neck, his dimples, and the water that glistened like jewels on his pale skin.

As quickly as it had come, our moment was broken.

Felix moved out of the way and the diving board snapped back into place. And then he climbed back on top of it, his ass flexing in his wet pants, to start the process all over again.

Over the course of the next hour, up and down, over and over, Felix fell and fell and fell.

And every time he did, he found me in the crowd, he smiled, and he laughed.

Like we were sharing a private joke.

A private moment.

Like we were the only two people here.

I wasn't sure my heart had ever really worked properly, not till that night, with Felix's joy directed at me. For a man that was taking my punishment, he sure didn't seem all that upset. I wanted to know *everything* about him. I wanted to know why he hid behind his hats, why he covered up a face so pretty even the angels would be jealous.

I wanted to know why he killed.

Why he didn't often cry.

Why he cared about me when all I'd ever done was complain about his lawn and accidentally steal his packages.

I wanted to know why he kept cats.

Why he had no repeat visitors.

Why his house was a time capsule.

I wanted to know every last, intimate detail about him.

In my life, I'd often lost interest in things. People were boring, their stories repetitive, their emotions confusing and uninteresting. I learned skills because I needed them and not because I cared. I observed, because to stop was to risk revealing myself.

There was no losing interest in Felix Finley.

Every time I saw him, I only wanted to know more.

The only other thing I'd ever cared this much about was killing—and that was saying something.

When it was finally time for Felix's shift to be over, I began making my way through the crowd to meet him. A couple, dressed in matching couple shirts—horrendous—blocked my way. Irritated, I tapped my foot at them, waiting for them to move—only to catch the tail-end of their conversation.

"He looks familiar, don't you think?" One of the men asked, clinging like a horny koala to his partner's arm. "Super familiar."

"Huh," the other agreed, a thoughtful frown on his face.

It was odd. I'd had the very same thought. That was the only reason I paused to listen at all—to see if they would have any more relevant, somewhat helpful information. They didn't. Instead, they started talking about clocks—or apps—or some other drivel I cared very little about. So I moved on.

Once again, someone got in my way.

"Christ," I muttered, more than a little annoyed. *Could they not see the flowers?* Had they not seen the looks Felix and I had been sharing? It was very obvious where I was trying to go—and yet everyone was determined to get in my way.

"Who is that?" one horribly dressed, brunette woman asked, right as Felix moved out of the little changing booth that was parked next to the dunk tank itself. My eyes were immediately drawn to his damp hair— pushed back and away from his face, and the way the light played across his rather perfect cheekbones.

"My god, it's Felix Finley." The other woman—who wore a pair of khaki overalls and a smart watch she couldn't afford—cackled, clearly delighted. "You know it's odd to see him out like this."

"I've never even seen him before."

"I only recognize him because of Barry's party last summer—"

Jesus god, could I not go a *day* without someone mentioning the damn party? It was like the general population was determined to punish me.

"You know there's rumors about him—"

"Oh, I know."

"They say he never leaves his house."

"I heard he's on the run," The second woman laughed, and I was officially annoyed. Well, I mean, I'd been annoyed before that moment too. I lived in a constant state of annoyance. It was my comfort zone, and I liked it there.

"Excuse me," I said, aiming for pleasant and landing somewheeeere close to murderous. "But I am trying to get through, and if both of you don't shut up I am going to scream."

"Hi, Marshall," both women swiveled to face me, clearly not cowed.

"Goodbye, Marshall, you mean." I waited, foot tapping, flowers still clutched in my hand. Their eyes widened and they both laughed again, glancing at me, then the flowers, then me again.

"Are you here on a date, Marshall Warden?" Khaki woman asked. *Was I supposed to remember her?* Because I definitely didn't.

"I am trying to be," I countered, foot still tapping. Arching a brow, I waited for them to get the hint. Was I being subtle? I didn't think so. I thought the whole *goodbye-Marshall* bit was rather obvious—especially when paired with me very clearly stating that I was trying to get through.

"With who?" Brunette's eyes were wide. She glanced over me, her gaze falling to my chest and the muscle there. She bit her lip, staring rather offensively. "Do I know them?"

"No, but apparently you know *of* him," I was quick to respond, "as you are gossiping about him like a couple of nosy hens."

They laughed, once again not cowed.

Was I not scary anymore?

Was it the sweater vest?

I didn't like this one bit.

"Felix Finley is your date?" Khaki asked in disbelief. "Oh my."

I didn't know what to do. Why weren't they moving? I'd been clear, hadn't I? How much clearer could I be? Steam was practically coming out of my ears as my brain stuttered to an awful, screeching halt.

Once again, I was saved by Felix, because of course I was.

He was my night with a shiny smile, after all.

A chilly hand met my elbow, tucking inside it. It gave me a tight squeeze as Felix easily inserted himself between me and the loud, terrifyingly brave women.

"Is he bothering you?" he teased, voice light, eyes sparkling. I melted, tucking into him immediately—flowers forgotten. I dipped my head down and tried to surreptitiously sniff his lemon-y hair. I knew first-hand just how soft it was—and despite being wet, Felix still smelled like I remembered.

Inhaling greedily, I gave up on being subtle and instead crowded greedily against his side. It felt second-nature to curl over him protectively with my bulk—despite the fact that at the moment, he was the one doing the protecting.

I knew what he was doing.

He was deflecting, working the crowd in a way that I had always known people could do—but never managed myself. Like a politician, or a celebrity. He seemed to know exactly what to say to get what he wanted.

People-wrangling was not a skill I possessed.

I hadn't known he did either.

Till now.

The women laughed, *delighted*. "Oh, that's just Marshall for you," one of them grinned. "Always grumpy."

The other snorted out in delight.

Who in the hell were these people? And how did they know me?

"Do you mind if I steal him?" Felix asked, giving my elbow another squeeze. Like a gentleman, he did not point out the fact that I was sniffing his hair and practically purring. Felix's body felt comforting and cool in my arms—not overstimulating, loud, and *smelly* like the rest of this place.

"Go ahead," the women grinned, ice broken, before turning away from us and finally—*finally*—leaving us alone.

Felix directed me out of the cluster of people who were beginning to disperse—almost like they'd been there to watch him, and him alone— and not the other volunteers at the booth. That in itself was odd. Was the population of Beach Town really that nosy?

Yes.

Yes it was.

Leading me through the crowd, Felix only paused when we found a less populated alleyway between vendor tents. At the end it led to what looked like a giant sheet suspended high in the sky, a movie playing on it. There was a crowd of people lying on blankets clustered beneath it, watching it, enraptured.

When I saw a square-headed grumpy old cartoon man yell at a child to get off his lawn, I recognized the movie immediately.

Without prompting, Felix laughed. Apparently he'd seen what I had. I was so startled by the sound, I jerked a little in his grip. Twisting to get a better look at him, my heart thudded unsteadily as a sunny smile split across his face. I hadn't noticed when—but he'd put his wet hat back on.

The sunglasses, however, remained blissfully in his pocket—or missing, wherever they'd ended up.

He was in a dry t-shirt now, the same kind they'd had him in the booth. It was odd seeing him in something so casual and modern. But I liked it. Maybe a bit too much.

"What are you laughing at?" I asked, more than a little curious.

"That's *you.*"

"What's me?"

"That old man," Felix pointed at the screen—exactly where I'd just been looking. *Flabbergasted*, I stared at him, then the screen, then him again. His eyes were crinkled at the corners, clearly delighted as he teased.

"That—what—" I'd seen that movie. Of course I had. I was unfortunate enough to have nieces and nephews—and this was not the first time I'd been compared to the cranky old man on screen. However, this *was* the first time it made me blush.

My cheeks flushed, and my heart thundered—an odd feeling—but not…unpleasant.

"If you're trying to insult me you've failed. All I see up there is a man who knows how to protect his property." My chest puffed up, pride bursting inside it. "He's a good man," I added, in case Felix hadn't seen the full movie and needed the cliff notes. Felix cocked his head at me. I answered his unspoken question eagerly, "loyal, even after death."

I didn't really understand the look Felix was giving me, but I liked it. In an odd way it felt like…crepes. Complicated. Buttery soft, delicate but hardy enough to hold fruit. Sweet, doughy. Powdered and covered in sugar.

"You're old-fashioned," Felix said.

"Is that a bad thing?"

"No. Not at all." Felix's small, secret smile as he turned back to the movie, felt like a prize I'd won. Bigger even, than the stuffed creatures that hung above the game booths we'd walked past. When he gave my elbow another squeeze, and my heart soared. "Quite the opposite."

So he *liked* old-fashioned.

That was nice, right?

Yes.

Yes, it was.

I licked my lips, cheeks still burning as I imagined what *that* might be like. A traditional life with my non-traditional hermit husband. Our children could be his cats. I would resent them, quietly, but buy them Pedigree cat food. On the weekends I'd mow our lawn and prune our garden. At night we'd dance beneath the stars beside the grill that sat on our back deck.

I'd feed him, *anything* to make him happy.

He'd crochet gifts for my sisters for Christmas, and they'd laugh and giggle when they saw what delightful things he'd come up with. We'd share stories beneath his telescope—look up at the stars, and wonder what was beyond them.

I'd go to work. My coworkers would ask me what I'd done for the weekend—and I'd tell them "nothing" but secretly I'd know that "nothing" with Felix was better than "everything" with anyone else.

Perhaps a little less traditional, I thought about my...*hobby*. About what that might be like to share with him. I could tell him about Alberta, maybe. Could take him to my hunting grounds. We could write the world's wrongs together. Perhaps he had compulsions of his own—compulsions I was still curious about, but was patient enough not to ask about.

We could go together, stalk our prey together.

The night would be our cloak.

We'd revel in it. The hunt. The victory. The relief, when that itch was finally scratched once again. I'd watch the blood splatter his lovely alabaster skin, and I'd *want* him. I'd want him so badly I wouldn't know what to do with myself.

Felix and I watched the rest of the cartoon movie. We sat on the grass on a blanket I bought. The vendor had been stationed at the back of the group of people that populated the grass. I bought us popcorn—popcorn that Felix pretended to eat, though I didn't understand why he felt the need to lie. *Did he think I wouldn't notice the fact he was throwing the pieces behind him instead of eating them?*

I gave him the flowers, and he flushed—a shy, nervous little thank you, the sweetest reward I could've ever received. You'd think he'd never received flowers from a date before, but I knew that wasn't true. Still though, his reaction made me happy.

The movie was enjoyable, the popcorn too.

As we finished the film, Felix stroked the petals of the flowers I gave him.

When I bought him a new hat—one less *horrifying*, and less wet than the last one—he smiled at me again.

For the first time in my life I knew *why* people spent all their time fantasizing about relationships, about love, about partners and families. I understood why they'd struggle through dating, through the awful Google searches, and the existential crises. Why they'd learn the social cues, the order of the bases—not goals. Because if *this* was at the end of *that*—I could suffer through more dates like this.

And we all know I wasn't suffering.

Chapter Ten

THE REST of the date was…dare I say, fun? At one point, I even ate a funnel cake. Which was something that I'd never had before—as I avoided fairs and amusement parks at all costs. I didn't even allow myself to feel guilty, as for the most part, I ate healthy enough that I could afford to have sweet treats when I decided I'd earned them.

I certainly felt like I had today. Even though Felix was the one that had truly sacrificed, I was still here—in a place I abhorred. Doing something I never thought in a million years I'd enjoy.

Dating.

It was quite good.

The funnel cake, not the date.

Though the date was also good. Very good, actually.

Felix ate nothing—even though I offered and even got him his own plastic fork. Instead, he beamed adorably up at me—all boyish good looks, and bubbly excitement. Like he genuinely couldn't believe how lucky he was to be here. With me. At a carnival, of all places.

No matter what he did, he managed to look out of place, even wearing the new hat I'd bought him, and the t-shirt from the booth. Like there was something *off* about the way he walked, or talked. He was part of the crowd but separate also. Like I'd plucked him straight out of a time machine from the black and white television era my mother had loved.

Felix's eyes *sparkled*.

Like one of those horrible romantic comedies.

He didn't seem to notice the looks we received as he wandered around, playing games—germ factories, the lot of them, thank God for hand sanitizer—and dodging gaggles of teens and gossiping moms that wore matching running shoes.

Felix was *good* company.

My first impression of him when we'd gone body dumping had been that he talked too much. But I found now, as he chattered at me about how lovely the rides were—and "oh, gosh, Marshall, look how swell that stuffed dinosaur is!"—that I had been wrong.

He didn't talk too much.

In fact, I wished he'd talk more.

Every time I tried to pry sneakily into his past he'd casually sidestep the questions. It was fun. Even more fun than the funnel cake and seeing him drenched and sparkling had been.

Which was saying a lot, because…*wow*.

I didn't think I'd ever seen anything as pretty as Felix dripping wet, with his blond hair pushed back, and his eyes shining red. Contacts again. I was certain of it. I'd Googled it and I was quite certain that shade could not be natural. It wasn't as though he could have color changing eyes.

Ha!

What a ridiculous notion.

Almost as ridiculous as the fact that I heard the word *vampire* muttered at us at least five different times as he wandered through the nosy crowd. I hated everyone here. I hated the noises, the sounds, the lights. I hated the way the smell of popcorn and frying oil cluttered my nose and blocked out the pine needle scent that had drawn me to Beach Town in the first place.

There were a lot of things I hated.

But I didn't hate Felix Finley.

Maybe I never had.

At one point, I'd paid a good chunk of change so that Felix could play one of the stupid games that populated the fair. It was one of the ones where you had to throw rings over bottles. He was surprisingly good at it, and ended up winning a fat cat stuffed animal that's eyes were slightly too far apart. He clung to it tight, before ultimately giving it over to me so that he could play more games.

I didn't even complain, either.

Because he'd been so *damn cute*, cackling like a maniac as he tossed the rings. I'd been unable to even blink for fear of missing a single moment.

After each game he played, Felix reached over, gently stroking a finger over the cat's derpy face with a fond smile. He'd tip his head up so he could see me better, and though his eyes were shadowed, blocked by the brim of the baseball cap I'd bought him, they were bright.

I much preferred this cap to the floppy monstrosity he normally wore. Mostly because I could see his ears better.

God, they were cute ears.

I'd never thought that about someone else's ears before, but at this point I wasn't surprised.

Felix was my supernova. A phenomenon that was so bright it blinded, but rare enough one may never see one, in all their life.

We stayed till they turned the rides off, and the last dregs of the once thriving crowd began to wander toward the exit gates. Felix and I were one of the last couples left. We lingered at the back as the few remaining guests gathered their belongings, prizes, and leftover popcorn in hand before heading home.

Felix's hand was cool inside my own—warmer now than it had been when I'd first taken it, almost like he was leeching heat from me rather than exuding his own.

It was odd, but I didn't question it. Not when his skin felt so good against my own. Not overstimulating the way most people felt. If I was Goldilocks, then he was *just right.*

A couple walked in front of us, their fingers laced together like ours were. They grinned at each other, walking so close they might as well be one person.

"What are your views on marriage?" Felix asked me out of the blue, staring at the couple just like I had been. I hadn't expected the question, so it took me a second to respond. Glancing down at him—having to crane my neck, he was so short—I frowned.

"What do you mean?"

There was clearly something on his mind. He'd had fun too, I could tell—but there was always this...*distance* between us. Perhaps this was what had been bothering him?

He had his secrets.

I'd asked him out, despite the fact he didn't leave his house hardly ever. Maybe he worried I wasn't...serious?

"Would you ever get married?" Felix asked, his eyes searching mine, his hand still clutched protectively in my own. He felt so...small. Despite this, the presence he had was unmistakable. Confident. Like he knew exactly who he was—though he hid it away from prying eyes. "Not everyone nowadays wants that."

"No," I scoffed immediately, shaking my head. Marriage was not something I had ever contemplated. Even though the fact that I was a thirty-eight-year-old single man was apparently *appalling* to some people—people who did not hesitate to comment about it. But then...*then*...I stopped thinking about *those* people. I stopped thinking about the unwelcome questions, the judgmental looks. The dating apps. The strangers. The people who would ruin my home's carefully cultivated ecosystem.

Instead, I thought about Felix.

His eyes had clouded over—the lovely swell of his lower lip and the dip at his throat both looked particularly soft. I licked my lips, heart racing.

"*Yes*," I amended my statement, voice rough. "With the right person. Maybe."

All the while, I was completely unable to stop staring at the lovely splotchy flush that blossomed across Felix's throat—reacting to my words like he knew *exactly* who I'd been thinking about.

Felix shuffled forward, and I reacted immediately, willingly following his lead. The smile he offered me in exchange for my obedience was ridiculously sweet. The look in his eyes was so full of longing it made me ache.

Felix knew he was my exception.

It was written all over his face.

"What about you?" I asked, suddenly anxious to hear his answer.

"About…me?" He played it cool, and I glared at him till he laughed.

"Would you ever marry?" I reiterated, waiting eagerly for his response—though I did my very best not to look like it. His hand remained clutched in mine, the stupid cat stuffed animal tucked beneath my other arm.

Felix was quiet for a long, long time.

Long enough we passed through the gates that led to the carnival. Long enough that we had time to walk the path that led round the property to the parking lot. There was a…melancholy expression on his face. It was an expression I didn't truly understand, though I recognized it.

It reminded me of my father's face after my mother had died. As though Felix was mourning me before I'd even died.

Once again, I felt the distance between us keenly.

What was he thinking about?

There was a puddle in the way, probably from the rain shower that had splattered the crowd a few hours before I'd arrived. I'd been caught in it on my way home from work and was grateful when it passed. However, puddles were inevitable. This was a large one, and Felix had tiny legs.

Without thinking, I picked Felix up and carried him over it before setting him back on solid ground as though nothing had happened. The cat remained tucked safely in my grip.

Felix stared at me for a beat, obviously shocked and delighted by the manhandling. *Had no one ever picked him up like that before?* I'd have to make a habit to do so more.

Finally, when the parking lot came into view, Felix finally answered my question. His voice was sweet as honey and buttery smooth.

"I would marry," he said sadly, his hand once again tiny and perfect tucked inside my own. My heart fluttered, but my stomach swooped.

I didn't know what *that* tone of voice meant.

I wasn't sure I wanted to.

It wasn't rejection—but it wasn't…well, it wasn't good either.

"But I don't think that's in the cards for me," Felix tipped his head back, staring up at the stars as his lips twisted into a sad, flat line.

His declaration was so inaccurate I nearly scoffed, thinking he was joking at first. He didn't look like he was joking, however. And…I realized he was *serious*. For whatever idiotic reason, Felix—the actual embodiment of sunshine—thought he was not…worth committing to.

Was it because of the murders he'd committed?

As always, my mind immediately went to the bloodiest option.

No, no. That didn't seem…quite right.

There was something else there.

Something I didn't understand yet, but I wanted to.

"I think it is," I grunted. He'd made it clear how little he liked prying, so I wasn't about to push his buttons, not when he'd given me more than he'd probably intended to already. Not when the gravel crunched beneath our feet, quiet and unobtrusive. Not when he was holding the flowers I'd bought for him. And not when I had hope that perhaps…*perhaps* I'd kiss him tonight. Here, surrounded by trees, stars, and the empty parking lot.

The secrets were piling up. The pile growing taller and more wobbly by the second.

One day, they'd all come tumbling down like a fucked up game of Jenga.

They'd spill on the floor, just like the condoms Winnie had sent me.

I'd see him for what he truly was behind the masks, behind the deflection.

Every part of him would be mine.

The pieces he was ashamed of. The pieces no one else had ever known. The parts that made him vulnerable and soft. The parts that made him human.

I'd see him, and maybe, when he knew how easily I bore his weight he'd realize how badly he needed me to do so.

He'd had a lot of opportunities recently to show me his strengths, but at the end of the day there was no forgetting that Felix was a deeply unstable person. I'd seen beneath his skin. Seen how pitiful and wretched he was. Brittle, broken, scared.

He *needed* to be loved.

I wanted to hold his secrets.

I wanted to keep him safe.

"I'm glad you think so," Felix laughed, and I jolted, unsure why he'd found my reassurance that he was marriageable—god, that did not feel like a word—funny of all things. He should've been *relieved*, right? Or happy? Not…*amused.*

An owl hooted, hidden somewhere in the line of trees that reached scraggly and dark above the parking lot.

I wasn't sure what the next socially acceptable thing to do would be.

Quick, do something romantic, Marshall.

Food was romantic, right?

I should give him more food.

He *had* to be hungry.

If I went more than six hours without eating, my stomach started to eat itself. He was small. Way too fucking small. Did he cook? He needed someone to cook for him.

Does he like chicken? God, I hope so. That's the only thing I know how to make.

Brow furrowed, I offered Felix the last of my bucket of cotton candy.

He shook his head, but gave my hand a squeeze instead of taking the treat. "No thank you," Felix said softly. "I'm full."

Full of shit.

He hadn't eaten *anything* all night.

I struggled with the container, trying to get it open without dropping his cat. Then I popped a bite into my mouth, chewing it pointedly in his direction with one of my brows arched.

Felix's laughter once again echoed through the night. This time was louder than before, less masked. I could tell the difference. I could recognize it in the way his shoulders relaxed, in the way his throat bobbed, in the crinkle at the corner of his eyes and the way his dimples appeared.

The distance between us began to close, inch by inch.

There were only a handful of cars left in the parking lot. Mine was at the edge because I didn't mind walking, and despite running late, I hadn't trusted the plebeians that populated Beach Town not to scratch it. The people who parked at the back of the lot tended to be more careful, they gave more space.

"Where are you parked?" I glanced around, eager to see what car Felix drove—only to be—oh.

Oh.

Completely fucking stalled when he gently tugged me toward a vintage 1955 Studebaker Lark. It was…Jesus god, it was gorgeous. I'd always been a car guy. It was one of the things I'd inherited from my dad, along with my appreciation for sweater vests and my general hate for any and all people.

"This is yours?" I dropped my cotton candy bucket, pressing close to the vehicle with hearts in my eyes. "It's…"

"Pretty, right?" Felix hummed, voice obviously pleased. I twisted to look at him in disbelief.

"*Pretty* is what you'd call a chapel, or a potluck table at a barbecue. *Pretty* is for the flowers I gave you—or a newborn calf standing for the first time." I scoffed. "This is not *pretty*. This is…wow. This is *gorgeous*."

"Gorgeous?" Felix repeated, obviously amused at my expense again.

Shithead.

"Majestic."

I couldn't even be mad because apparently Felix was gorgeous and had a gorgeous car—and wow. Yes. Yes, yes, yes.

I'll marry him, I decided suddenly, thinking back on his recent question.

If I got this car in the bargain, I'll marry him tomorrow.

"Marshall," Felix laughed, leaning against the vehicle, his head tipped so I could see beneath the shadow cast over his eyes. They almost seemed to glow even in the dark, maybe especially then. I knew it was my eyes playing tricks on me—as I was currently half blind after witnessing one of the Seven Wonders of the World.

"What?" I asked, though I was paying more attention to the frankly magnificent shade of turquoise the exterior paint coating the car was.

"Would you like to drive it?"

Yes.

Yes.

I was marrying Felix.

I was marrying him, secrets be damned.

Chapter Eleven

I DIDN'T KISS Felix. And I didn't get to use the condoms Winnie gave me. Not that I was ready for that, as we've already established. They sat in my pocket, a silent promise that while *tonight* was not the night, someday…it would be. The thought should've frightened me—because it was new, and scary, and foreign—but it didn't.

It felt right.

As right as Felix had in my arms the first time I'd held him and the monster inside me had opened its eyes.

The weight of the unused condoms was almost soothing. It was a reminder that we would have more nights like this. That the tragedy Felix thought his life was, wouldn't come to be. The clouds opened up above us, blocking out the stars, and rain poured down on the night-black roads. Ignoring the rumble of thunder, and the shimmery slick reflections that danced on the quiet streets, Felix and I sped through town late into the night.

The rain fell and fell and fell.

Lightning flared along the treetops.

Felix took off the hat I'd bought him. He tipped his head back against the headrest like he'd done in my car. He didn't speak. Just closed his eyes, and relaxed in the silence. When the torrent of rain softened, he rolled the window down—manually with the lever on the door.

I pulled to a stop at a red light, my mouth dry as I took the opportunity to watch water droplets slip through the open window and decorate his ivory skin.

He was porcelain perfect, like a doll almost.

Angelic, even at times like this.

Times that should've been ordinary, but weren't. It was only Friday. It was only rain. But it was…more than that too. Felix elevated everything he touched. The more I looked at him, the more certain I was that I'd never tire of those soft, sweet lips. Never tire of the shadows beneath his eyes, or the little mole beneath his eye—the one I *really* wanted to kiss.

Felix's dark roots hadn't grown back in, but the nearly black shade of his brows made it obvious, even now, that blond was not his natural color.

It suited him, but I couldn't help but wonder what he'd look like without the bleach. Would the raven-esque strands make him appear paler than he already did? Or would they lend his milky complexion color?

Why dye his hair at all? Was it another part of his disguise?

Felix was so *still* as he listened to the rain.

Deathly still.

So still, if he'd been lying inside a casket he would have looked at home.

His chest didn't move, and no breaths slipped from his lips as he remained relaxed against the vintage leather of his frankly fantastic car.

He fit in more here than he had at the fair. More than he did even in his own home. There was something about this car that rang…*true* somehow.

Once again, I got the feeling that I was missing something.

Something vital.

But…as I stole glances to the right, memorizing the way the flashes of thunder lit him up—I realized I didn't care. I didn't care about the murder. I didn't care about the secrets, the rumors, or the fact I'd never wanted someone before.

I wanted Felix.

I wanted him so badly there was nothing I wouldn't give to have him.

My sanity included.

When Felix finally opened his eyes, *relief* flooded my body. It wasn't that I'd actually thought he'd died while sitting in the passenger seat. It was just reassuring to know he hadn't?

For a man that often fantasized about death, I was sure frightened of Felix's.

I knew better than anyone how quickly a life could end.

Intimately, even.

I decided then, as I watched his lips curl into a soft smile, his pointy teeth flashing—that I would rather die than let something bad happen to Felix. *He was mine.* He just…maybe didn't know it yet.

And at the end of the night, when we returned to the parking lot to split ways, I didn't kiss him even though I wanted to.

I didn't kiss him because, though I knew I wanted to keep him, I didn't know how exactly to make that happen yet. I wasn't ready for the physical side of a relationship. Tonight had been a dream, really truly, even before I'd driven the car of my fantasies. Tomorrow, the cold harsh reality of my inexperience would come rushing back in.

I'd do more research.

I'd plan better.

I'd continue to carry these condoms and maybe—one day—when I was ready, we'd need them.

Over the course of the next few weeks, I spent a frankly obscene amount of time on porn websites. Yes. Me. Marshall Warden, the proudly self-proclaimed prude—was watching porn. And not just a little of it—no. No. I was watching so much that when my office got pizza delivered on a particularly busy Friday, I immediately reached for the mace in my desk, ready to fend off the delivery boy should it be necessary.

It wasn't.

But still.

When I closed my eyes I saw dicks behind my eyelids.

So. Many. Dicks.

It was horrifying.

Porn was ridiculous. It really was. I didn't understand why people seemed able to just…walk into a room—in this case, on set—look at another person, and immediately want to tear their clothes off. I had never felt that about *anyone*. In fact, most of the time when I saw people out in the wild I wanted to put more clothes on them, rather than take them off.

I'd never looked at someone and thought about *fucking* them.

At least, until now.

I tried that a few times, during periods of research, putting myself in the shoes of the "characters" I was watching on screen. I *wanted* to understand. And I figured the best way to do that was to expose myself, the same way I'd exposed myself to cat sounds. Perhaps if I became desensitized, I wouldn't look like a fool when the time finally came to share physical intimacy with Felix?

That was the plan anyway.

And the plan went awry rather quickly.

On the first night, actually.

Sitting at my desk in my home office that first time the night after the carnival, with a water bottle and an aspirin—should the sounds prove irritating—I prepared to become a new man. I had a few weeks before our next date—Felix was once again acting *cagey* and like his social calendar was quite full, so I had time. I had tissues on hand—not because I intended to masturbate, but because I always had tissues at my desk. Because I was a planner, like Winnie had said, and even planners needed tissues.

Unfortunately, when I imagined fucking my fake stepmom, the delivery man, or the mechanic that worked on my car—instead of having a positive physical reaction, I became violently uncomfortable.

This was clearly not working, so I switched tactics.

I thought about Felix.

And *well*, that was a different story.

The idea of Felix without clothing made something shivery and needy awake inside me. The thought of unbuttoning his trousers made my breath unsteady. Heat coiled in my belly, my cock twitching to life.

I could free his cock. The one I'd—maybe—stared a bit at during the carnival, bare. Slick. Pink. See just how big it was in real life. Touch the silky skin and watch his face scrunch with pleasure. Would he push it inside my mouth? Would he hold me steady, plunging in and out, whimpering and whining above me like a needy beast in heat?

When I thought about slicking up my fingers—about slipping them inside him—about…about…*shoving* him onto his belly. And pushing his legs open and tasting him where he was filthiest, I just—

Fuck.

Yes.

Okay.

That was better.

It was wrong, wrong, wrong for me to want to touch someone else like that. To want to violate their body with my own. Sticky sweat. *Naked.* The slap of our hips meeting as I forced my cock inside his cherry pink hole and grabbed his ass cheeks like I often grabbed his face. Would the back of his neck taste like salt? Would he *cry* when I fucked into his sweet little hole?

I hoped so.

I wonder if his tears would taste better if I was the one who had caused them.

Perhaps he'd take charge like he had at the fair and with Barry? Perhaps he'd push me onto my back, straddle my hips—and with no complaints from me whatsoever—slide himself down onto my cock. Would he get *violent* with me?

The thought made me shiver.

Would he bite and choke—would he attempt to kill me as he had his other paramours?

The beast inside me paced in circles.

He was a twisted, hungry thing. Desperate for praise and touch. Frothing at the mouth the moment Felix came to mind.

Locked away, I hadn't even known such a creature existed inside my psyche before, but I became achingly familiar with him as my days, my nights, my weekends spent mowing Felix's lawn—were filled with thoughts of fucking him.

I masturbated a lot more over those few weeks than I had in all my life.

When I was doing laundry, I thought about having Felix over the dryer.

When I was doing dishes, I thought about having him over the sink.

When I was mowing his lawn, I thought about having him on his front porch, bent over, trousers pushed down his legs, his desperate needy cries echoing through the air as I fucked him till he cried.

When I wasn't thinking about sitting Felix on my cock, dodging Winnie's well-meaning but annoying questions, and ignoring Harold's teasing…I went on dates.

Felix was a hard man to pin down. I couldn't get him to text me back for the life of me. Our dates were spread out—and always, unfortunately, happened after I'd seen men and women alike over at his place. I knew I was one of many suitors, but I was determined to be the only one who crossed the finish line so to speak.

If I had to bludgeon every last one of them to make that happen—so be it.

Though my time with Felix was infrequent, each date was more perfect than the last.

One warm, sticky summer night a few weeks after the carnival, I went over to Felix's home. It was a redo of the night we should've had, and I was excited to say the least. Armed with my new knowledge and confidence, I couldn't wait to spend the night with him. Felix had opened the door wearing his ridiculous disguise again, but—before I even had to prompt—he took his hat off and hung it on the hook by the door.

"No hat, right?" He smiled.

My heart fluttered.

Dolly and Tiffany glared at me the entire time I prepared dinner, their beady little eyes following my movements. Felix helped me set the table, a polite little gentleman—because of course he was.

Felix and I sat in the formal dining room, surrounded by his clutter. At one point, when I tripped over a stray dusty radio and nearly brained myself—I'd had enough.

"I'm cleaning your house," I declared. Felix stared at me from across the room where he'd been setting the plates in their places.

"You are?" He blinked.

"I am."

A flush spread across his face, and rather than get offended, a happy, fizzy smile escaped. "Thank you, Marshall."

It was clear that Felix was trying. Every space in the house that was clean—was also full of his crocheted wisteria—but it was obvious that there was too much junk for one person to be able to fully manage.

Clearly he liked vintage things, judging by his clothing and his hoarding. But it seemed he'd slowly begun to siphon them out. Almost like…he didn't need to cling to the past anymore.

Perhaps one day I could convince him to learn how to text.

"Do you really need all this stuff?" I asked, sweaty, a lock of hair slipping into my eyes. I was lucky I hadn't fallen. I probably would've crushed the reading glasses in my pocket.

"I thought I did," Felix answered honestly, eyes trembling and far away like they often were. "But…" he glanced around the room, at all the lost, old things—then his gaze met mine and all I felt was warm, warm, warm. "I don't anymore."

I cleared my throat. "Okay," I said simply, even though my heart was pounding.

"Out with the old, in with the new—" Felix added, lips tipping up.

We finished setting the table together in silence. As I carried dinner in I couldn't help but wonder what had caused him to collect so much in the first place. There had to have been a lack in his life, right? A hole that only items from the past could fill.

Before I'd even come over, it seemed he'd begun to change, however.

Ready to move on.

And now that I was here, I could help.

Felix had an entire ornate dining room table, bedecked in dripping candles. It was far longer than any one person would ever need it to be, even considering the amount of visitors he had. There was only one chair at the table, however, which made it clear that he didn't often bring guests here.

I could so easily picture him sitting there, quietly eating his dinner, the giant house far too quiet. As alone as he'd been on Christmas Eve, a silent, solemn figure.

When the candles dipped low, I asked him about his cats.

Part of me was curious, because I couldn't fathom why anyone would keep cats indoors. We'd had barn cats growing up—kept around for the mice, of course. They served a purpose.

These cats…didn't.

Dolly was a fat, fluffy, white thing who Felix told me had a penchant for hiding atop the fridge and spooking him when he least expected it. Tiffany was her slimmer, friendlier counterpart. Which wasn't all that friendly—as neither cat did anything but glare at me like the intruder I was.

I supposed I could understand their reluctance to trust me.

I didn't trust strangers either.

"Two cats," I said, by way of conversation starter.

"Two cats," Felix repeated, obviously amused. "What about them?"

"Why—" Do not be an asshole, Marshall, you are trying to woo this man. "In God's name would you subject yourself to that? Twice over."

Christ.

Fuck.

Felix laughed, his eyes dancing with mirth, head tossed back. The long line of his throat bobbed, those extraordinary twin scars on his neck flickering as his delight filled the room.

I'd gone to a symphony once in the city. The trill of the violins had lit my soul on fire, and the smooth crooning of the bass had buzzed beneath the surface of my skin. At the end of the performance, I'd been tempted to cry. Which was unlike me, as I couldn't recall ever crying. Not once.

That was one thing Felix and I had in common.

Our aversion to tears.

Felix's laughter was far more beautiful than the symphony had been. I'd thought then, sitting in my assigned seat, surrounded by the lithe dance of notes flitting through the air, that I would never hear anything prettier in all my life.

I committed his laugh to memory, locking it away in the back of my mind. Deeply hidden inside the space where I sometimes retreated when my thoughts were a mess and I needed a reminder that the world carried beauty as much as it carried filth.

When he dropped his head down to look at me, his expression was…
fond.

I locked the memory of his laughter away, replacing the symphony
as my new favorite sound—settled, precious, and perfect into its space
inside my head.

Unaware that he was the second coming of Christ, Felix spoke, "I found
them," he said simply—referring to the mongrels that were currently
giving me what Winnie would refer to as "side-eye". "There was this shop
I drove past when I was coming home a few years ago. My car broke
down. It was raining, so I went inside," Felix continued.

A far away expression crossed over his face as he described the shop he'd
stumbled upon by accident. It had been a stormy day—like the night we'd
driven around town in his car. The clouds had been dark and angry, a
torrent of cold rain spattering his windshield. The moon had been hidden
between the gaps in the trees, and Felix had been frightened.

He'd entered the shop looking for a good Samaritan and was lucky
enough to find one. It was a book shop—or what appeared to be one.
Tall, musty bookshelves. A dust-coated snack counter with a closed sign.
The narrow aisles and two checkout counters he described struck a chord
within me, but it wasn't until he talked about the thin but tall shopkeep
who worked the floor of the shop that I realized *why*.

I'd *been* there.

"Both the cats were sitting in a little basket behind the counter, and
before I left, the owner asked me if I wanted to take them home." Felix
smiled wistfully, like remembering Dolly and Tiffany as children made
him blissfully happy. I would've found it adorable, if my thoughts were
not spinning. "Turned out I just needed gas!" Felix laughed again, tinkling

and bright. "He was happy to provide that, as well as the two kittens."

"I think I've been there," I said, quiet and curious. It was an *odd* thing. Not because visiting the same store as someone else was all that odd, but because—for the last ten years I'd tried and *tried* to find that shop again. After my first visit, no matter how hard I looked, it was nowhere to be found.

It was almost like it hadn't existed at all.

As a very logical person who is quite rooted in reality, I found it more than a little concerning that I had memories of a place that didn't seem to exist. After doing some digging, I discovered that there was no reference to the shop on social media or any sign of it on my map app.

Searching for it every time I left town became a compulsion I could not ignore. For years, I'd done just that, hunting the winding roads for a place I was certain I'd once been.

After a while, I'd been forced to face defeat.

I knew my mind was not what most would consider "*healthy.*" Part of me wondered if I'd imagined the entire encounter—but that was unlike me. When I dreamed, normally I saw violent visions, memories from a past I'd tried to forget, or worked mundane jobs at a variety of boring places.

I was not the kind of man that simply made things up.

I always remained firmly rooted in reality.

For example…one time, while I was dreaming I'd given a prescription to a customer at the pharmacy. The next day, I'd Googled the medication I'd filled, only to discover that it was somehow very *real*. I'd never been certain how my brain knew about it, only that it did.

Which was why the "shop" in my mind had become somewhat of a demon.

Now though…

Now I knew I hadn't made it up at all. If Felix had been there, it had been very real. Which didn't explain where the hell it had gone.

I still had no idea how the shop had disappeared.

"Oh," Felix responded, clearly not understanding how monumental the fact that he had been *inside* the missing shop was. "How fun! When did you go?" As a person who very rarely left the house, I could see why he'd be curious. There was no reason for him to believe anything was amiss if he'd never tried to hunt for the shop in vain himself.

"It was ten years ago. When I was passing through this area to visit my sister, Melissa," still feeling a little shell-shocked, I was certain my expression looked off. "*Before* I'd moved to Beach Town."

"Huh." Felix cocked his head to the side, regarding me curiously.

At the time, I'd still lived with my father and Winnie in the city, and I'd been looking for independence.

"It was how I found Beach Town in the first place. I'd been wanting to move away from home, but I didn't want to live in the city with Winnie and my dad. I love them, but not enough that I want either of them popping their heads into my business. Besides, I missed the small town life we'd left behind when we moved away from the farm." Realizing I'd gotten off track, I realigned. "The owner of the shop was the one that pointed me in this direction. He said I'd like it here. That I'd find what I was missing."

A town off the beaten path.

A town with a club for murderers.

A town where Felix lived with his cats, his secrets, and his pretty pointy smile.

Though, I'm almost certain the owner of the shop hadn't known that last tidbit. Unless…of course…he had. *Maybe disappearing shop owners were matchmakers who could see the future? What a joke!* I was too shell-shocked to muster any mirth, despite how fantastical that thought was.

"Are you okay?" Felix asked, frowning at me. "You look as though you've seen a ghost."

"It feels like I have." I stared at him, then the cats. "Have you ever tried to go back?" I asked, curious.

"No. Why?" Felix laughed, eyes crinkling at the corners. "I don't often leave, as you know."

"I…" I was acting irrational. "Never mind. I suppose I found it odd. There are a lot of things I'm finding odd lately. Perhaps you feel the same?"

There was a strange expression on Felix's face…almost guilty? Though I could've been imagining things, because the next moment it was gone, and he was peering at me like he always did, red eyes soft.

I'd stopped questioning their color and appreciated it instead.

"I do," Felix said, honesty quaking in those two simple words. "So much has changed in such a small time. I don't know how to wrap my head around it."

"The murders?"

"Yes, that too." His expression pinched and he curled into himself, before glancing at me through his lashes. "I never expected to have you here," he admitted, voice low and sweet. The candles flickered, and my pulse skittered. "At my table. In my home."

"I never expected this either," I replied, just as honest. "But I like it."

"You do?" Felix perked up. If he'd had a tail, it would be wagging. I wanted to reach across the table and touch him—but he was too far away, and I was too much of a coward to leave my seat, surprised once again by the compulsion to comfort him when I'd never felt that way about anyone before.

How he could be so powerful one moment and so vulnerable the next, I couldn't understand.

"I do," my voice was rough, my pulse racing. His gaze snapped to my throat, almost like he could hear the way my heart galloped, attracted to it like a siren song.

"Do you ever get lonely, Marshall?" Felix asked. He looked so small all of a sudden, sitting at his end of the table with his dinner untouched in front of him. There was such raw vulnerability on his face, I couldn't bear to look away.

It was beautiful.

Devastating.

As lovely as an avalanche destroying everything in its path. That's how he made me feel. Like he'd come into my life, rolled through everything I'd known, and pulled it into him. Remade it into something bigger, and better—and twice as terrifying.

His question was an interesting one.

Loneliness wasn't something I often contemplated. I was too busy with my rituals. Too busy planning my next kill. Too busy helping Harold with his messes. Too busy warding off Winnie's nosiness, and trying to figure out what to get my sisters for Christmas. There wasn't *time* to be lonely.

At least…I hadn't thought so.

But then I thought about all the nights I sat at my dining room table, eating the same meal, listening to the same songs on the playlist I'd created specifically to cultivate peace. The lulling twists and trills of the same symphony I'd attended all those years ago. Chasing a feeling I hadn't thought I'd ever feel again.

Until now.

I thought about the emptiness in my home the moment Winnie left after visiting.

The silence I'd always loved, but now felt…hollow knowing Felix was across the street, sitting silent on his own.

It hadn't occurred to me before that I might be lonely.

But…perhaps I was.

"Yes," I admitted just as softly, answering his question after what was probably an awkward pause. Felix didn't say a word about my awkwardness though. Instead, he just nodded, that same faraway look in his eyes. "Do you get lonely, Finley?" I countered, gripping my fork tight.

"I can't remember a time when I wasn't," Felix admitted, voice tight. He swallowed, and I watched his throat bob with fascination.

I was a bad person.

I knew that.

Because the idea that I could fill that gap in Felix's life made me fizzy with *elation*. I should've felt sad for him, probably. Pity. A normal person would've. Instead, I was excited for the opportunity this offered.

An opportunity to be everything for him.

To make him need me even more than he already did.

"Why?" I asked, curious. "You're often having guests over."

"They mean nothing to me. Friends at best."

The beast inside me reached toward his. *Hungry.*

"Nothing?"

Felix nodded his head in agreement. "Sometimes…when they're here they make me feel even lonelier than I did before," he admitted, a sad twist to his lips. "They remind me of what I've lost—of who I used to be."

"Then stop inviting them over," I huffed—totally not biased or anything at all.

"I wish it were that simple," Felix's eyes danced. "I need them, so that I can see *you*."

Well, that made no sense.

"Why?"

Felix mimed zipping his lips shut, and I sighed, frustrated. Another secret to add to the ever-growing pile. "What about your family?" I asked, thinking about that Christmas he'd been all alone. "Your actual friends?"

I suppose I could allow him to have his paramours for now. At least… until I was ready to fill in the gaps they left behind. If he needed them to spend time with me, then I would let him have them.

Though that wouldn't stop me from imagining running them over with my car.

"Everyone I've ever cared for is dead," he said simply, like that wasn't a horribly depressing thing to say.

"My mother is dead," I told him, in an attempt to relate. "My sister too."

"Do you miss them?" Felix blinked, shaking his head a little to clear it, his eyes centered in the present once again as he turned to look at me.

This felt like a trick question.

I should probably say yes.

Instead, I settled for the truth. "Sometimes." I shrugged. "When I remember them." I remembered Alberta most, once a year on her birthday. After the first time I'd enacted my ritual, it had stopped being the worst time of year, and quickly became my favorite part of it. I'd right the wrongs committed against her, and until it rolled around again the following spring, I'd feel the itch beneath my skin settle.

Right after their deaths, I'd thought of them more often. But as the years passed, the instances I recalled of them grew farther and farther apart. Sometimes I could go days or weeks without thinking of either of them at all.

And sometimes—like lately, I thought about them often.

Felix tipped his head to the side, watching me curiously, so I added, "Mostly I miss my mother's pie," in an attempt to make him laugh again.

He snorted, face scrunching up with delight as he shook his head. "Gosh, that must've been a *swell* pie."

"It was."

"What kind?"

"Rhubarb."

"Rhubarb?" Felix snorted again, fingers tapping a happy dance on the table as he shook his head. "You look *exactly* like the kind of person who likes rhubarb."

"What is *that* supposed to mean?" I asked, mock offended. "First I'm an old cartoon man, and now I look like I like rhubarb."

Felix grinned. "It means whatever you think it means."

"An insult then. And here I was, about to tell you that the next time you felt lonely I'd come over," I scoffed, surprised to find how fun it was to *play* with him this way. Like our beasts were circling one another. "Offer rescinded."

"The offer you didn't make?"

"Exactly."

Felix's grin never fell. He leaned against the table, almost like he was trying to get closer to me, despite the wood barrier between us.

"Would you like to know my most closely guarded secret?" Felix asked out of the blue, his eyes still dancing. Immediately I nodded, my heart skipping a beat. He took a fortifying breath. "When I'm with *you*, I'm not lonely," he said softly, lips twisting up. "I don't feel like a ghost."

I had no idea what he meant by *that*, but it was a nice statement all the same. It was comforting to know that I was not lumped in with the other people he had over, but special. Separate. The cream of the crop. The only one that offered him true companionship.

"I should be here all the time then, shouldn't I?" My pulse raced, my hands sweaty as I waited for his answer. "So that you don't feel that way."

"As often as you can," Felix countered. The need simmering in the air between us was palpable. "Until you can't anymore."

That was a morose statement.

I didn't plan on dying anytime soon.

"What if I want forever?" I offered, voice a little hoarse. We were getting more…*personal* than I'd expected for a second date, but it was nice all the same. I'd always struggled with people. I hated them. I avoided them. I found them tricky, obnoxious—annoying.

Felix was none of those things.

Talking to him was *easy*.

My masks fell away.

I was Marshall, in all my prickly, unpalatable glory. And Felix seemed to like that.

"Nothing good lasts forever," Felix countered, that faraway look threatening to overtake him again. To take him *away* from me. To steal him, despite the fact that I was right here—in front of him—physically present when the demons that lurked in his head were far, far away.

"One day, you'll tell me why you say that," I countered, voice low.

"Will I?" Felix's eyes were present again, and I nearly sagged in relief as his attention flickered back to me. Those lovely red eyes almost seemed to glow in the dwindling candle light.

"You will," I commanded confidently, voice soft. "You'll tell me all your secrets." It was a promise. Felix knew that as well as I did, because he hummed back thoughtfully. "I'll know why you lock yourself up in here. I'll know why you hide. I'll know why you kill. I'll know all your wants, your needs, your desires."

"And what will I receive in return? You're getting an awful lot from me in this hypothetical future."

"Only the truth."

"My secrets are all I have," he countered.

"And your cats."

"And my cats." Felix blinked. "So. Make it fair, Marshall. Wow me. What great, wonderful thing will you offer me in exchange?"

"Hmm," I mulled this over, tapping my lip. What could I offer him? What could I give him that might make him laugh, but wasn't a promise I couldn't keep? I'd already offered forever. He hadn't responded to that the way I'd hoped when I made the statement. Almost like he didn't trust my words.

Maybe…huge declarations were not the way to Felix's heart.

Ah. Yes. I knew what to do.

If he didn't respond well to big declarations, a small one would do.

Simple, but to the point.

Perfect.

"Marshall?" Felix waited, impatient. I clucked my tongue at him, but responded to his cajoling anyway—confident that for the first time in my life, I knew exactly what to say.

"Two eyes, two hands…" My cheeks hurt, and I realized—once again—I was smiling. "And a grin."

The bare minimum.

But everything all the same.

I promised him my attention, my help, my humor.

My presence in its barest bones.

"How *generous* of you," Felix joked—but I could tell he truly meant the words. Like my promise to be present in his life was the best gift I could've offered him. Like he understood the subtext so subtly offered. Like he spoke my language, when no one else ever had.

"What, did you think you were special?" I scoffed, pulse racing, as we both pretended I hadn't offered him everything I had.

Felix's face pinched playfully as he *hemmed* and *hawed*, before shaking his head. "That would be presumptuous of me." He nodded, faux seriously. "It's not like you mow my lawn for me every Saturday—or are quite doggedly trying to go steady with me or anything."

"Exactly." I shrugged. "I do this for all my neighbors."

"Even Barry."

Gagging, I was tempted to throw my napkin at him. "Never say that to me again, you little floppy-hatted bitch."

Felix cackled. "If *I'm* a floppy-hatted bitch, I wonder what you call Barry in your head. It'll be colorful, I'm sure. Creative."

"You don't want to know."

"Fluffy-haired ass kisser?" Felix blinked innocently. I snorted out a laugh. "Nosy, inconsiderate floral-pattern-wearing-asshole?"

"What is it with you and asses?" I leaned my chin on my hand, staring at him, my heart thumping unsteadily.

"Pink-cheeked—"

"Oh god."

"Hawaiian-shirted gremlin man?"

"No, that would be you." I grinned, and Felix grinned back.

My heart was full.

I didn't think it'd ever been full before.

For five minutes, Felix came up with more and more Barry-themed insults. We traded barbs back and forth. I never stopped staring, reluctant to even blink for fear of missing even a second of his smile. Every time he cackled, I logged the memories away for the future. Drops of sunshine saved for rainy days. It seemed my head would be full of his laughter, his smiles, and his jokes. I couldn't bring myself to be mad about it.

Not at all.

Not even a little.

Not one bit.

Chapter Twelve

AT THE BEGINNING of this—after the first body I helped Felix dispose of, I'd thought that Felix was too daft to be an evil mastermind. I wasn't so sure of that now. He certainly had me wrapped tightly around his finger.

Felix often reminded me of a politician. He knew exactly what to say to dodge questions. Exactly how to give enough, without sharing too much. Like he'd been trained to unite masses of people—but didn't know what it was like to be genuine when he was alone.

Despite this, lying did not come easily to him like it did to me.

He was an enigma.

People who were natural saviors didn't tend to be brutal murderers on the side. At least…I didn't think they did? I'd consulted *The Club*, and all I'd gotten were odd looks. Allen had slapped me on the back and told me not to be so closed-minded. That things weren't always as they appeared.

Whatever that meant.

There were pieces I was still missing in this story, and I couldn't wait to fill in the gaps.

I'd promised him I'd find out his secrets, and I *meant* that.

But I was content to wait till he told me himself.

Right now, I wanted to pay attention to Felix. He looked quite lovely in his spiffy white button-up. It hugged the contours of his chest, and clung almost obscenely to his biceps. There was a light in his eyes that flickered ever-changing, as unsteady as the flames that dwindled on the table.

After our laughter had died down, I'd done something rather insane.

I'd asked him to dance.

"How do you feel about waltzing?" I asked, voice quiet, hushed. Felix's expression shuttered and he sighed, lips pinched like he was deciding what to say. His earlier ease was forgotten as he slowly rose from his seat at the table.

"It's alright if you don't like to," I promised, eager for the little crumbs he sometimes dropped. Seeds of truth that felt like gifts. I rose to mirror him, the table still between us, my heart in my throat.

I knew exactly what song to play.

I had no idea if he knew how to dance at all—but part of me, something deep down, suspected he would. That he would perfectly mirror me in this like he did in everything else.

"I…" Felix's eyes felt very far away again. "I do. It's just…been quite some time since someone asked me."

"About time then," I answered, crossing the distance between us. "Felix Finley?" My voice was low, soft, as I latched onto his wrist and gently pulled him close. My nose brushed the shell of his ear and Felix sighed, melting into the embrace like butter on a warm day. Like he'd *needed* this as much as I had.

Like he could feel the distance between us too.

And hated it as much as I did.

"May I have this dance?"

Felix inhaled a sharp, overwhelmed little sound. He nodded, his soft golden hair tickling my nose as he did so. "Yes, Marshall Warden, you may." The teasing lilt in his voice was addicting. So full of life. *Vibrant.*

Nothing like he'd sounded when he told me he felt like a ghost.

He led me to his living room.

The walls were cluttered with movie posters I didn't recognize in gilded frames. The most prevalent of which was called "The Emperor". Dark wallpaper from what appeared to be another era entirely lined the walls, nearly navy blue in the softly twinkling light that hung from a chandelier that dangled above. More crocheted wisteria hung from the ceiling. A cat perch ran along the wall, with a staircase that led all the way to the floor for the felines to frolic. It was ridiculous. Almost as ridiculous as the line of hats that hung along one back wall.

We moved the couch and coffee table aside to make room.

I tried not to stare at the way Felix's arms flexed when he did so—or the fact his breaths remained even, not labored at all.

He stared at mine in return, and I admit, I maybe flexed a little more than was necessary—just to see his eyes darken.

Was this flirting?

It felt like flirting.

There was an odd buzzing feeling beneath my skin, like fluttery little winged ants. Reminded me of the ant hills I used to drown when I was a child—but…less creepy crawly. Softer, somehow.

When we had the room in order, furniture spread to the sides, a makeshift dance floor cleared, I turned toward the record player in the corner of the room. I'd intended to use my phone speaker—but this was far better. I'd never had one of these, though I'd always wanted one.

I moved to sift through the stacks of vinyl records, and a startled laugh escaped me when I saw one of the albums he'd collected.

It felt like fate.

"You have *Tchaikovsky*?"

Felix blinked. He'd been waiting, leaning against the wall behind me, watching me move. He acted as though I was the only person who had been inside his home in years. Which I knew was a lie.

But, I was, apparently, the only guest who made him less lonely.

And that meant something, didn't it?

"Of course I do." Felix's lips twisted into a merry little smile and I beamed at him, pulling the record out with barely concealed delight.

"You are perfect, aren't you?" I said the words without thinking, and the moment they came out I wished I could take them back. They were too honest. Too much. Even without my masks in place, I hadn't expected this sort of…open affection to pop free.

"I thought I wasn't special?" Felix teased, eyes dancing.

"You…uh—" I tried to quip back, to set us back on the right, bitter path. But…the words didn't seem to want to come. "I lied," I admitted, face hot. "Maybe."

"I see."

Because this was awkward, and I didn't want him to ask me any more questions, I held the record out to him. With ease, as if he'd done this thousands, if not millions of times, Felix took it from me, then pulled the vinyl record from the box. He lovingly cleaned the disk before putting it in its place on the record player with a graceful flick of his wrist.

I had never been jealous of an inanimate object before, but I certainly was now.

Perhaps if I got dirty, Felix would dust me off too?

The veins on the back of Felix's hands flickered as he moved. He was tiny, yes, but there was an effortless masculinity to him—especially now. Like he knew exactly who he was. When he wasn't overthinking or rambling, he moved as fluidly as a dancer—unafraid to take up space.

The moment the pin settled in its place, the soft, melodic croon of "Waltz of the Flowers" filled the air. The music was so…*warm*. Almost as warm as Felix's eyes. Or my cheeks, still flushed, as I reached for him, unable to help myself.

I latched onto his face the same way I had many times before, fingers pinching the supple skin as I leaned down to see him better.

That little mole beneath his eye taunted me, begging for kisses. His lips were still chapped, and I ached to bend down to taste them. Felix's eyes flooded with heat. Something electric zinged through my body as I stepped into his space, our toes tapping, torsos brushing.

God, he was gorgeous.

A classic sort of handsome. Timeless.

Perfection—in a world so full of flaws.

"The way you look at me is so…" Felix's lips parted, and I squished his cheeks harder till he laughed.

"So?" I wanted to bite him, he was so damn adorable. He made my teeth ache. I'd often looked at small animals and thought the same thing.

Rabbits on the farm, baby calves, foals as they waddled. It was a primal feeling, wanting to tear into cute creatures. To devour them whole.

"Intoxicating," Felix admitted, voice deliciously husky.

"How do I look at you?" My hand slipped from his cheek, down his throat, caressing the cool skin as my heart threatened to pound right out of my chest.

"You look at me like you…" My thumb skimmed over his Adam's apple and he gasped, lashes fluttering.

"Like I?" I echoed, voice throaty and low.

"Like you never want to look away." That was accurate, so I didn't deny his claim. "Like I am…riveting."

"You are."

Felix flushed. His lips wobbled up, his throat bobbing beneath my hand as I gave it a gentle squeeze. He had such a long, lovely throat. I'd thought so before—but now, touching it, I knew firsthand how right I'd been.

There was no pulse fluttering beneath my fingers, which…should've struck me as odd. But in that moment, all I could think about was touching him more—about the lilting music—about the fact that there were condoms burning a hole in my pocket and I wanted to *kiss* him.

I wanted to kiss him so badly I felt insane because of it.

I dipped my head down even more, my bangs brushing against his forehead as we shared a single, solitary breath. Barely a centimeter separated our lips and it felt like too much. Too much, too much, too much.

"You look like you want something, Marshall." Felix's voice was sweet, so fucking sweet.

I nodded, a needy sound building up in my throat as I continued to hold his neck tight. His voice vibrated against my palm, a tantalizing buzz that made me equal parts want to squeeze till he was silent, and make him speak again just so I could feel it a second time.

"Is it terribly forward of me to kiss you?" Felix asked, his lashes fluttering as he stared up at me with those luminous, lovely eyes.

Distantly, I recognized how *real* they looked. That they didn't look like contacts at all. But I was too distracted by his mouth and the promise of the kiss I'd been aching for, to really think too much about it.

"*Please*—" My voice was rough. The beast inside me clawed at its cage, whining for the gift Felix was offering. "It's not too forward. I want it. I want you so badly I—"

"Then bend down here, so I can reach."

I bent.

And Felix kissed me.

He kissed me and the world ended. Everything I'd ever known whittled away to nothing but scraps. The soft brush of Felix's lips sent me spinning. I moaned.

It was a chaste kiss.

No tongue. (Thank God. I wasn't ready to be French, just yet.)

There were only soft, flickering little brushes as he parted his lips and coaxed me to do the same. I knew I was too rigid. That I was stiff as a board—but I'd never done this. I'd never *wanted* to do this. I didn't know how.

There wasn't time to worry that my inexperience would be ill received. Because Felix's lips never ceased teasing mine, sweet and patient. Tender in a way I didn't know kisses could be. I ached, pressing into him with a *hungry* sound that made Felix shiver.

"That's it," he urged, his words fluttering between our lips. His voice vibrating my palm where it still encased his throat. "Relax for me, Marshall."

I relaxed.

As if it had been that easy all along. As if all I'd needed was Felix's gentle command to do so. Something settled inside me then. A screw that had been knocked loose so long ago I'd forgotten it had happened at all.

With a sigh, I pressed harder against him, holding his throat captive with my palm as my fingers gently pinched. Greedier, *rougher*, our lips slid together. Over and over, a mating dance that caused shivers to run up and down my spine.

His mouth was cool and slick. The longer we kissed, the warmer it became, almost like he was stealing my heat again. Like we were sharing it between us. And that thought—that something I exuded could become one with him was just…

"*Fuck*," I hissed out, pulling away, panting.

My chest was heaving and I couldn't seem to get it to stop.

"Not today," Felix countered, voice low, as rough as my own. His eyes were dark. The pupil had swallowed them whole. "But…"

"But…?" My pulse skittered. I squeezed his neck tighter, watching his lashes flutter as a needy little moan left his lips. He melted, like butter in my grip. The tighter I squeezed, the more docile he became.

"Soon," he croaked, lashes fluttering.

Soon was now my favorite word.

Felix and I danced. We danced for *hours*. Well past my bedtime. The stars flickered outside his living room windows, the lamplight from the street casting an orange, homey glaze around his living room as I led him through steps I'd memorized years ago. Back and forth, swirling, dipping, gliding.

The way my mother had taught me back when I'd been young and anxious and needed a guiding hand.

We went through Felix's entire record collection. Through the old rock music he favored, through the symphonies, through Sinatra.

The cats watched us curiously, like they didn't know what to make of what we were doing. They attempted to trip me once—the bastards—but for the most part, left us alone.

And by the time I went home—dear God, *who was I?* Staying up this late!—I'd been touching Felix for so long his body was *warm*. He'd looked dazed as I paused on my way out his front door, twisting to say goodbye.

There'd been a single, awkward moment when I wasn't sure if I was allowed to kiss him again. But he quickly remedied it. Hopping onto his tiptoes, Felix pulled me down by a gentle fistful of my vest and answered my unspoken question by kissing me soundly.

"Goodnight, Marshall," he said, eyes alight.

"Goodnight, Felix."

If he noticed it was the first time I'd used his first name, he didn't say.

I didn't either.

Some things didn't need to be said out loud.

Chapter Thirteen

I HAD the most *brilliant* idea the day after our second date. I'd always been a bit…obsessive. Call it what you will—but it was part of who I was. After visiting Felix's home, it was like a dam had broken and I …*couldn't seem to turn it off.*

I could not stop thinking about him.

All day.

When I was writing spreadsheets, I thought of him. When I was warding off Harold's well-meaning lunch invites, I thought of him. When I drove home—and passed a cop car—I thought of him.

My head was in the clouds. But it wasn't until I received an unexpected visitor that I knew what to do with my newfound obsession.

It was after dark. I'd been meal prepping for the next week at work, and the doorbell rang. Immediately, my hackles raised. The only person who visited me this late was Barry (the bore). I'd already received the note on my door inviting me to his annual Summer Bash at the end of August, and I worried—like with the fair—he would try to rope me into doing something to help him.

I'd rather eat my own leg.

If he asked me to bring coleslaw I was going to scream.

It was different if I brought something on my own. That only meant that I'd decided to be generous that day. Or that I'd had extra time on my hands. If *Barry* asked me to bring something it became an obligation and I hated those. So much.

Teeth gritted, my brow lowered into my most intimidating scowl, I made sure my apron was tied before wiping my hands off on it and heading to the front door. When I yanked it open, I was prepared to yell.

That became unnecessary the moment I saw who my guest *actually* was.

"Felix," I perked up, my scowl melting away, despite how hard I tried to keep it in place. I couldn't have him realizing how giddy he made me, could I? That would give him too much power over me.

"Hi, Marshall." Felix smiled at me. "I like your apron. You look…very domestic."

"Domestic?" I frowned down at my apron, unsure if that was a good thing. It was frilly. Winnie had given it to me as a gag gift one year, but I liked it, so I often wore it when I was cooking. I hadn't brought it to Felix's house the night before. But that was because we weren't apron-level-lovers yet. At least…we hadn't been, until the end of the night.

Now we'd gotten to first base.

So I supposed it was alright if he saw my frills.

"Yes," Felix nodded, biting his lip, his sharp little incisors flashing. "Domestic."

It felt like a compliment, so I let it be one.

"You look…" I scanned him, head to toe, my own cheeks flushing as I tried to come up with a compliment of my own. "Soft."

Felix's smile widened. "Soft?"

"Cuddly," I added, clearing my throat, my entire face hot. "Like a baby horse." We'd had a few throughout my childhood and their fur always looked like that. Fuzzy. Downy. Sweet.

"Thank you." Felix's shoulders looked particularly delicious today. His sweater was pale pink, a perfect complement to the baby blue I was sporting. It clung to his frame, highlighting every curve, the collar dipping low enough I could see his collarbones.

The way it swooped reminded me of his pajamas.

Damn. I should've paid more attention the one and only time I'd seen them.

What a waste.

I wish I could see them again.

Felix's hair was curling around his slightly pointed ears, his hat perched on top of his head. There were still dark circles under his eyes, but the sadness that normally lingered was missing. Instead he looked…*excited*? Huh.

The scent of something buttery and sweet filled my nose, and I cocked my head at him, gaze finally swiveling from his face down to the box he carried.

"Is that…" I blinked, flummoxed. "A pie?"

"Rhubarb!" Felix held it out to me, looking incredibly proud of himself. "I didn't bake it. I can't bake—" he laughed, self-conscious. "Or cook. I never learned. Never had to. Always had staff on hand for that. Never had to learn to clean either. Did you know there's such a thing as pie delivery?"

I shook my head dumbly, reaching out to take the pie from him, shell-shocked. "The modern world never ceases to amaze me."

"It's full of wonders," I echoed, only half-listening.

Because pie.

This blind-sided me even more than the murders he'd committed.

Bodies I knew how to handle. Pie? Not so much.

"A friend recommended it to me," he said—still talking. My eyes narrowed.

"What friend?"

"No one special, caveman," he snorted out. I eyed the label on the box curiously. I'd always had a sweet tooth. It was something I should've tried to curb—especially as I got older—but I'd never seemed to manage.

My three vices.

Murder, sugar, and Felix.

"Special enough they told you about pie delivery," I wheedled. The box was warm in my grasp.

"Maaarshall." Felix laughed, an almost guilty twist to his lips.

"Is this another of your secrets?" I cocked my head to the side, the sweet scent of fresh pie filling the air between us. Felix seemed to debate with himself, before he ultimately nodded.

"I feel like you're lying," I said, unable to bite my tongue.

"Okay, so maybe calling them my friend is a stretch. Acquaintance is more accurate." Felix bit his lip. "A fan of my work? A guest."

"What work?" I had never seen him leave his house. "Are you an artist?" That would explain…a lot actually. Perhaps he had one of those online shops where he sold his wares. His crochet-creations. The memorabilia he collected from the 1950s that littered his house.

"Of a sort," Felix answered vaguely. "Depending on who you ask."

"I'm asking *you*," I frowned.

"Right." Felix inhaled sharply, an almost forlorn expression crossing his face. "Then yes…I think what I made was art." His lips tipped up. "I don't do it anymore. I can't."

"Does that make you sad?"

"Sometimes," Felix offered me a soft little smile. "It helps that you asked."

"Oh. Well. Good for me then."

"Good for me too." Felix laughed, and it was the prettiest thing I'd heard all day.

I nodded, relaxing. "An acquaintance told you about pie delivery."

"Yes." Felix's face was bright red. "I called him up and asked. Because you mentioned yesterday that you missed it."

I would've rather he never called anyone other than me ever—but I suppose I couldn't be too angry. Because he'd bought me a pie.

"You called up your acquaintance," I repeated, trying to parse this together. "And what? Asked if he knew of any places where rhubarb was made?"

"Yes." Felix's splotchy flush was lovely. He licked his lips. "Was that… okay?"

He peered at me through his lashes, and I softened, unable to hold onto my ire.

"Of course it was okay. You may buy me pie anytime."

Felix's hypothetical tail wagged.

If he was a chihuahua, I was the doberman panting after him. Willing to jump through hoops for him—my doggy brain fully set on breeding him into the ground. He certainly made me want to howl.

It was like he'd reprogrammed the way my brain worked. And I couldn't even be mad about it—Especially after what we'd shared, and how many times he'd jumped to my rescue.

He was mine, silly pies and all.

And I didn't want to share him—just like I didn't want to share my new treat.

I was half-tempted to hunt down every person he'd ever slept with and eliminate the competition entirely.

"Do you like it?" Felix asked, his hands slipping into his pockets as he rocked onto his toes, then back onto his heels. He looked like a needy puppy, all fluffy blond hair, his eyes searching mine.

"I love it," I said simply, because it was true. I squeezed the box, my heart fluttering. "Would you like to come in?" I cocked my head to the side again, jerking my chin backward. Felix twisted a little, his eyes alight with curiosity as he glanced down the pristine hallway, gaze flickering to the line of Italian loafers on a stand by the door.

Good.

Gaze at my shoes, Felix.

See how well I take care of the leather and know I'll take care of you too.

"Are you cooking?" he asked, sniffing the air.

I nodded, twisting my body to allow him a view of the archway that led to the kitchen. Almost like it was perfectly timed, the timer above the stove beeped. Quickly, I shut the door on Felix, hurrying down the hallway to deal with the chicken before it burned.

I set his pie down, put my oven mitts on, and bent over.

Chicken saved, I leaned back to admire it, hands on my hips.

It was only then that I realized what I'd done.

Oh.

Oh no.

Oh no, I had not meant to do that—to shut the door on him—oh fuck.

I sprinted back to the front door, yanking it open, mitts still on. Felix was miraculously still there. He blinked at me and my now frazzled expression. Then he laughed. It was a glorious sound, soft and husky.

"You stayed."

"I'll let you cook," he said—in answer to my earlier invitation, the one I'd given him before I'd slammed the door in his face. "I just had something else I wanted to give you. You mentioned that you might want to clean my house, and I know that's weird but I…"

I hadn't mentioned so much as I'd demanded that he let me do it. But it was cute of him to soften my words.

"I *do* want to clean your house," I blurted. "Very much." And then, because he deserved an apology, I added, "I am so sorry for shutting the door in your face. And running." The words tasted like ash on my tongue as I waved my gloved hands at him.

"Don't be." Felix grinned even wider. He crossed the distance between us, slipping between my outstretched arms and tipping up onto his tiptoes for a kiss. I leaned down immediately, answering his silent command.

The kiss was chaste and soft.

It tasted like cherry chapstick. The one I'd given him last night before I'd left. He tucked something into my pocket, something small and light. "In case you need it to get in." Then he kissed me again, and every thought in my head fled.

My stomach filled with butterflies, my socked toes curling against the tile.

When we parted the second time, Felix reached up to gently swipe his thumb over my lip, probably to clean off the leftover chapstick.

"Goodnight, Marshall," he said, following our usual pattern.

I swallowed the lump in my throat, heart pounding. "Goodnight, Felix."

He looked pleased that I'd used his name again. It was written all over his face as he stepped back, swiveling gracefully on his heel before hopping down the steps. When he was halfway across my yard, he twisted back around to wave.

I waved back.

But I didn't stop watching him. Not until he'd crossed through the white picket fence that marked the end of my property. Not until he strode across the street to his own home. Till the door shut behind him, and I saw his shadow move up the stairs.

Later that night, I had my brilliant idea.

My brilliant, amazing, wonderful idea.

Innovative, really.

I'd been checking the camera footage from the security cameras like I did every night when a familiar, floppy-hatted man showed up in the feed. I paused it, zooming in on his face with near manic glee.

Cameras.

Yes.

Cameras!

I could see Felix's pajamas again if I used this to my advantage, couldn't I? And I wouldn't even have to wait until we slept together. I could keep my eye on him. Make sure he was safe. That no one—cough—Barry—cough—would be bothering him throughout the day while he was sleeping. I could make sure his "friends" were treating him with respect. And if they weren't? I could step in. Yes. Yes. *Yes.*

I was a *genius.*

An absolute fucking genius.

I should win an *award* for this.

I was only forward thinking. Protecting Felix was noble, wasn't it? Not *creepy*. I shot down Winnie's voice in my head—chest puffing up with pride. Never mind the fact that I had rather gleefully taken screenshots of the parts of surveillance video that had Felix in them, and saved them to my phone.

I was Suburban Serial Killer Batman.

Protector of tiny, lonely hermit men.

Not a lovesick stalker who would tattoo Felix's face on my ass if I wasn't terrified of needles.

It wasn't until I was changing into my pajamas that I remembered the second gift Felix had given me. It spilled from my pants pocket onto the floor, and I grinned—*evilly*—when I saw what it was.

A key.

A key to Felix's house.

So that I could go over and clean.

Unfortunately, I had to wait until I was off for the weekend to enact my evil plan. Which was, A: clean up the dust and cobwebs in Felix's home. And B: install the cameras I'd purchased to spy on him.

He'd sleep all day—I already knew that—which meant I had plenty of time.

Cleaning his house, on top of helping him, offered me the perfect alibi.

Bright and early, I headed across the street to Felix's murder-mansion, feeling like a giddy child as I used the key he'd given to me for the first time.

Dolly and Tiffany hissed at me where they lurked at the base of the stairs, and I waved them off with a positively sunny grin.

"Oh, hush," I hummed, shutting the door behind me. "I'm helping your father, so behave."

Never mind the fact that I was spying on him too. But they didn't need to know that.

I tried to be quiet, despite the fact that Felix had assured me that he was a deep sleeper, because it was only polite.

From six a.m. to noon, I worked my way through the first floor, the kitchen, the dining room, and living room. From noon to five, I scrubbed my way through the second floor—which, to my mounting horror, housed a whole plethora of rooms that were filled to the *brim* with junk.

The clutter that lined the halls was just the tip of the iceberg, and that only became clearer with each door I opened.

Letters, paintings, posters. Old, dated furniture. Portraits and pictures of people I didn't recognize in black and white, that I could only assume were Felix's family. A tarot deck that looked about a thousand years old. Knick-knacks and memorabilia from what looked like the mid 1900s. And in the back room at the end of the hall, I found a very memorable, very large coffin tucked away in a surprisingly dustless corner.

The cats watched me as I worked around it, but I found I didn't mind the company. At least…when Dolly wasn't swiping at my head.

"You've got a very pretty father," I informed them as I worked my way through the coffin room. "You're very lucky. Mine is quite a bit uglier than yours is."

They both seemed to approve of this statement, and left me alone when

I headed into the next room.

I didn't throw away any of Felix's things, as that wasn't my place. But I *did* clean them up, organizing them as best I could, and freeing them from cobwebs and dust.

I avoided the third floor where Felix's bedroom was, so that I wouldn't wake him. I was quite curious what his sleeping face would look like but that felt rude—and I didn't want to disturb him. Especially when I was about to install cameras in his kitchen and by his front door.

I chose both locations for specific reasons. Most importantly, I was unlikely to see anything inappropriate with either camera—I wanted to observe him, not violate his privacy. The camera at the front would allow me to see people coming and going. And, the kitchen camera meant when Felix ate dinner, I could join him, even from my computer at work.

Finally, around six p.m., when I was dust-worn and gritty, I made my way back downstairs. Pulling out the box I'd brought that housed the surveillance equipment, I tugged on my apron—the cleaning one, not the cooking one—and got to work.

Felix had *never* been awake during the daylight hours before, and I hadn't expected that to change. He was a creature of habit as much as I was. Perhaps I'd been too loud when I was cleaning and disturbed him?

Or perhaps it had been the chipper way I'd whistled while I worked. Either way, like usual, my guard was down when Felix was in my general vicinity. Which was why I hadn't realized he was there.

"You know, if you wanted to take photos of me you would've been better off installing the camera in the living room," Felix said, startling the bejesus out of me and nearly making me fall on my ass. "I'm hardly ever in here."

I paused, rigid—and very, *very* slowly turned my head to look at him.

I knew what I probably looked like. A kid with his hand stuck in a damn cookie jar. *Don't freak out, don't freak out, don't freak out.* But…my guilt melted away the second I actually saw him.

"Thank you for cleaning my house, Marshall." Felix was sleepy-soft, wearing the pajamas that had sparked this idea in the first place. "It hasn't been this nice in years." There was a dazed sort of look on his face that reminded me of the first time that I'd come over here, like he was still half-asleep. Felix leaned against the doorway, his cats looping through his legs as he blinked blearily up at me, a soft smile on his lips.

I checked my watch. Seven o'clock.

He wasn't supposed to be up yet.

I squinted at him, annoyed.

"Why are you awake?" I accused him. "You shouldn't be awake for hours."

Why wasn't he freaking out?

That did not look like the face of a man who had just discovered his neighbor-lover putting cameras up in his home.

Felix yawned, stretching his arms over this head. The hem of his pajama top lifted up, flashing me a delicious peek of his pale, flat belly. *Do not get hard, Marshall. Not while installing cameras in your boyfriend's kitchen.*

"Why are you putting a camera in my kitchen, Marshall?" Felix countered sleepily, not sounding nearly as offended as he probably should have. Touché.

His lips curled up into a sly little smile. "Did you miss me?"

I scoffed, "As if."

"Uh-huh," he nodded, lowering his arms, that lovely span of naked belly covered once again. I licked my lips, my pulse skittering. His gaze snapped to my throat, and I must've been imagining things because it almost sounded like he groaned. "I'm not mad, Marshall."

I squinted at him, sure he was lying.

Hell, I'd be mad if I caught someone putting cameras in my house.

"You're not?"

"No."

We were at a standstill. Like an old Western film. Two cowboys in a duel. Felix waited me out, his lips twitching—like he was amused, even though his silence was apparently a weapon he could use against me.

It wasn't fair. What happened to the bumbling nervous man I'd walked in the woods with? It was like he could see right through me. See the way I ached for him. And like a switch had flipped, Felix's nervousness melted away. His true confidence began to shine through and it was... god, it was heady.

It felt like a century passed before I spoke.

"I'm protecting you."

He cocked his head to the side, assessing me. "I see." He scratched his pec, and my eyes snapped to the movement, my mouth suddenly dry. "So you're not spying on me?"

"I mean...I am."

"Right."

"So that I can protect you."

"Right." Felix laughed. It was a lovely, tinkling sound. "It's not because you're obsessed with me or anything."

"Of course not." Even I knew that sounded like a goddamn lie.

"It would be okay if you were," Felix said, voice low and fluttery. "I'd like it."

"You…would?"

"Yes." His eyes were such a striking shade of red. I didn't understand why he'd chosen to wear colored contacts, but I didn't mind. Not when they were so damn pretty. "I miss…being watched," Felix admitted, and his words were fragile and soft. "Being adored."

"Oh."

He offered me the grace of God then, because he didn't ask me any more questions about the cameras. In fact…he kept me company while I finished installing the second one, then followed behind me like a sleepy little duckling as I showed him where the first one was.

"So, you're telling me, that if I stand here—" Felix guided me back into the kitchen, then stood in the corner of the room facing the camera. "You'll be able to see it?"

"Correct." I showed him the app on my phone, a little, tiny Felix and Marshall showed up on the screen. I looked massive when standing next to him. *Ginormous.* Like a fucking mountain troll. My cock ached already, staring at the first *ever* photo of us together.

I screen-shotted it while I was looking, just in case.

I'd need to frame this.

Just imagine all the pictures I'll get!

There were so many wonderful opportunities.

"Okay," Felix said, smiling up at me. "This is going to be fun."

I didn't know what he meant.

At least…not until the next day when I was going through the first day of footage and saw Felix walk to that same corner of the kitchen I'd shown him. He raised his hands, made an odd shape with them, and paused there for a solid minute or two—probably to make sure the camera captured what he was trying to do.

It wasn't until I'd screen-shotted and zoomed in that I realized what symbol he'd been making with his hands.

A heart.

For me.

For the next week, every day like clockwork Felix would wake up and wander into the kitchen to give me a heart. On Tuesday he even blew me a kiss. Aside from that, the cameras didn't catch much.

Just him bringing in his delivery and blocking the contents of the box with the fridge.

I was starting to seriously wonder whether he needed to eat or not because the most I ever saw him do when he went into the kitchen was fill a mug with some sort of juice from the fridge. At least, I assumed it was juice. Because the liquid looked dark when he walked close enough for the camera to pick up the contents of the cup.

It never even occurred to me that Felix's appetite was a little more complicated than mine.

Maybe it should have.

Chapter Fourteen

THE NEXT TIME we went out, I took Felix to a vintage car show. It took pulling some strings—through my boss Harold, damn him and his toupee—but I managed to get the venue to give me access the night before a big show opened. Which meant…we had the *entire* place to ourselves.

Felix had been nervous to go out—but it seemed after the fair, the dam had broken and though he was nervous, he was incredibly excited too. After I'd told him we'd be the only ones there, all his nerves had melted away. Like an excitable puppy, he bounced around the room, hopping between vehicles and exclaiming every time he saw one he'd seen before.

"God, I used to have a car just like this," Felix said dreamily when we'd reached the end of one of the rows. He leaned lovingly along the hood of a Studebaker Champion, fanning his fingers along the paint with a sigh. The vehicle had a distinctive bullet-shaped nose and rounded fenders. The large windows on the car gave it a spacious feel, despite being smaller than my own SUV. I loved it, honestly, and the fact that he did too made him even more perfect in my eyes.

"What happened to it?" I asked, curious.

I expected him to clam up, but instead he sighed.

"Gone. I couldn't keep all of my old stuff, though I obviously tried." His voice was wistful, a sad little twist to his lips. I cocked an eyebrow.

His words were unusual. Just another item to add to the long list I was compiling of things that made no sense about Felix. Once again, I was forced to be content that I'd get my answers some day.

Maybe not today.

Because my main goal today was to steal more kisses.

And I accomplished it.

Because by the end of the date I'd stolen forty-six kisses. Felix's lips were swollen pink. They tasted like cherry chapstick—as did mine. I was sure I looked a mess too—as he'd taken to running his fingers through my hair. He'd been both ravenous and shy—wary, like he didn't know it was okay to want me as badly as I wanted him. By the end of the night, I'd remedied that.

It was hard not to feel confident after I'd spent all night kissing him against whatever vehicle was closest…and the walls…and the doors…and also the passenger seat in my car.

The evidence of our greedy touches was obvious. Both our shirts were untucked, our hair rumpled, and a boyish, giddy smirk was mirrored on our faces as we finally said goodnight.

Felix stood on his porch steps bathed in the golden light from the open door behind him. He was nearly as tall as I was when standing two steps above me. His eyes were as warm as they'd been when we'd danced—and as a cool breeze ruffled his hair, I ached to kiss him again.

Forty-six kisses, and it was still not enough.

His mouth looked *so soft*.

I wanted to kiss him so badly.

So I did.

Thoroughly.

Out in the open—where anyone could see, neighbors be damned.

When I retired home for the night, the front door shut behind me, I groaned and slid my hand down my pants to fist my hard cock. Felix drove me insane. With greedy flicks of my wrist, and my precum slicking the way, I jerked myself off, remembering the way he tasted and felt in my arms.

So small, so solid, so perfect.

Twisting, I stared through the peephole on the door, my hand still working, my cock dripping onto the floor as I watched the house across the street for any sign of the tiny, wonderful man inside. When I saw his shadow in the upstairs window, I came with a needy, desperate growl.

Harold gave me shit the next morning at work, but I found that asking him for help had been worth it. It seemed half the office—who am I kidding, *all* of it—knew about me and my new romantic adventures. Normally, I'd mind. Normally it would piss me off. Normally I'd guard my privacy like a rabid wolf guards his steak.

But…I was too busy to be annoyed.

Too busy spending my nights watching penises bounce. (In preparation, of course.)

Too busy spending my days reading spreadsheets. (Because I needed money to provide for Felix, and art.)

Too busy spending my evenings with Felix. (Whenever his schedule permitted it, his other paramours aside.)

Too busy being in *love* with a tiny, pastel-wearing gremlin man, to find the energy to care about anyone or anything but him.

I was a lovesick fool and *everyone* knew it. They could see it on my face, probably. Though my new screensaver didn't help. I had, rather proudly, turned my desktop screen into a homemade collage of the pictures I'd been collecting of Felix. Most were from the security feed I had going in his kitchen. He'd posed for those, which I found just…ah. So *sweet*.

I'm not going to insult your intelligence by pretending this was "normal" behavior from either of us. I knew I was odd. Possessive. *Obsessive*. I'd just…never met someone who not only didn't care about my more unpalatable personality traits, but maybe even liked that I had them.

Some pictures were more sneaky than those were. For example, I had covertly taken several of Felix at the car show. And there were a few extra fun pictures of him walking his cats outside. Last but not least, I'd collected a rather gorgeous photo that featured Felix crocheting while sitting on his couch.

That one was my favorite. It'd been tricky to get it—and Felix nearly caught me lurking in his bushes, my camera out. My heart had been pounding so loud, I'd worried it would give me away.

He looked so…*forlorn* in the photograph.

Do you get lonely, Finley?

I can't remember a time when I wasn't.

"That's a bit creepy, you know," Harold hummed as he passed by my office around noon. I already knew why he was here. He was going to invite me to lunch like he did every Thursday. I'd decline—like always. Then he would wander off to leave me alone with my chicken breast and asparagus filled Tupperware. It was routine. A pattern we stuck to.

This time, however, I was in a generous mood—aaaand I didn't have my Tupperware.

"Lunch?" Harold asked like he hadn't just insulted me.

"It's not creepy," I replied, while still staring wistfully at Felix's *lovely* face. "And yes."

"Yes?" Harold blinked, obviously surprised. "As in…?"

"Yes, I will go to lunch with you." I turned my computer off and rose from my seat, sliding my laptop into my satchel.

"No chicken today?" He squinted, clearly confused. For ten years we'd done this exact dance and this was the first time I'd ever changed the steps. I was a fan of routine, as was he.

I supposed it made sense that he was concerned.

"No," I answered, slinging my bag over my shoulder. "No chicken."

He blinked.

He blinked again.

And then a slow, wicked smile spread across his face. "Were you out too late to meal prep last night, Marshall?"

"And if I was?" I sniffed, adjusting my bag. Technically, I would've had time when I'd gotten home to cook. But…instead, I'd spent the last hour of the night before bedtime creating the masterpiece that was now sitting prettily as my desktop screensaver. I hadn't had enough pictures before the car show, and now it was perfect.

"Good for you, buddy." Harold laughed, shaking his head with obvious delight. "Now how do you feel about cheeseburgers?" My face pinched, and he redirected. "Pizza?" Again, my face pinched. "What do you even eat?" Harold frowned at me in mock concern. At least, I *thought* it was mock concern. *Maybe it was real?* I couldn't tell.

"Chicken."

"Fucking christ, Marshall."

We went to a local diner.

I ate salad, ice water, and a giant slice of rhubarb pie.

It didn't taste nearly as good as the one Felix had bought me.

For the first time in my life, I couldn't shut up. While I shoveled pie in my mouth, and changed my phone screen to Felix's face, I told Harold about our date. About Felix in general. About his pretty eyes, and how short he was, and the fact that he was clever, and silly, and lovely, lovely, lovely.

When Winnie visited me again she remarked—rather unhelpfully—that she had "never seen me more zen."

I didn't know about *that*.

Zen people did not feel like they were about to vibrate out of their skin.

Zen people did not buy binoculars so they could peer inside their neighbor's windows when he had visitors over.

Zen people did not hoard said neighbor's mail—because they'd waited too long to give it back, and now it was *awkward*.

Tampering with packages was a felony. I knew this. We all knew this. But of the felonies I was guilty of, *this* was the one I was least concerned about. I was lucky that my kill for the year had happened during spring, as that itch in and of itself was hard to ignore.

My full focus was on Felix now.

And I'd never been more satisfied—or *hungry* in all my life.

Visions of fucking him assaulted me at the most inopportune times. As did fantasies of dancing with him, of playing with him, of lying beneath his big telescope and watching him gaze at the stars. I wanted to share *everything* with him. Every waking moment we had left.

There were rings in my shopping cart.

I bought a t-shirt with his face on it to wear as pajamas.

I doodled his name on my notes at work like a lovesick teenager.

And when my coworkers asked me what I was doing for the weekend, I grinned so wide and so creepily that they all left me alone.

I was so *obsessed* with Felix that I nearly forgot about the disappearing shop we'd both visited in the first place.

Nearly.

I *had* spent a solid two hours immediately after that first dinner date hunting the internet for signs of it—to no avail—but aside from that, yes. *Forgotten.* Totally, completely forgotten.

The next time I saw Felix, he was leaving his house well after ten p.m. It was late, but I was curious. And when I inquired what he was up to, I was informed that it was time for his cats' yearly check-up at the vet.

I offered to carry them, and forty minutes later, with cat carriers in each hand, we strode into a twenty-four hour clinic in a town called Elmwood. The receptionist eyed me curiously, but didn't say a thing, though she was rather friendly toward Felix.

Suspiciously friendly.

I didn't like it.

"Back again?" she asked with a happy hum. Her nails clicked on the counter and it grated on my nerves.

"Tiffany had a stomach ache a few months ago," Felix explained to me. "So we're back sooner than usual."

"She feeling better?" the receptionist asked, tapping away on the computer like she was taking notes. The cats were surprisingly docile as I held them aloft in their carriers. They stared up at me through the gaps in the cages, almost like they appreciated my presence here.

As they should.

I was protecting their owner after all.

"Much better," Felix replied. He had his hat on, and his sunglasses, and he looked adorable and *tiny*, dressed in a cute little vintage shirt-pant combo that looked like it came straight out of a black and white film. His biceps were on display, and I had a hard time not staring at them. They looked particularly…lickable today. As did his ass, which flexed rather prettily as he shifted from foot to foot.

It was tricky to stare up close like this without being caught, so I switched tactics.

Figuring I wasn't needed, I retreated to the waiting area with the cats where I could ogle a little less obviously. However, I did stick close enough that I would still be able to hear Felix and the woman as they spoke.

I kept my attention half on them as I took in our surroundings. Pristine, white paint. Posters that were probably meant to evoke a feeling of calm. A wall lined with portraits of animals. Boring.

The street was bursting with life outside the large glass window in the waiting area.

You'd think the town would be asleep this late at night on a weekday. Couples held hands, waltzing down the sidewalk together. And at the end of the road sat a diner. It had a lively glow, and a line practically ran out the door.

Beach Town was not this active at night, that was for sure.

Perhaps that was why Felix had opted to come here for his "cat care." I had a hard time imagining many vets kept their doors open past midnight.

"That him?" The receptionist asked, her voice quieter than before. I glanced around covertly, trying to see *who* she was talking about, only to belatedly realize that she was probably talking about *me*.

"Yes," Felix laughed, a sheepish sort of quiver to his words. "He insisted on coming the second I said I was leaving town."

"I see."

"For protection." Yep. They were definitely talking about me.

There were a lot of sickos out there. Believe me, I knew. There was no way in hell I was letting Felix out on his own. He was far too oblivious. I may not be gifted emotionally, but I was quite street smart, at least in the ways that prevented an altercation.

He'd get robbed or worse if left to his own devices.

Normally, I hid behind my sweater vests, but today I'd abandoned the second layer entirely. Felix's eyes kept gravitating to my chest where a bit of hair peeped through the collar of my button-down, as well as my arms—staring at me the same way I stared at him.

I hoped, with my size and musculature more obvious, people would be less likely to bother him. I folded my arms over my chest, a cat on either chair beside me as I glared at the receptionist, willing her to find fault in my words.

"For protection," she repeated, her voice wobbling with a laugh.

Rude.

"He *insists* I need it," Felix added, sounding oddly delighted.

"I see." She flashed me another knowing look, her gaze gliding appreciatively over my body. "Good for you," she added, humming to herself as she stared at my pecs.

I nearly slapped a hand over them, scandalized.

"He is." Felix covertly stepped in front of her view, and a little thrill flipped inside my belly. I licked my lips, doing my own ogling as my gaze traveled down the surprisingly long line of his back to his pert little ass.

My cock perked up, and to preserve my dignity, I folded my leg over, resting my ankle on my knee to hide it from view.

It wasn't until later that I realized the fact that the receptionist had known who I was meant Felix had been *talking* about me. Probably far longer than we'd even been together.

I probably hadn't needed the stroke to my ego but it was lovely, all the same.

Two weeks or so after we visited the vet, I received a frantic call from Harold. The summer was winding down.

We were only a month away from Barry (the blight's) annual Summer Bash. Something I was dreading, though Felix was surprisingly excited. This year, the theme was "weddings". Which, if you asked me, was frankly ridiculous. Felix told me he wanted to go together.

As grooms.

And wasn't that…just the stupidest thing I'd ever heard?

I was going to enjoy it immensely.

I'd already ordered my tux.

I was getting ready—a button-down and no vest today—to take Felix out again, and of course, because everything sucked, Harold called.

"Marshall…" He sounded apologetic.

Why did he sound apologetic?

"No, Harold."

"Yes, Marshall."

"No, Harold." I groaned, rubbing my temple. "No." He made an apologetic sound. "But—it's date night."

"I know. I'll make it up to you?"

"Fuck."

Apparently—sparing you the gritty, boring details—someone had been an idiot (big surprise there) and something had been logged incorrectly—and blah, blah, *blah*.

A giant, expensive, pain in my ass.

In a tizzy, I walked over to Felix's home. It was brisk out, chill for a summer night. The woods creaked, and down the street, Barry's lights were off despite it only being eight p.m.

I'd been flying on cloud nine all day, imagining what Felix and I could get up to tonight.

I'd had it in my head that I might touch his ass.

I know! Me?! An ass toucher.

I'd never wanted to touch someone's ass before.

I had been psyching myself up for it all day. And if things got a little frisky, I'd also figured I might throw a little tongue action in for the first time. I was a goddamn *adventurer*. Obviously I'd take Felix for food he wouldn't eat first and park us in the woods in what I now affectionately referred to as "our spot" in my head.

It was going to be so *romantic*.

Which was *why* I was pissed-angry-annoyed-irritated that I'd have to call off our date. Damn, Harold and his burger-pizza-eating, polo-wearing bitch-face.

Luckily…my ire was for naught.

Because when I told Felix what had happened, instead of sending me home to bitch and moan alone, he invited me inside, laptop, spreadsheets, foul mood, and all.

We sat together on his couch in silence for hours while I put out metaphorical fires and Felix crocheted some more wisteria for the parts of the house I'd cleaned.

He graciously left me alone, which allowed me to focus.

I'd never understood the phrase "comfortable silence" until I'd met him. Now I knew it intimately, and I never wanted it to end.

The occasional brush of Felix's cool feet beneath my thigh served to remind me that I was here—and not at home. As did the lovely lemony scent of his hair, and the quiet whisper of his needle looping through yarn.

At one point, Felix abandoned his project and switched positions entirely. No longer sandwiched at the other end of the couch, he scooted into my side almost…*shyly*. He glanced at me through his lashes to gauge my reaction to his closeness.

A pleased little smile flitted across his lips when he saw my face.

I wasn't sure what it was doing, but apparently it was favorable because only seconds later he was settling his head against my arm, his fluffy hair an absolute mess.

He dozed sleepily, like he wasn't curled up with a predator.

Like he wasn't a predator himself.

My monster ached.

Felix drooled against the sleeve of my button up, his crochet forgotten. Docile. Sweet. He looked so…soft like this. Covertly, I took a picture, logging it away in the album on my phone that was dedicated to him, and him alone. Then, because his hands looked rather lovely where they rested almost demurely in his lap, I took a picture of them too.

And his feet.

And his collarbones.

Fuck, his collarbones were pretty.

He was asleep, so I tried to be quiet—even when Dolly, the white-haired, bug-eyed beast tried to climb onto my lap, ignoring the presence of the laptop there at all. I pocketed my phone quickly to free up my hand in case I needed to defend my honor.

"No—" I hissed out, trying not to flinch. "Do not step on my spreadsheet—"

She blinked at me, lifting one soft little paw above the keys threateningly. It hovered, pink toe beans flickering into view. Using my free arm, I tried to push her away. Instead, somehow—witchcraft probably—the violent shove I'd planned on giving her somehow morphed into a gentle pet. My fingers fanned along her back, stroking the—*oh wow, that was so soft!*—fur with reverence. "You are a plush, little beast, aren't you?" I murmured, surprised by how much I liked how her fur felt beneath my palm.

I was going to have cat hair on my nice slacks, dammit.

Like the devil had overtaken me entirely, I found myself gently guiding her to snuggle up against my other side. She purred, rumbling against me as I gave her head one last, awkward pat, before retreating back to my laptop.

Because, apparently, things could get worse—that was not the last of it.

"Fuck my life," I muttered under my breath, as Tiffany—only a few seconds later—hopped up onto the couch and joined Dolly at my side. "I'm not your emotional support human," I chided both of them under my breath, though I tucked Tiffany in too with an annoyed grumble.

This was awful.

So terribly awful.

Almost as awful as the fact that Felix wanted to wear matching suits with me and pretend to be husbands for the entire neighborhood to see.

Bundled up as the rather tall center of a Felix sandwich, I worked through the last of my work. When I finished, I stayed, still reluctant to wake the three sleeping beauties who had made me their bed.

The stuffed cat Felix had won at the fair sat on his mantel, staring at me, but I didn't mind.

And when Dolly and Tiffany—movie characters, I'd Googled when Felix had told me their names—awoke and fled their spots on the couch, eyeing me like the intruder I was. I didn't mind that either.

"Acting as though you didn't just use me as a pillow for an hour and a half," I snorted as they climbed onto their ridiculous cat tree, far more graceful than any creature had a right to be. "Spoiled things."

Felix yawned, alerting me that he was awake. He gave my arm a little kiss that sent my pulse skittering. Then he wiggled, his chin digging in— and he peered up at me through the dark fringe of his lashes. His blinks were slow and sluggish.

Without thinking, I reached down to stroke a hand through his hair—

like I'd done to the cats.

Felix smiled, humming softly as he tipped into the touch. "I've never slept beside someone else before," he admitted.

My heart skipped a beat.

He was so damn pretty, he distracted me from the train wreck that was about to happen. God, his lips looked soft. Kissable. I wanted to lick them like I'd planned. Very badly.

Then his sleepy smile flickered in confusion—the same time he glanced at my laptop screen and saw—oh shit.

He saw my collage.

The one Harold had called "creepy."

And my life flashed before my eyes.

Chapter Fifteen

MY PULSE SKITTERED.

My heart lurched.

Abort, abort, abort.

He found out. He found out! He's seen it. He's going to freak out. I'm screwed, I'm screwed, I'm screwed.

I was so certain at that moment that I'd somehow inadvertently found his limit. That there was no way he'd be able to see the collage for what it was—a declaration of affection. Instead, he'd see it like Harold did.

He'd think I was a creep.

He'd be done with me.

I'd have to move.

Why hadn't I thought of switching my screen over before I came here? I was a planner. How could I have been caught so horribly off guard? Oh god. Oh-god-oh-god-oh-god. Cameras were one thing—but collecting and using the photos? That was something else entirely.

"Don't blow your stack, love," Felix grinned.

"Don't blow my…what?"

"Your stack. You know? Have a conniption?"

I blinked, cocking my head again. Him and his weird phrases again.

"It's cute," Felix said, still grinning. "Your little…collage thing. I suppose I didn't know what you'd do with the pictures you were taking, but I…like it."

"It's…cute?" I blinked, my brain officially broken. It was very clear that I had taken quite a few of these pictures without his consent. And instead of creepy, he was calling me *cute*? I squinted at him, flummoxed. Sure, I hadn't *wanted* him to think I was creepy—but I was seriously beginning to question his sanity.

My pulse raced.

My belly flipped.

Maybe we were even better suited for one another than I'd thought.

"*Yes,*" he laughed, nuzzling my bicep with a happy hum. "It's cute. You must really like me, huh?"

My cheeks flamed, my head spinning. I scoffed, but I knew he didn't believe me. I didn't even believe me. "*You?* Not likely."

"Because I'm not special," he hummed, eyes dancing with mirth.

"Exactly."

Felix kissed my bicep, once, twice, three times. The same biceps he'd complimented the first time we were together. I flexed, and he hummed, nuzzling into the hard muscle happily, almost like he'd been wanting to do that for years.

Then his kisses climbed, up, up, up. Over my shoulder, across my trapezius, and up my neck. His breath puffed tantalizingly against the shell of my ear as his body hovered carefully against mine.

"You know…" Felix said, lips fluttering against my skin.

My cock throbbed.

When I glanced down, I was mortified to see it pushing rather pointedly against the seam of my pants, thick and needy. I surreptitiously tried to shift my laptop over it, so that Felix wouldn't see.

"In case you forgot, I like how obsessed you are with me." Felix's voice was a throaty purr. He kissed the shell of my ear, and I whined, unable to help it. It was the second time he'd said something along those lines, and this time, I was inclined to believe him.

"Oh."

I tried to think about chaste things. Tried to calm the beast inside me that ached to grab him and pull him right into my lap. I wasn't sure what to do with him once I had him there—but god. My dick hurt. I just… wanted to rub it on him a little.

Was that really so bad?

Felix's slippery tongue slid along my ear and I whined again, hips jerking up, searching for something to fuck.

"Take whatever pictures you want, Marshall," Felix said, licking a cool slick trail behind my ear where he settled, his teeth worrying the skin of my throat. "I promise I don't mind."

"Nnng," I gasped out, tipping my head to give him more room. Slick and tantalizing, he flicked his tongue needily against my throat—like a kitten would lap at a bowl of milk.

Then suddenly, he was gone.

I blinked my eyes open, and Felix was on the opposite side of the couch.

His eyes were wide. His lips were pressed into a flat line. And he was staring at my throat like it was *taunting* him. His throat bobbed, and I panted, staring at him with mirrored hunger.

From a safe distance, Felix's gaze trailed over my body appreciatively. His hands flexed into fists. When I glanced from his broad shoulders, down his supple chest, to his tiny little waist, I *groaned.*

It wasn't fair.

The bones in my hands practically creaked as I squeezed them into fists, struggling to control myself. Struggling not to toss my laptop to the floor and shove him into the leather, inexperience be damned.

"Let's cool down, yeah?" Felix said, voice rough. There was a noticeable bulge in his pants, and I ached. I ached, and ached, and *ached.*

I wanted to yank his pants off and taste him.

Wanted to lick up the salt and cum, and make him sob.

"Marshall," Felix's voice was a gravelly soft warning. "My eyes are up here."

"I know." I jolted, surprised by how low my own voice had gotten. I hardly recognized it. It was like the beast inside me had risen to the surface and taken over entirely.

I gritted my teeth, sucking in a steadying breath.

It was difficult, but I managed to tear my eyes away from Felix's cock. My gaze dragged upward, ravenously taking in every gorgeous, provocative inch of his tiny, compact body.

"You make it so *difficult* to be a gentleman," Felix said, his lovely, pointy teeth flashing. "And I already have a hard enough time not losing control when you're here."

I knew what he meant, so I didn't push.

My own control was hanging by a thread even thinner than the yarn he'd been using earlier.

Doing my best not to defile him with my gaze anymore, I forced my eyes away, looking for something distracting. My gaze fell on the cats again—and blearily, I tried to refocus.

"Is Tiffany a…calico?" I asked, curious. I had no idea if "calico" was even a breed. Only that I'd heard the name here and there over the years, and was desperate to think about anything other than fucking Felix into the couch. When I twisted back to look at him, Felix shook his head. He stretched his legs out, his hats hung up on the wall on his side of the couch. He hadn't even put one on today. Not once.

Felix's eyes were soft as he reached a hand out. The cat wandered closer, Tiffany's lovely—awful, I mean, *awful*—head pushing into his palm. "Tortoiseshell actually."

"Tortoiseshell," I repeated, storing that information for later.

I shut my laptop, figuring it was time for me to head home.

Mostly because my cock would not go down—and I was not ready to cross that line yet. Or embarrass myself further by pointing my dick at Felix for the rest of the night. Besides…it was getting late.

I hadn't gotten to tongue him—or touch his ass.

But he'd certainly tongued me.

So I was calling the night a win.

Later, which was apparently the next day, when I was Googling cats and how to care for them—I had Tiffany's picture up on my phone for inspiration. Harold walked by, because of course he did—it was Thursday. He peeked over my shoulder at the screen, head cocked to the side.

"Ah, a calico," he hummed, leaning over my shoulder to get a better look. "Cute."

"*Tortoiseshell*, you bitch." I sniffed.

Harold laughed, slapping my back affectionately. "This the famous cat?"

"One of them." Flipping through the forty or so pictures I'd taken last night for research, I showed him a picture of Dolly.

Harold looked at me with a peculiar expression, but I didn't notice.

Staring at the two cats gave me an idea for my next date with Felix, however, so it ended up not being a waste of time after all.

My own discomfort was well worth it when the following Thursday—after I'd done some more extensive research—we arrived at our destination and Felix's eyes went wide with wonder.

"A *cat* cafe?" He asked, flabbergasted. "What does *that* mean?"

Proudly, my chest puffed up as I held the door open for him. I'd worn my favorite sweater vest— a sacrifice, as you can probably guess, as cat hair and fancy sweaters did not mesh well. Actually…perhaps they meshed too well. If the wiggly, stubborn hair that never fucking came out after it had snuck into the grain of the fabric was any indication.

I'd wanted to look my best because I was bound and determined to touch Felix's ass tonight.

Over clothes, you whore.

I had thus far been unsuccessful in my mission, but that was going to change.

Felix was dressed like he normally was, a soft pastel sweater and crisp trousers. The only difference was the fact his bare ankles were showing above his leather loafers. *No show socks, what a slut.*

That little strip of bare skin made me weak-kneed every time I saw it. The entire drive I'd been panting after him, gaze flicking down over and over, spying on the skin for later appreciation.

The inappropriate looks didn't stop. In fact, they only grew more frequent over the span of the next two hours—as we sipped coffee and sat amongst a harem of frisky, furry beasts. Every time one touched me, I jumped, and Felix laughed, seemingly as delighted by my antics as he was the cats.

We were the only couple there. Which I knew would be the case, as once again, I had bought out the cafe for privacy.

Only the best for Felix.

Winnie said I was ridiculous—seeing as he'd been fine when we'd gone to the fair. But I was nothing if not thorough. And besides…I had…maybe—a lot of money. Okay, fine. I was loaded. That's what happens when you become CFO in your twenties and put all your money into stocks.

I didn't mind spending my small fortune on Felix.

Hell, I wasn't going to spend it on myself.

Aside from my wardrobe and my Mercedes, I rarely spent money at all.

Most of it went toward Christmas, and even then, I was never exorbitant. My sisters had always been the kind of people that valued quality time and handmade gifts over money. Which was incredibly frustrating, as I didn't like to offer my time—and I hated getting my hands dirty with anything but blood. Which I suppose…was the point.

Probably.

Anyway—

There was a mangy cat that sat in one of the ridiculous boxy enclosures in the corner of the cafe. The woman who worked the desk informed us that they were called "cat igloos" and I was…morbidly fascinated.

He was skinny and weak, with a patchy pelt and large brown eyes. He reminded me of some of the barn cats that had wandered free around the farm when I was a child. There was a wild, wicked look to him—almost feral, though still skittish. Felix tried to coax him out multiple times to no avail.

Unfortunately, the one and *only* time I beckoned him closer—to try to help, obviously, not because I wanted to touch the cat—he'd come immediately. Felix was so delighted he practically danced next to me, vibrating happily as he watched enraptured as the small cat sat his bony ass right down in my lap and started to purr.

"He's got good taste," Felix hummed, grinning at me from where he sat cross-legged on the other side of our small, round table. He'd barely touched his coffee and I'd been the one to eat his croissant. He was going to waste it. I wasn't sure why I'd bought it in the first place when I knew that.

"He does?" I blinked, holding stock-still.

"You've got a lovely lap, Marshall." Felix blinked, faux-innocently, the cad. "If I was that size, I don't think I'd ever leave it." His voice was a slow, sweet purr. Even sweeter than the little thing buzzing on my lap. His damn ankles mocked me, and I swallowed, my cock threatening to jerk to life.

"You're such a whore," I told him immediately, cheeks flushed.

Felix cackled, head tossed back in delight.

"You've been waiting all night to call me that, haven't you?" I glared at him, eyes narrowed. "You keep staring at my ankles like I'm walking around naked."

"Because you are."

"Huh," Felix blinked, head cocking to the side. His eyes were dancing, so I knew he was teasing, even though he really was a slut with his damn ankles out like that. "I thought I was wearing clothes?" He plucked at his very nice, very soft sweater thoughtfully.

"You're ridiculous," I scoffed unhappily, the cat still purring in my lap.

"You're the one that's getting hot and bothered because I've got my ankles out."

I scoffed again, cheeks beet red.

"Just imagine if next time we go out, I decide to wear *shorts*."

"Don't tease."

"You'd see my knees, Marshall. I don't know if you could handle that."

"I bet you don't even own a pair of shorts," I countered—because the idea of seeing Felix's knees was definitely going to make me hard. Which was not something I wanted to be when I had a mangy cat in my lap.

Felix was entertained.

I was not.

I returned my focus to the creature using me as a cushion, desperately willing my cock to behave. The damn thing had been dormant for ninety percent of my life. Why'd it have to wake up now? I wish I had an off-switch for my libido. Though, realistically, it wasn't bound to do shit. Because if I had an off-switch, that meant I had an on-switch too—and I was certain Felix would be constantly flipping it, just because he was a little shit who liked to watch me squirm.

Stop thinking about your libido, Marshall.

Cats.

Think about the cats.

Unsure what to do with my hands, I sort of—hovered them over him—till Felix coaxed me into petting the damn beast.

The moment I touched him, something clicked into place inside me. The part of me that had always loved the desperate and weak.

And I…well.

I took him home.

Even though he quite effectively cock-blocked me, and instead of getting to touch Felix's ass, we spent an hour shopping online for cat things together.

I tried to rationalize it.

Cats were useful beasts, surely. They ate…mice, didn't they? Not that I had a mouse problem—but still. Mice. Yes. That was why I took him. Not because he was ugly and old and had a knick in his ear.

Not because he hated everyone but me.

Not because he needed me.

No.

That would be ridiculous and sentimental—and I was neither of those things.

Which turned out not to be true at all, because the next time Felix and I went out—a few days later—I took him to see a meteor shower inside our local botanical garden.

There were lights that lit the path that led through groves of fickle flowers, the rich scent of pollen permeating the air. It was a bee's paradise, and yet…Felix's eyes never left the starry night sky above.

He wore his hat, as he had for all of our dates out. No shorts, thank God. I could not be held responsible for what I would've done if Felix had flashed me his knees.

When I reached out and pulled his hat off his head, he didn't fight me. He just laughed, eyes crinkling. Then he cuddled into my side to hide behind my bulk.

There were only a few other couples that dotted the garden, so it wasn't like we were totally surrounded. Still though, I curled protectively around him, blocking him from view so he could focus on the meteors above without worrying about prying eyes.

I wasn't sure what it was about being observed that bothered Felix so much.

I'd always known he was hiding something—hell, *two* somethings now. But this was…well, *this* was different.

I had a feeling his murders and his reluctance to be seen had nothing to do with each other.

This was our…fifth date? Sixth? If I counted that time I'd brought him "lunch" at ten p.m. on my way to bed.

Which meant…maybe we'd been dating long enough I could ask?

Bolstering myself forward, I took a steadying breath. Felix was still staring at the stars, so tiny, but perfect as I curled around him. Snaking a hand around his back, I gently, slowly slid it lower—lower—lower.

It took strength to ask, when I'd told myself I wouldn't.

But…things were different now, right? This wasn't like the first time I'd been in his house. There was no body to burn. There was no blood to clean up. We were…something, weren't we? And "somethings" were supposed to be able to talk to each other, right?

Felix had told me that his secrets were all that he had, and while I understood that, had I not earned at least a little trust?

I'd been patient.

I could *keep* being patient.

But I just…wasn't sure when it would be time to cross that line. If I never asked, would Felix ever speak? He wasn't the best at offering truths unprompted—or at all. Was I supposed to initiate this? I had a feeling I was. Just like I suspected I was supposed to initiate sex between us.

I was *aching* for it.

Which was odd to admit.

But damn.

I wanted him so fucking badly.

Perhaps speaking came first? Emotional intimacy. Maybe Felix was like me. Maybe he didn't feel comfortable crossing the physical finish line before we'd reached a certain point emotionally. Which meant I needed to suck it up, buttercup, and ask him.

So I did.

"Why do you hide?" I asked, face pressing into his buttery soft hair as my fingers toyed with the hem of his sweater. I was only one solid drag from grabbing his ass for the first time, and it taunted me. Though, I quickly forgot about it as soon as the question slipped free and I waited, with bated breath, for Felix to reply.

I worried he'd brush me off like he had before. I thought he'd deflect, or lie, or pretend like I was making things up—like his hats and his glasses weren't shields from the general population.

But he didn't.

Instead…he gave me a brilliant, beautiful gift.

The most beautiful gift I'd ever received.

Better even, than the time my dad gave me my own hacksaw for Christmas.

Felix told me the truth.

"I used to be quite well known. I'm worried about being recognized," Felix said honestly. "I used to be a lot more…concerned about it? But time has passed and people have started to forget." I blinked, surprised. It was strange—because truthfully I had recognized him. The moment I'd seen him without his hat and glasses, there'd been something about him that struck a chord with me.

I still hadn't figured out quite what it was.

However, it was now evident that I'd been correct to find him familiar.

"One day my exile will end," he said softly, the perfect size where he settled into my arms. The longer I held him, the warmer he became. His eyes were full of stars as he stared up at me, the light show reflected within them. "I'll walk the streets like you do—" He gestured at the other couples that had begun to move, their heads tipped up like his was. "Like they do. I'll stay home, not because I have to, but because it is my sanctuary." Felix's voice was soft.

The air tasted like rose petals.

His hair smelled like lemon, and I *wanted* him.

I wanted him so badly I could feel it aching in my very bones.

"I'll be forgotten," he added as the meteors danced above, sparkling and bright, but not as bright as he was. "And my invisibility will be my freedom as surely as it will mean I've finally died."

I didn't know what *that* meant.

I didn't think I was supposed to.

So instead of asking more questions, I told him a truth of my own.

"I've never seen a star that shines as bright as you do," I admitted, and it was the scariest thing I'd ever said.

Felix hadn't put his hat back on.

He didn't hide from me.

He just…smiled.

His eyes shone, and I thought…if I could have this—

I would give up anything.

I would *do* anything.

If I could have him, I'd be whole.

Chapter Sixteen

IF I'D KNOWN the bloodbath that awaited me at Barry (the brainless's) Summer Bash, perhaps I would've been more excited it was coming. As it was—three weeks out, with my tux now sitting pretty in my closet, I was dreading it like I always did.

Every day, I waited for a note to be left on my door last minute, changing the theme. Barry had done it to me once before, I wasn't paranoid to expect it a second time. I worried…because this was the first time Felix and I would be going to one of these events not as neighbors—but as boyfriends. Lovers. Partners. Whatever the fuck your preference is. We hadn't talked about it yet, but I was certain this would be our suburban debut.

It had to be *perfect*.

Or I was going to "blow my stack."

"Another date tonight?" Winnie's voice echoed through the speaker on my phone as I finished getting ready for the night. I had several packets of lube tucked into the pockets of my corduroys and I felt like such a whore my cheeks would not stop burning.

Somehow, somewhere—out in the city—I wouldn't doubt that Winnie's Marshall-is-embarrassed sense was tingling.

Which was why she'd called.

Obviously.

To torment me.

"Yes." I grunted at her as I pulled my sweater over my head. Fanning my hand along the pale blue fabric, I frowned, tugged it off, then reached for a different one. Yes, yes. This one was better. When it was on, I twisted to check out my back in the mirror, pleased to see the soft fabric clung rather nicely to my broad shoulders.

Thank you, home gym that I had installed when I moved here.

I'd been…so close to touching Felix's ass on our last date.

Literally less than a hands width away.

But after he'd admitted to me why he was hiding, I hadn't felt it appropriate to grope him. So instead, I'd snuggled him along the path, and listened to him prattle on and on and on about "St John's Wort" and "Pussy Willows".

At the end of the night, when I'd dropped him off on his doorstep with a long, searching goodnight kiss, Felix had pulled back and grinned.

He'd acted *electrified*—like going outside his home obviously energized him.

"You know, for a man who claims he never leaves his house, you sure like leaving your house," I groused, stealing another kiss.

Felix just cackled and kissed back.

But that was as far as we'd gotten.

Long, searching kisses.

Drugging, toe-curling kisses.

No tongue.

No butts.

No dicks whatsoever.

I needed to change tactics. Subtle was not working. I needed to go on the offense.

"What are you going to do today?" Winnie asked, interrupting my rather inappropriate thoughts. Vladimir, the cat I'd adopted, scurried by my feet, crawling onto my bed with a quiet meow.

"No beds, Vladimir," I chided him, hands on my hips. "We've talked about this."

He meowed again in protest, so I left him alone.

Before I could answer her question, Winnie interrupted me. "Is that a cat, Marshall?"

How the hell had she even heard that?

Was she even human?

"We're going to watch a film at the drive-in a few towns over," I answered her first question, then the second, "And yes. His name is Vladimir."

"You…have a cat." It wasn't a question, but it sure felt like one. "Named… *Vladimir.*"

"Yes. Vlad the Im-paw-ler."

"Marshall—" Winnie laughed. "You *hate* cats."

"Do I?" I squinted, staring at Vlad where he lay peacefully at the foot of my bed, his tail swishing. "I suppose I do."

"And yet…"

"How about you poke your nose in someone else's business? I heard

Melissa is pregnant again. You can offer her my condolences," I threw our elder sibling under the bus. Winnie laughed.

"Been there done that. What, you think you're my first call of the day?"

"Fuck off." I clipped my favorite pair of cufflinks on as I spoke.

"So. The drive-in?" Winnie smoothly segued. "Also, I need pictures of the cat, like—yesterday."

"Yes, and fine."

"Really?"

"Yes, really." I had about a thousand pictures of Vladimir on my phone. I'd taken them because I knew something like this would happen the second my family found out I'd adopted a beast of my own. They were nosy like that.

I had not taken the pictures because he was cute.

I wouldn't do that.

If I had a gallery of him in a few little cat outfits, that was only because Winnie was bound to ask if I had any. And the second she knew I did, she'd demand to see. I was saving myself time. Being efficient.

"You use those condoms I gave you?" Winnie asked, inappropriately.

"God, you're nosy today." I picked up the phone, taking her with me as I headed into the bathroom to wash my face and shave. I whipped up the cream with a brush in a bowl as we talked, only half-listening to her as I applied the cool, fluffy substance to my face.

Damn. I should've done this before I got dressed.

I hadn't realized I'd begun to grow stubble though.

I wanted to be clean shaven. I had plans, dammit. And giving Felix beard burn was not in them—at least…not till I'd gotten a chance to stick my tongue in his mouth. I wanted him to be thinking about how sexy I was and how slick my tongue was, not that my beard hurt.

"What are you doing now?" Winnie asked, clearly amused as she listened to me rattle around.

"I'm shaving."

"I thought you shaved in the mornings."

"I did. I do. But—" I hated that she knew that about me.

"Marshall…" Winnie laughed, amused. "Why are you shaving twice? It's not like you're a werewolf. You couldn't have gotten that hairy."

"Maybe it's not necessary."

"Yeah, maybe."

"But I don't want to scratch him with my beard." Oh shit. I had not meant to say that. Oh fuck. I'd never hear the end of this. I'd be ninety years old, still getting ribbed.

"MarMar—" Winnie gasped, delighted. "Are you planning on making out with your boyfriend?"

"Stop. No. Ew. Winnie—"

"You're worried about beard burn." Winnie cackled, the riotous wheezing laugh she rarely used. "Oh god. Baby Martian's worried about beard burn! I never thought this day would come—"

"Shut up, shut up, shut up."

"Are you going to give him tongue, Marshall?"

"Shut up, shut up, shut up."

"Do you even know *how* to French kiss?"

"La-la-la-la." I spoke loudly, trying to cover up her teasing. As I reached for my razor, I debated hanging up on her entirely. We hadn't spoken since she'd visited me after the car show—and I missed her, even though I hated her more than I hated Walmart. Which was saying something.

Harsh, I know.

"Marshall and Felix sitting in a tree—" Winnie sang, "K-I-S-S—"

I hung up on her.

She tried to call back so I blocked her.

I finished shaving in peace—though I did go down a mini anxiety spiral and spent a solid half hour watching video tutorials about French kissing because she'd been right. I didn't know how. I'd never done it. Swapping spit had seemed incredibly disgusting before—

And now it was…

Ugh.

Fuck.

The idea of licking inside Felix's mouth was just…*yes.*

I was still flushed and flustered by the time I pulled into Felix's driveway to pick him up. I opened his door for him, and his eyes flashed with warmth as he settled into the passenger side, the seat already programmed into position to fit his short gremlin legs.

He smiled at me, leaning over the console by the time I slid into my seat, so he could give me a long, lingering kiss.

"Hi, Marshall," Felix said, voice low and sweet.

"Hi, Felix." I grabbed his face, holding him still so he couldn't pull away. All nervous thoughts fled my head as I crowded in and kissed him a second time. And then a third. And then a fourth.

I wanted to ask him about the woman I'd seen going over to his place the night before—but I was too distracted by how soft his lips were to do so.

An hour later we were parked at the back of the drive-in lot. An old black and white movie was playing, and Felix was…distracted. He kept glancing at the screen wistfully, then at me, then the screen again.

"I remember this one," he said softly as I passed him the blanket I'd brought for us to snuggle under. I'd shown him how to shift his seat into position, so we were both reclined while we snuggled under the comforter. Lights danced across Felix's face, and his eyes were far away again.

"You've seen it before?"

"I've lived it," Felix sighed, shifting closer to me, though the console was—annoyingly—in the way. I shifted closer too, half-tempted to pull him over it entirely and tug him into my lap.

I didn't know what he meant. This was a ballet film. Older than his car, probably. As far as I knew, Felix had never been a professional ballerina. Though, now that I thought about it, he *was* a good dancer.

And he had said that he was frightened of being recognized.

Perhaps he really had been?

There was a man on the screen that looked oddly familiar, but I ignored him for now, twisting to give Felix my full attention as I tried to figure out an appropriate—and not too forward—way to ask him if he would like to sit in my lap while I sucked on his tongue.

The car to our left—that was visible through Felix's window—rocked subtly, the glass already foggy.

Horndogs.

It wasn't fair.

I wanted to do that.

I just…didn't quite know how.

I squinted at Felix, and his attention moved from the film to me. He cocked his brow in question, the lovely muscle in his jaw flickering as his lips twisted up in amusement. "Is there something you want, Marshall?"

I cleared my throat, prepared to be suave. To seduce him with flowery words and declarations. Instead, all that came out was a garbled whine.

Felix's expression softened even more, a frankly smitten look on his face as he turned away from the film entirely. "What is it, darling? There's no need to look so distressed."

Darling.

God, I loved that.

"I want to kiss you—" There. I'd done it. Amazing! Fucking, finally.

Fuck you, brain.

Felix nodded, shifting over the console gracefully, his fingers curling around my shoulder to steady himself. "Okay," he leaned down, pressing a soft, delicious little kiss against my lips. Electricity zinged down my spine. Victorious, I languished in it, a muffled groan escaping me as our lips slid together, soft and slick.

Only…Felix pulled away.

Sure, a few minutes had passed—but that was not enough. It would never be enough. When he started to move back into his own seat, my life flashed before my eyes. I was old and grayer—and Felixless. It was *awful*.

I snatched him.

Yanked him right into my lap again—exactly how I'd wanted to only a few minutes prior. He was a solid weight, despite being small, and a startled sound escaped him as his eyes widened. We were so close. Intoxicatingly so. The scent of his lemony shampoo filled the air and my nostrils flared. Need curled hot and tight in my belly.

"Marshall—"

I kissed him again.

No more games.

fae.loves.art

No more playing.

I might've been awful at it, but I didn't think so. Because when I slipped my tongue inside Felix's mouth for the first time, he melted like butter in my arms. His fingers kneaded at my shoulders, a muffled groan escaping him as my tongue bumped up against his peculiar, sharp little teeth, and one of my hands tangled in the back of his hair, holding him in place.

Felix made a hungry sound—mirroring my own—as I disappeared inside him with each slick, needy flick of my tongue.

The beast inside me howled.

He kissed back. It took him a moment to get over the shock of having a tongue in his mouth, probably. Hell, I was quite shocked by my own behavior too. But…the moment he did, he was kissing back with fervor. His tongue slid along mine, cool as always, rubbing, rubbing, rubbing as my cock perked up beneath his ass and I struggled not to rut against him like a fucking animal.

His scent was heady.

It filled my head, my lungs, my heart.

When I finally broke away, it wasn't because I wanted to stop kissing but because I needed to breathe or I was going to pass out.

"Fuck," I hissed out, head thumping back against the headrest. Felix made an affirmative sound. And god…his lips were swollen and pink, abused from the rough kisses. I wanted to muss him up more. Which was a wild thought from a man who ironed his t-shirts before wearing them.

"Marshall," Felix's voice was a quiet warning. "We shouldn't—"

"Why not?" I asked, genuinely flummoxed. "I want you." I blinked. "You want me."

A horrible thought occurred to me.

What if he doesn't want me?

And that horror must've been written all over my face, because Felix made a quick sound in affirmation, diving in to kiss me again before I could fully panic. "I do. I do want you," he agreed, voice low and rough. "I want you so badly."

"Oh thank God." I hadn't meant to say that out loud, but as soon as it was out, I was glad I had. Felix laughed, a melodic little chuckle.

"I'm just not sure if I can control myself. I'm not hungry right now," he admitted, lips still brushing mine, "but…"

"If you get hungry I'll feed you." I did not understand him and his aversion to eating in front of me. Did he think I'd care if he got food stuck in his teeth? Or spilled—or…I don't know, burped? Even though the idea was unappealing, I was quite aware by now that there wasn't anything Felix could do that would make me less enamored with him.

Felix laughed, though the sound was brittle. "What if I want to eat you?" he joked, a wobble of real fear in his voice. "What then? Would you forgive that?"

"Are we talking cannibalism?" I blinked, trying very hard to listen to his words when he was sitting in my lap and his lips were right there. One of my hands crept up his thigh, making him shiver. Up it slid, over the groove where his leg met his torso, and back toward—

So close

So, so, so close.

"Cannibalism is not a hard limit for me," I told him honestly, my hand twitching. Touch the butt, Marshall. Touch the butt. Do it.

"Really?" Felix looked surprised, I didn't understand why.

"If murder doesn't bother me, why would eating people?" I blinked at him, distracted from ass-groping by talk of murder.

"I'm talking about eating *you*, Marshall."

"If you killed me, I would think it kind of rude if you didn't."

"Fuck." Felix laughed, head tossed back, his eyes dancing. "You're adorable."

I was not adorable. Maybe he was blind.

"Do you kill everyone you sleep with?" I had not thought of this, obviously. Perhaps that was Felix's MO. I couldn't blame him. I had one of my own. My kills were repetitive. Ritualistic. I followed the same formula every time. Perhaps he was the same? I killed bullies. Bullies that reminded me of the man who had tormented my sister.

While my kills had never involved sex, I could see the appeal.

I wouldn't have been able to before—but after meeting Felix, after helping him clean up after his own murders, I'd thought many times how lovely it would be to fuck him while adrenaline was still high. We'd both be buzzing. Maybe there'd be blood. And god, he'd taste so good—vicious and gorgeous and terrifying.

Was I willing to die if it meant sleeping with Felix?

If it meant having him?

I knew then that I was crazy. Because the answer was—without a doubt in my mind—yes.

"That's also not a hard limit for me," I added, breaking the awkward resulting silence.

"Oh, Marshall." Felix melted, falling forward into another, longer, greedy kiss. This time it was his tongue that was in my mouth, flicking along mine, teasing, teasing, teasing. He coaxed me and I followed—a helpless dog chasing his master for scraps of attention.

Felix hadn't answered my question—but I didn't care. Whether he killed me or not at the end of this, it would be worth it. I slid my hand lower, mirroring the movement with my other hand, so that both of them finally—blissfully—fanned around Felix's ass.

It was *perfect*. Perky. Bouncy.

Better than I'd imagined.

I gave it a squeeze and Felix groaned, sucking ravenously on my tongue, his sharp teeth pricking my lip. They pressed hard—hard enough they split a little and blood spurted between our lips.

I was about to pull back—to apologize, even though I hadn't done anything wrong—but there was apparently no need. Felix *whined*, a needy sound as he sucked greedily at the blood, his fingers scrabbling at my body, nails digging into my shoulders.

I'd be bruised. I could already tell.

Was it odd that I liked that?

It seemed I'd finally broken Felix. Because there was no more pausing, no more waiting, no more games. His monster had finally been drawn to the surface. He pushed his ass back into my hands, fingers scraping over my chest as his hard cock pushed against my belly.

Fuck.

Yes.

I understood now why everyone seemed to be obsessed with sex.

If this was sex—if all I'd needed was to wait for the right person to share it with—then I was sold. S-O-L-D sold. Felix was a ravenous, greedy little thing. He scratched and sucked, licking, biting, pressing into me like a beast in heat.

It was like the dam had broken.

All his control evaporated the second he drew blood.

God, I loved him.

I kneaded his ass possessively, squeezing and rubbing, listening to his gasping little whines as his cock pushed into my abs. I flexed to give him something hard to fuck against, urging his hips in a steady, swiveling grind as my own dick shoved against the space behind his balls.

This was heaven.

I'd thought that about Felix's smile before—and I'd been right then too.

But now I was…oh fuck.

Yeah.

I rutted harder, rolling my hips to meet the rhythm we'd set as Felix shoved his tongue into my mouth and I groaned around him.

I knew I wasn't going to last—and neither was he.

And that was what made this all the sweeter.

Because there would be more opportunities to play together. Infinite really.

So long as he didn't kill me.

When he came it was with a broken little howl. It was muffled between our mouths, but earth-shattering all the same. I bucked against him, grinding against his sweet little body, my hands forcing his ass down, over and over, to give me something to fuck against.

I bit his lip, hard, holding tight to it as he gasped against my mouth, his red eyes glowing.

Glowing.

What the—

Oh.

Oh.

Oh.

Felix shifted back a little, parting his legs. He pressed his hand to the ceiling for balance, holding tight, his other hand digging into my shoulder as he bounced on my lap. There was blood smeared across his lips, cherry red. My blood. My blood-my-blood-my-blood.

"That's it, darling," Felix urged, riding my lap, his eyes dark with heat. "Fuck me, sweetheart. C'mon. I know you need it."

"Please—" I gasped out. I'd only ever begged once in my life, and I'd sworn I'd never do it again. Apparently that had been a fat fucking lie. Because all I needed was Felix's sweet ass grinding onto my hard dick and I was prepared to sell my soul to come against him. "Please, please, please—"

"Fuck me," Felix growled, head tipped back as he watched me through his lashes. He looked powerful like that—gorgeous and inhibited. A sexy god. A sex god.

Aphrodite's tiny, delicious brother.

"Look at you," Felix's hand ran over my chest, pushing against my hard nipples as I grit my teeth and panted. Up, up, up, I fucked against him, planting my feet into the floor so I could make him bounce. There were too many layers. Too many layers—why had I brought lube and condoms if we weren't going to use them?

Why-why-why?

"Please—"

"Look at that big fucking chest heave." Felix squeezed one of my pecs, pinching it in his hand tight enough that for a moment I couldn't breathe. "You're all hot and bothered, aren't you, Marshall?"

I nodded, my jaw clenched tight, my lip no longer stinging—like it'd never been torn at all.

"You like to act scary, don't you?" Felix pulled his hips up and away, and my own pelvis jerked, trying to meet him—to no avail. Somehow, someway, he was stronger than me. It didn't make sense. *It didn't make sense*— "But you're really just a big, sweet puppy dog."

I growled at him, baring my teeth, and Felix grinned.

"You play bad, but deep down you're a good boy." I sobbed, the words bouncing around inside my head. "You're *my* good boy, aren't you?"

I nodded, though my jaw remained clenched tight.

His eyes were dark with heat and mischief, and I didn't think I'd ever seen anything prettier.

"You *need* to fuck me, don't you?"

"Yes—" I managed through gritted teeth. "Please—"

"Okay," Felix dropped his hips back down and I growled, head tossed back, my neck bulging. I clutched at his ass cheeks, yanking them apart, fingers dipping into the sweaty fabric-covered crease between them as I jerked up, over and over, and over. "Okay, Marshall."

"Felix—" his name was a swear and prayer on my tongue. Panting, I stared at him—enraptured all over again.

"I know—" Felix released the handle above the door, both hands pressing hard to my pecs. "I know." He squeezed and I sobbed, fucking into him as his palms scrubbed against my hard nipples. "Take what you need from me, my *good boy*. I want you to."

It was that last little purr that set me off.

My head tossed back again, hips pumping, eyes squeezed shut. Pleasure, unlike anything I'd ever known coursed through my veins. He felt so good. So warm, and solid, and fuck-fuck-fuck. I came inside my pants, sobbing as I chased that pleasure, rubbing my hard bulge against the sweet swell of his ass, fingers still clutching him open.

It took a while, but when I finally came down from my high, I opened my eyes.

Felix was still in my lap. He was warm—probably because he'd stolen my heat, the little thief. His eyes were soft, and his fingers were rubbing distracting little patterns over my heart and shoulders, and up my neck.

He looked…at peace.

But guilty too.

Like he knew he'd done something wrong—even though I'd wanted this.

"Are you going to kill me now?" I asked, voice low and hoarse. It was the only thing I could think of that would make him look at me like that.

Felix laughed, the sound startling out of him. "Ah. No." He smiled, though there was a bit of strain around his eyes. "Not today."

"I have a request." His fingers danced up my throat again, and Felix nodded, biting his own lip as he waited. Behind him the movie on the screen was winding down, the credits rolling, their light casting him in a rather spectacular halo.

A name caught my attention at the top—if only because it was one I'd seen before.

Lucky.

Huh.

Just a simple name. No last name attached.

But then my attention flitted back to Felix, and I smiled, hoping I didn't look as manic as I felt. There was cum drying in my pants. I had a crick in my back. And my legs were beginning to cramp. Logic dictated that I should not have been as blissfully happy as I was.

But logic was a bitch, and I was ignoring her today.

The only thing that mattered to me right now was Felix.

"What's your request?" Felix asked, sweetly. There was a dazed sort of look on his face, docile—like his orgasm had sucked the life out of him too.

"If you're going to kill me, at least let me fuck you a few more times first."

Felix laughed.

And it was sunshine, sunshine, sunshine.

I leaned up to taste it, gathering him close because if I didn't, I worried he'd slip away again. There was a lot I was willing to lose in this life, but Felix wasn't one of those things. And I knew I would keep him forever if he let me.

Even if my forever was not nearly as long as his was.

On account of the fact he had not confirmed whether or not he'd kill me.

The odd thing?

I'd let him.

Chapter Seventeen

THE NEXT TIME I saw Felix, I showed up with a plan. I'd spent all summer researching, thank you porn writers, and I was ready to take our relationship to the next level. Which was why I purchased a pizza delivery man uniform from Amazon.

And also why I bought an actual pizza to go with it—in preparation.

It'd been difficult to find something in my size, but I'd managed.

I was supposed to be going over to Felix's house for the night. We were going to watch movies. Movies he told me would be…enlightening. You know what is also enlightening? My dick. This pizza box. And the box full of condoms Winnie had given me.

I rang the doorbell, pizza in hand, feeling ridiculous-stupid-idiotic-in-love as I waited for him to answer. Like usual, it was after dark. The block was quiet aside from a house a few down. A couple kids were out playing basketball by porch light. The *thump, thump* of the ball hitting the ground

SEX

filled the air as I waited.

If Barry saw me I'd never live this down.

At least from a distance it was impossible to tell that I was not, in fact, a real delivery man. But Marshall, the block's resident "thirty-eight-year-old-grump."

When Felix pulled the door open, he had a sunny but nervous smile on his face.

That smile died a slow, painful death as he stared at me. His eyes flickered up to my pizza cap, my polo with its logo, and down to the box that I was holding. "I…don't understand." It seemed I'd broken Felix's brain.

"Hello, neighbor." Fuck. Shit. I wasn't supposed to say that. I wasn't supposed to acknowledge that we were neighbors. Fuck. Retract. "I mean—customer."

"Um." Felix stared at me some more, stepping back inside to make room for me, his brow furrowed in confusion.

"I am your delivery man." Why was he not getting this?

Hopefully he did not have mace.

I didn't know how much more obvious I could be.

Was sex not the obvious conclusion to take from this? I was a delivery man. Therefore, Felix should be inviting me in—telling me how hot I looked—and trying to hop on my dick. I squinted at him, trying to figure out if he was teasing me or not.

Maybe I needed to pose sexier?

I stepped inside the house, making sure to check behind me. When I'd confirmed that no one was watching from the street through the little stained glass window at the side of his door, I leaned against the wall on my elbow and struck—what I hoped—was an enticing pose.

Felix did not look enticed.

He still looked confused.

"What is happening?" He laughed, eyes dancing with mirth. "Did you get a new job—?" He blinked. "Speaking of, you've never told me where you work."

"I'm CFO of a pharmaceutical company," I answered automatically. "And no. This is not my job." How was he not getting this? I had thought this was a fool-proof plan.

I wanted to fuck him, dammit.

Why hadn't he fallen for my charms?

I squinted at him some more. "Why aren't you getting naked?" I asked, point blank, pizza box still in hand. "I'm seducing you."

Felix blinked at me like I'd grown a second head. "Is that what's happening?"

"Obviously," I gestured with my free hand to my pizza outfit. "I'm the delivery boy. You're supposed to swoon and ask me in."

"I am?" Felix blinked, then his lips curled up into an amused grin. He was dressed for the day, unfortunately. Not in that silky, slinky pajama set that shouldn't have been as sexy as it was.

"You are." I waited for him to correct his behavior, but it seemed to be taking him a moment. Maybe he needed more instruction? God knows, I did. "You're supposed to let me in, swoon—" I repeated, more slowly this time. "And then…when I've successfully wooed you…" My gaze dragged over his shoulders, down his supple chest to the tiny waist I knew— firsthand—was tight and the perfect size to grip. I licked my lips. "I'm supposed to get to fuck you."

Felix's eyes flooded dark, a sharp little exhale leaving him.

He'd had a visitor the night before.

Hopefully he still had an orgasm left in him?

I was starting to really hate all his so-called "friends." One of these days I was going to sit in the entryway with a shotgun and see who tried to follow him to bed then. Still though…I was the one with a key—so I knew I was different.

I just…

I wanted to be everything for him.

Was that so bad?

Felix's expression did not inspire confidence. He still did not look seduced. I blinked, confused. Perhaps I'd done this all wrong?

"I'm supposed to fuck you…right?" I blinked again, brow furrowed.

"Seems fair." Felix cut me some slack. Even though he apparently did not watch porn—as I couldn't see there being another explanation for his ignorance—he stepped in close. His fingers curled in the hem of my polo, pulling me in close as he tipped his head up for a kiss.

I met him in the middle, melting with a happy groan.

I dropped the pizza box.

But neither of us seemed to care.

Immediately, my hands slid to his face, clutching it in a tight grip as I sucked and licked, and whined into his mouth. His lovely little teeth threatened to tear into my lip again. I'd thought I'd imagined it the first time, as there hadn't been even a scratch left behind before—but I was certain now that they were sharp enough.

They pricked, and I shuddered, clutching him even tighter, his blond hair fluttering against my fingertips as I ate him the only socially acceptable way I could.

When we parted—it was only because I had to breathe.

I sucked in a ragged, needy pant, our lips still brushing, his face still clutched in my grip.

"You put a lot of effort into this, didn't you?" Felix murmured, lips bumping mine as his fingers gave my outfit another gentle tug.

"Of course I did," I kissed him again—now that my lungs were full, I was excited to empty them again. "I'm asking you to let me have you. The least I could do was put in a little effort."

"Mmm," Felix hummed as I dove in for another, longer, greedier kiss. One of my hands slid to his throat, fanning along it, dipping beneath his collar. The way he shuddered lit me up from the inside out. I had no idea what the fuck I was doing, but Felix didn't seem to mind.

Apparently my unpracticed groping was good enough for him.

That only became even more clear when one second I had my tongue in his mouth, sliding hot-wet-cool-slick along his, and the next, his hand was latching onto my cock for the very first time and he squeezed.

I growled, hips thrusting up into his grip, my cock aching as I felt his fingers close more surely around it, his palm pushing against me to give me something to fuck against.

Bliss fluttered behind my lids, and a frankly horrifying sound escaped me as I pulled away from the kiss—too blind-sided by pleasure to do anything other than stupidly flex into Felix's grip. Led by my dick. Like a fucking plebeian.

And I couldn't even be mad about it.

"As romantic as this is," Felix said, plucking at the hem of my pizza-polo at the same time he gave my dick another pointed rub. Precum leaked from the tip immediately, making my boxers sticky and wet and uncomfortable as I panted against his lips, mindlessly pushing into his grip. "I hope you know it wasn't necessary."

"It…wasn't?" I managed, even though my brain had taken a vacation.

"No, Marshall." God, I loved it when he said my name. He gave my dick another rub, and my toes curled. "I've wanted you since the day you moved across the street."

This was news to me.

Mind-blowing news.

And yet…my dick still won the battle with my head.

Stupidly, I gasped against his cheek, the hand that had been toying with his collar, slipping down to grip his ass tight. Felix gasped, and I felt like I'd won the lottery. God, his ass was nice. So supple. I gave it a greedy squeeze and he laughed, a throaty, rough sound. "That's…" I managed, pausing again to grunt when Felix gave my cock another pointed rub.

"Ten years, Marshall," Felix said softly, like I wasn't wrapped around his finger. "Ten years, I've wanted you, just like this. Sitting in my kitchen. Sharing our nights—sharing my bed."

I didn't know what to do with a declaration like that.

No one had ever said anything more perfect.

"I was raised differently," Felix continued, toying with me—his grip lightening to the point of madness. I squeezed his ass, and he sighed, lashes fluttering. "Where I'm from, we wait till marriage to share what you so clearly want."

"I'd marry you tomorrow."

Felix laughed, startled. "You can't mean that."

"I do."

"Marshall—" I could tell he was about to release my cock. And I didn't want him to. I didn't want that. For the first time in my life, I understood the appeal of sex. I understood why people might chase this. Why they might go out in public hunting for one-night stands if this kind of pleasure was at the other end of the long, overstimulating evening. Though…once again, I was forced to face the fact that I'd never be comfortable having sex with someone other than Felix.

It was him and me. The only equation that made sense in my head.

The only reason this sort of intimacy felt comfortable at all.

I'd never had an interest in it before.

And now…I…well…

I was insatiable.

"What if you don't know…the truth about me?" Felix asked, voice wobbling. "Because you don't."

"It doesn't matter."

"How can it not matter?" He didn't understand.

He didn't understand—

But…that was my fault.

That was my fault, because I hadn't told him, had I?

I'd shown up with a hard cock and a pizza box, and expected him to know how I felt.

"I hate the world," I told Felix, my voice shaky. "I hate going out. I hate people. I hate *touching*. I hate pop music. I hate Nascar, fried chicken, olives on pizza, pickles, picnics, and pastels."

"Marshall—"

"I hate Christmas in July, buying presents, bullies, flip-flops, sand, soda, and Barry (the blockhead)." I sucked in a steadying breath. "I hate sunscreen, SPF50 specifically, those popsicles that always break before you can get them out of the bag, dogs that are brachycephalic." Another breath. "I hate people that say good morning to strangers, hot sauce, and when my sister, Winnifred, calls me Marshall the Martian."

I had never laid myself bare like this.

It was terrifying.

Awful, awful, awful.

But if it meant I'd get to keep Felix... If it meant he'd understand that *this* wasn't only physical for me but that it was *more*, that it was... *everything* I'd never offered anyone before, perhaps, he'd say yes. Perhaps, he wouldn't be lonely anymore if he knew that he was my supernova.

My obsession.

Steady as the stars.

"I hate so many things that I can't possibly keep track of them all," I said, voice quaking. "But, Felix...I..." *Just do it, Marshall. You've already laid your heart on the line. What's one more truth?* The biggest truth. The most important truth you've ever hoarded. "I don't hate *you*."

My heart was pounding.

Nerves tingled at my fingertips, twisted around my insides, and tied my gut into knots.

"I could *never* hate you. Not ever. Not even a little. Even if I tried."

Chapter Eighteen

FELIX KISSED me then, and it was *different* than before.

It was like the distance that had been between us had finally fallen away.

He was here.

Present.

My greatest gift of all.

I grabbed his ass in both hands, hefting him up and shoving him into the wall in one swift movement. His legs tangled around my hips, our cocks aligning at the same time our mouths met and I—fuck. Fuck.

I didn't even care that I had to hunch to reach.

Because he was a cool, solid weight in my arms. He felt like heaven, his body quaking against mine as I scrambled at his clothing, struggling to free him from its confines. Felix tried to help, but he was too busy biting a trail down the side of my neck to be anything but a hindrance. He worried the skin there, his sharp teeth threatening to break through—

almost on purpose, it seemed. Meanwhile, I was actually productive, and managed to get the buttons undone on both of our pants.

"Bed?" Felix gasped out, his breath fanning along my neck, his spit slick as he pulled off with a wet little sound.

"Bed," I agreed.

As fun as rutting against him in the hallway was, I wasn't about to lose my virginity there. I deserved a bed, not rug burn, thank you very much.

I didn't let Felix down.

I didn't think he'd let me, even if I wanted to. He clung to me like the gremlin he was, kissing and sucking at my neck the entire time I struggled us up the stairs.

"Why the hell is your bedroom on the top floor?" I complained, out of breath by the second landing.

Felix laughed but didn't answer. He did lap at the sweat on my neck though—and that was…*mmmm* distracting.

When we got to his room, I was forced to struggle with the handle before pushing inside. It was just as I remembered it. Telescope in the corner. Wisteria hanging from the ceiling. Movie posters on the walls— like the ones in the living room.

Luckily, there were no cats.

Not this time, anyway.

I shut the door after us so that it would stay that way. The last thing I needed was performance anxiety because Tiffany and Dolly were nosy. And then, I was stalking across the floor—an arm full of Felix, wiggling and nipping at my neck—before I tossed him onto the mattress.

Dust bloomed up from the fabric, and it was a testament to how distracted I was by his body that I didn't immediately notice how odd that was.

Later, I'd mull over it.

But for now…

Oh yes.

God.

I licked into his mouth again, climbing on top of him—dust be damned.

"Should I apologize?" Felix murmured between greedy kisses, his fingers scratching over my shoulders, rather obscenely groping the muscles I spent years cultivating. He moaned appreciatively when I flexed, crowding into him, shoving his legs apart to make room for my body.

"You can't help that you're short," I replied without thinking, trying to shove him farther up the bed so I'd have ample room.

Felix cackled, his head falling back as he wiggled backward to help me in my mission. Ah, there. Now my knees were on the bed. Good. "No, I mean—that I didn't get your pizza thing."

"Oh," I'd almost forgotten about that already.

It felt like years had passed as we'd climbed the stairs.

Felix helped me grapple with my polo, and with an annoyed grunt, I managed to tug it over my head and toss it away. He grinned up at me, his hands lying flat on my abdomen as I knelt between his legs, chest heaving. His palms were cool. Confident. He petted over the muscle on my lower belly, before gently sliding upward, leaning up to chase his own grip.

The look on his face was positively filthy, lips flushed and swollen, his eyes blood red.

Fuck.

He was delicious.

"Naked," I commanded, tingling when Felix's fingers combed through the hair on my chest, before sliding over to pluck at one of my nipples. I shivered, and he grinned—wide and wicked.

"I'm working on it."

"Not me. *You*," I scowled at him, and he laughed, not at all cowed.

"We'll get me in a minute," Felix countered, voice as rough as my own. Normally he was all melodic, smooth edges. Now, however, his voice was crackly soft. "Let me look at you."

I shivered again, my nipples hard and poking up rather obscenely. The thin dusting of golden hair on my chest made me question for a moment if I should've shaved it—only to realize that I'd done well leaving it alone, because Felix seemed to like it.

He seemed to like it quite a bit.

At least, if the way he tugged at it was any indication, a pleased grin on his face.

"You're huge," he said softly, heat simmering in his tone. "So *fucking* big."

I shuddered. "Maybe you're just small?"

"No, darling," Felix's voice somehow dropped even lower. One of his hands slid from my chest, down, down, down, fingers fanning along the fat swell of my cock where it pushed needily toward him. "*You're* big," he said again, and it was very clearly a compliment. My hips bucked into his grasp, a needy whine escaping me. "My big, loyal sweetheart."

"You've ruined me," I gasped out, because he was right. My loyalty knew no bounds. "I can't stop thinking about you—" I shuddered again, the wet patch my cock had left on my boxers spreading to the fabric of my slacks, making it obvious how needy-horny-wet-wet-wet I was. "Not even spreadsheets are sacred anymore—"

Felix laughed, and that shouldn't have made me even harder than I was—but it did. And then he did something totally unexpected. He flipped me over.

Felix.

Tiny.

Fucking.

Little.

Itty.

Bitty.

Felix.

Flipped me over.

As easily as if I'd been a pancake. One second I was leaning over him, chest heaving—and the next I was on my back, and I had a lap full of artificial-blond. I gasped out, shocked, but not angry at all. In fact, his show of strength was *incredibly* attractive.

Goddamn.

My hips jerked against his ass, my lashes fluttering as I watched him, breath coming in rapid little gasps.

Felix reached for the hem of his shirt, arms criss-crossed, as he very slowly, very pointedly began to lift it. "Are you ready for this?" He teased softly, that lithe body perched atop mine. My dick bumped against his perky ass and I nodded, staring at his flat little belly with greed.

It took me a second to realize he was teasing me.

Probably because of how I'd reacted to him flashing his ankles at the cat cafe.

"Fuck you," I said, voice rougher than I'd ever heard it.

"*Soon*," Felix countered playfully, tugging up enough on his sweater that

I could see his—oh fuck. Yes. Pale, delicious skin mocked me. I wanted to lick it so bad, my mouth felt dry. There was a smattering of dark hair that led down his flat belly beneath the hem of his unbuttoned pants and I was—fuck-fuck-fuck.

Not going to last all that long at all.

"Felix, please," I managed, gritting my teeth as his red eyes took in every twitch of my body. Almost like he was a predator cataloging weaknesses. His gaze once again snapped to my throat, tracing along it almost reverently, before his eyes found my lips. He licked his own, before he pulled his sweater up the rest of the way—finally, *finally* ending my punishment.

Inch by inch, the fabric climbed, revealing leagues and leagues of gorgeous alabaster muscle.

There were a few tattoos smattered along the pale skin, and I read each one as it was revealed, enraptured by the beauty that now perched on my cock. One in particular stuck out to me, as it was so desperately Felix, that it made sense that it was permanently etched into his skin.

Unable are the loved to die, for love is immortality.

I didn't understand the context of the words, but I understood the meaning well enough. Especially when paired with the words he'd shared with me beneath the meteor shower.

"One day my exile will end. I'll walk the streets like you do—like they do. I'll stay home, not because I have to, but because it is my sanctuary. I'll be forgotten and my invisibility will be my freedom as surely as it will mean I've finally died."

The day *his* secrets would become *our* secrets was nearing.

And now…now I was going to fuck him.

I was going to *enter* him.

Become one with him.

Share each breath, each heartbeat, and pleasure.

Sex…was a vulnerable thing. I didn't need to have had it to understand that. It was personal. Intimate. It meant trust—and I had never been the kind of person who blindly trusted anyone. Trust, for me, was hard won. It took time to build, brick by brick. And even then, it easily crumpled.

Felix had earned that trust as surely as he'd earned my affection.

Every time I'd done something "odd" and he'd laughed rather than condemned me for my differences. When he'd looked at my camera, my idiosyncrasies, my prickly habits, and my frowns—and seen a man worth smiling for.

He'd accepted me in a way I'd never been able to accept myself.

Which was why I wanted this.

I wanted him.

Every last, beautiful, wonderful inch of his body.

I wanted to claim him. A primal thing. A thing the beast inside me had ached, and ached for since the day he'd found his mate. He was writhing, threatening to break toward the surface—but still, I held back.

I held back because Felix was a gorgeous, perfect creature.

And he needed to know how strong he was and how much power he held over me. The wretched, twisted thing he was needed to build confidence.

Even though it was torture to wait.

When his sweater fell to the bed, I groaned, eyes scanning over every last beautiful inch of his pale, muscular body. I took him in as surely as I took in fresh air during spring, sucking in greedy lungfuls of Felix, Felix, *Felix*, as I fanned my hands along his hips and dug my fingers in till I felt bone.

Felix's eyes were dark with heat as he spread his legs wider, my cock pushing against his ass as he undulated his hips. I wanted his pants *off*. Right the fuck now.

Whining, I bucked up against him, my brow scrunched.

"I know," Felix murmured, reaching down to cup my face as I panted up at him, chest heaving. "I know you want it, darling." He arched his back, grinding into me. Unable to help myself, I planted my feet into the mattress, bucking up into him—shoes be damned. Like I could fuck him through four layers of clothing just because I *wanted* it bad enough.

Illogical.

I was acting illogical.

But my head—and my dick—didn't care.

Felix is in my lap. Felix is in my lap. Felix is in my lap.

I'm going to fuck him.

I'm going to fuck him—

Oh fuck, I needed to stop thinking about that or I was going to come before I got inside him.

"You're so *needy*," Felix purred, and I sobbed, hips fucking against him again. The friction was good but not enough—not enough—not enough. "One second, sweetheart. I've got you." Felix's words were a balm on my soul, and I nodded jerkily, watching him desperately as he shifted away from my lap so that he could jerk his pants and underwear off in one swift motion.

His hard dick slapped against his belly and I—

Oh fuck.

Oh fuck.

Pop music, Nascar, pickles, pastels—I thought of all the things I hated so that I wouldn't come prematurely. Especially when I couldn't tear my eyes away from his cock. His lovely…long, pink cock. It flexed toward me, the tip glistening with precum, the vein on the underside twitching as Felix moved.

"Lift your hips for me, darling," Felix was moving, and his hands were at my waistband—but my eyes were…yes. *God.* I wanted to lick his cock. Wanted to taste the salt and sweat and suck him down till I could taste him behind my eyeballs. It bobbed between his legs, the sweet pink crown winking at me as he moved.

"There you go." I lifted for him, and Felix jerked my pants and underwear down and off, discarding my shoes as well. He even pulled my socks off. Which felt odd, as I'd never been sockless around anyone since I'd moved away from the farm as a kid. The city had felt too dirty…our new apartment after Mom died—too cluttered.

The world was chaotic.

It always had been.

But…I didn't mind. At least, not right now. Not when I was with Felix.

My dick was leaking, a steady stream slicking my belly as my hips flexed toward him, and Felix growled, low and rough. "Fuck."

And then he fell to his knees, pushing his face into my groin and I was—oh god. *Fuck.* Yes. Felix's tongue lapped at the salty skin of my sac, pushing against the velvety softness as he sucked and slurped—a man possessed.

I parted my legs, rutting against him, my cock head leaving a streak of precum along his cheekbone.

"Fuck," I gasped out, toes curling into the dusty comforter.

"That's it—" Felix groaned, flattening his tongue and rubbing a long, slick stripe up the center of my balls, then my length, till he could dig it into the weeping slit at the top of my crown. "You're such a good boy,

Marshall.”

I whined again, leaking onto the wet of his tongue, my eyes nearly crossing so I could get a better look at him.

“Let’s get you nice and hard.”

I huffed at him angrily. I’d *been* hard since I walked across the street—I didn’t *need* to be any harder.

“Then…I’ll let you fuck me. Okay, darling? I promise I’ll give you what you need. Just let me…get ready—” Felix was doing something with his hand—the one that wasn’t lying on my thigh, playing with the hair there—and I was too dazed by the wet mouth flicking at my cock and the vibration of his voice, to realize *what* exactly it was.

Not until I recognized the open lube packet he’d stolen from my pants sitting on the bed.

And the slick sounds suddenly made sense.

Felix was…

Felix was fucking himself.

Oh.

My.

Fuck.

My hips jerked toward his face. The knowledge that he was crowded between my legs, his own fingers up his ass, sent me spinning. My control snapped, the beast alive and well as I strained toward him, teeth gritted.

I growled, and it didn’t even remotely sound human.

Slick, twist, slick.

Felix’s fingers continued to work, his mouth tight and perfect as he slurped messily around the crown of my cock and I stared down the line of his back, desperately trying to see past his shoulders to his—

Oh.

Fuck.

I could see it.

The spread of his thighs, his perky ass poking up—thick and meaty. His hand twisting behind himself, the cause of the filthy sounds filling the air. I couldn't actually see the fingers disappearing inside him—but I could *imagine* it.

Pink, fluttery, needy, his hole caving for their searching caress.

The way he'd push in—and gasp—deep, deep, *deep*.

"Marshall," Felix's voice was sweet as he murmured against the spongy skin of my dick. It flexed toward his face of its own accord, and I reluctantly pulled my eyes away from his tapered back, his ass, and that *hand*—that fucking lovely hand. "Tell me you want this."

I didn't think he was asking for me to beg.

But I begged anyway.

"Please, please, please—" I gasped out, hips snapping up. Sweat beaded at my temple, slipping down my neck, and Felix's eyes blazed softly as he followed the movement hungrily. "I *need* it—"

"Yes," Felix removed his fingers, and his face pinched—a frankly delicious expression of pain that had me panting after him. "I know you need it. But do you want it?"

"Yes—" I gasped.

He rose onto his knees again, fumbling with his wet fingers for another lube packet. He slicked me up, long fingers spreading the cool trickle of liquid up and down my length. My head tossed back, my entire body trembling with need as he grabbed one of the condoms I'd brought. He held it up for me to see, brow arched in question.

"What about this, Marshall? Do you want to use one of these?" He asked softly, voice low.

I stared at the condom, suddenly…irrationally eager to be rid of it entirely.

"I'm a virgin," I blurted out. If Felix was surprised, he didn't show it.

"We don't have to use one," he said softly, wagging it at me. "But we can, Marshall. Virgin or not."

"I…"

"Tell me what you want," Felix said, voice gentle. The bossy, tiny Dom was gone, replaced by the bumbling fool I'd fallen in love with all those weeks ago in the woods. "I promise you I'll be happy either way."

Winnie was going to kill me.

Probably.

Her favorite phrase in the world was probably "no glove, no love." I swear she'd get it as a bumper sticker if she could. *Hey! Christmas idea. Wahoo.*

But…what Winnie didn't know wouldn't hurt her, would it?

And the idea of…oh fuck. The idea of spilling inside Felix—of marking him as mine from the inside out was just…yes.

Fuck yes.

"No condom," I said simply, more than a little satisfied when Felix immediately tossed it away. He straddled my hips and my brain short-circuited. There were no thoughts in my head at all as his lithe body poised above my lap, ass hovering enticingly over my hard cock.

All I could think about was pushing into him.

About how tight he'd be.

About the face he'd make if I pushed too fast, too soon. I wanted to make him cry as much as I wanted him to scratch me up. Would this be the time he killed me? If he was following his usual mode of operation?

I hoped not.

But the thought that Felix might try to end me after I finished only served to make me more aroused. Violence in any form had always fascinated me. It should come as no surprise that that extended toward sex.

"I might be a little rusty," Felix murmured, body taunting mine. "So bear with me."

My dick flexed, pointing up toward him, angry, ruddy red. I didn't think I'd ever been harder in all my life.

"*Look at you,*" Felix purred, positioning himself over my dick, the oddly lukewarm clutch of his ass, fluttering at my crown. "Just a big, feral beast, aren't you, Marshall?"

I hissed out a breath, too focused on how close I was to finally pushing inside him to care what he was calling me. I couldn't stop leaking. I could feel the sticky smear of lube and precum slipping down my cock as Felix pressed down a little harder and—oh.

Oh.

Oh.

Bliss.

Sweet, heavenly bliss.

His body was so tight—and wet—and surprisingly warm on the inside. My eyes rolled back as Felix's hands laid on my chest for support. He used his hold on my pecs for leverage, gradually sinking further, further, further—

"Oh fuck." I sobbed, and then—snapped my hips up.

Felix's face scrunched up like I'd hoped it would. He made a soft, startled sound, his dark brow knit—but I was too focused on the *tight, wet, warm, tight, wet* of his body to think about anything other than pulling out, and pushing back in again.

And again.

And again.

"Marshall—" Felix moaned, rocking his hips to meet my thrusts. There was no build up. No slow, long progression. No teasing. It was feral. Animalistic. Primal in the way only killing had ever been for me. There were no thoughts in my head at all, other than fuck, fuck, fuck—a command to invade Felix's body, to leave my mark inside him. To fuck him so hard and good he couldn't walk for weeks.

I grabbed onto his hips, nails biting into the skin—but not piercing—as I planted my feet into the mattress and rocked up with fervor. Felix swiveled his hips to meet each of my thrusts, a steady slap, slap, slap sound echoing through the room as I snapped into him—delighted every time I made him gasp.

"Fuck, you are so big—" he hissed out. It wasn't the first time he'd called me that. And it wasn't like I could control how long or thick my cock was. But still…pride filled my body. Virile and irrational—I preened, plowing into him harder, yanking him down into each of my thrusts as I chased my pleasure.

I should've reached for his dick.

I knew that.

But I honestly couldn't think about anything but pushing inside him—and Felix, lovely, wonderful Felix, didn't seem to mind. He stared at me like the fact I'd lost control was the sexiest thing he'd ever seen. Stared at my heaving chest, my hard nipples, the way my neck strained and flexed.

Stared at how big my hands looked when they clutched his hips. Stared into my eyes—long and hard enough I got lost inside his gaze.

As lost inside him as he was inside me.

I was so close.

I was so, so close.

And when Felix reached down and began stroking his own cock, bouncing eagerly on top of me, his cock bobbing, I just—

I just—

I couldn't.

It was my turn.

With a howl, I flipped us over, shoving him into the mattress with a ferocity I hadn't even known I possessed. Felix made a startled sound, though the hand on his dick didn't stop stroking the flesh.

"Yes, yes, yes," I chanted, biting at his neck, his shoulders, down his chest as my hips continued to snap a brutal, unforgiving pace into his body. *Tight, wet, warm, warm, warm.* Yes—fuck.

Down bitch.

Down, down.

That's it.

Take it, take it, take it.

"Nnnn," I whined, gnawing at his pec, my teeth worrying his nipple as I curled over him.

I'd fought hard to win Felix's submission, and I was going to take it.

"That's it—" Felix hiccuped, no longer quite so put together. He sounded as fucked out as I felt. "That's it, Marshall," he spread his legs wider, the submission making my blood sing.

That's it, I thought, mirroring his words.

Let me in.

Submit to me.

Let me have you.

You're mine, mine, mine.

I felt the hot splatter of Felix's cum before my own orgasm came. His face scrunched up, his brow knit. The tendons in his neck tensed as he tossed his head back, a breathy little hiccup escaping him as his pleasure spilled messy between us.

That was it.

All it took.

Once, twice, three times, I slapped against his ass, spilling inside him with a heavy whine of my own. I ground hard against the swell of his pert ass, my cum filling him up, marking him from the inside out. A wet, squelching noise sounded as I continued to grind into him even after my orgasm had ended.

"Fuck," Felix sighed, stretching a hand out—the clean one—and curling it around the nape of my neck. He hauled me up, mouth meeting mine in a searing, sated kiss. "Well, so much for being a gentleman," he joked softly.

I laughed.

I laughed and laughed and *laughed*.

We curled up together beneath the covers, naked, sticky, sated. I bundled Felix in my arms and he fit there. He fit there so well it was hard to ever believe there'd been a time when I hadn't known how good he felt.

Our monsters were sated.

I kissed his head, his ears, his cheeks—and he stroked my nape, traced my cheekbones, my nose, my brow bone. When he flicked the lamp off and the room was filled with darkness, my heart was as full as my arms.

I thought I wouldn't like this.

The prickle of our leg hair scratching together.

The way our sweat made us stick.

But I'd been wrong.

I'd been so wrong.

Because if I'd thought holding Felix was the best feeling in the world, fucking him was even better.

Twice more throughout the night, when I woke from my slumber, I slipped back inside him. Rutted into him while I was still half asleep, his fingers scratching at the comforter while I plastered myself against his back and bounced my hips against his plump ass.

I filled him up, over and over and over.

And once, around four in the morning, an hour or so before my usual alarm went off, I slipped beneath the covers so that I could taste where he was sore and loose.

His lovely ass gave beneath my tongue, his hole sucking greedily at me as I tasted my own cum inside him. I'd expected it to taste worse than it did, and was pleasantly surprised when the flavor didn't bother me at all.

Felix sobbed, whining into the mattress as he shoved his ass back against my face, a fresh rush of my cum slipping free as his pretty, pink hole fluttered a greeting at me.

I pulled at the little ring of muscle, enraptured as I watched the slick pale liquid slip free.

"Marshall," Felix gasped, embarrassed.

"Mhmm," I sighed happily, content—for once—to touch another person. I gave his messy hole a slurping, wet kiss, and he stopped protesting altogether.

There was something inherently wrong about licking someone's ass. And I supposed that's why it made me so damn hard. It wasn't something I ever would've expected to enjoy. But I did. Especially when Felix began chanting my name—hips swiveling back as I grabbed his ass cheeks, spread them wide, and ate his ass till he came all over the already cum-stained sheets.

With sloppy, flat licks, I soothed his sweet little hole, enticing it to soften again as Felix came down from his high.

"Fuck," he said, muffled into the mattress. "What the hell was that?"

Feeling incredibly proud of myself, I replied, "I believe it is called felching."

"Felching?" Felix echoed, voice dazed. You'd think I'd eaten his brain, not his ass. I'd once, uncharitably, thought he had no brain cells left to lose. It was amazing how wrong I'd been. This clever little creature seemed to know *everything*—which was why it was quite fun that for once, I knew more than he did.

"If I hadn't licked my own cum out of your pretty little hole—"

"Oh fuck," Felix's hips flexed, like my words were causing his already spent dick to perk back up again.

"It would be called rimming."

"Rimming?" He echoed again, sounding equally as dazed. "I didn't know you could do that."

Thank you, porn, for your service.

"Did you like it?" I asked, nibbling along his ass cheeks just to feel the bouncy flesh give. Felix shuddered, his hole clenching. Unable to help myself—because now that I knew what it felt like inside him, I wanted to be inside him at all times—I pushed my thumb inside his soft, well-fucked hole.

He whined again, and my dick attempted to resurrect itself.

"Loved it," Felix replied, arching his back a little. He gasped when I bit his other cheek, thumb sinking deeper. He was so velvety soft inside. I never wanted to leave. Ever. "How did you learn that?"

"You have your secrets, I have mine," I countered, not wanting to tell him how much time I'd spent researching for this exact moment.

"Mmm fair enough," Felix said. And then he did this lovely, amazing, wonderful little swivel, arching his back enticingly. "Got one more in you, big shot?"

"Fuck." I hadn't thought I did.

But apparently I'd been wrong.

Crowding overtop him again, my dick was honestly a little sore—it'd been used so *much*. But…the little bite of pain only made the pleasure sweeter as I lined the fat crown of my cock up with his hole and fumbled around the bed for another lube packet. Once slicked, I pressed in, slow and easy.

Felix half-dozed beneath me, muffled little gasps and groans escaping him as I bracketed his lovely broad shoulders with my arms.

"Arch your back," I murmured, fingers digging into his ass, pulling his cheeks apart so I could stare at where my cock kept disappearing inside it. It was ridiculous how sexy it was—his tiny little hole giving for the thick length of my dick. It should not have fit inside him—but it did.

I came with a grunt when he did as he was told, staring in fascination as my own cum slicked the last few thrusts inside him.

We slept again, my spent cock drooling against his hip, our legs tangled.

A few hours later my alarm went off—the one I'd set for later than usual, as I had anticipated spending the night. Felix was still sleepy soft—as it was his bedtime now that the sun was up. But that didn't stop him from disappearing under the covers to clean my dick with his rather dexterous tongue.

He only licked it once—and we'd both gone…

A little feral.

When I was forced to retreat to my house to get ready for work, visions of long, pale muscles assaulted my senses every time I closed my eyes. My smile refused to die. And my sore cock became—*officially*—my favorite body part.

I couldn't wait to use it again.

I couldn't wait to see Felix again.

Perhaps I had finally sated him? Perhaps he would no longer have his nighttime visitors. Maybe his beast had settled, the way mine had.

Maybe.

Chapter Nineteen

HOPE WAS a cruel, heartless bitch. I know this because after Felix and I shared a perfect wonderful, amazing night together, reality—of course—came crashing down. Though not before I had some sweaty, dirty, *amazing* sex. For the remaining few weeks before Barry's party, I spent as much time as I possibly could inside Felix.

I neglected my laundry, and instead, fucked Felix over the dryer.

I neglected my dishes, and instead, rutted into him over the sink.

I didn't have him on his front porch like I'd pictured—but I *did* push him to the floor in his front hallway one night and eat his ass till he cried.

I fucked him on every possible surface I could, in every possible combination I could think of. And when I wasn't humping Felix's ass, my dick somehow always found its way inside the wet, slurping cavern of his throat. He liked it when I choked him. He liked it even more when his little spiky teeth nicked my cock and he could suck the blood at the same time he fed on my cum.

He'd sucked my dick so many times I almost forgot what it felt like to not have my cock buried inside him in some way or another.

And every *single* time he was a bossy little bastard. Climbing on top of me. Biting me. Scratching me. Leaving hickeys and bruises. Commanding me to "go faster, Marshall." "To the left, Marshall." "That's it, my good boy. Fuck me harder, big shot." "Come *inside* me—I want to feel it." "God, you're so big. Fucking bruise me, Marshall. That's it. Yes, yes, *yes*."

We never did watch the movies he'd told me would be "enlightening." But I figured there was time.

Felix was as insatiable as I was—but even we eventually…reached a limit.

It took several weeks to get there, yes, but it happened.

I was nearly forty, goddammit. I should've been surprised it didn't happen earlier. I'd been spending my nights frolicking around both our houses like I was learning how my dick worked for the first time.

Like all good things, the manic sex-fest came to an end.

There was a moment, two days before Barry's party, that Felix and I were making out in my kitchen while I meal-prepped. For the first time since I'd lost my virginity neither of us pushed for more. Our tongues danced, playing, searching, rubbing. And then the kisses petered off, slow and sweet. Immediately, a comfortable warmth filled the room.

Warmer even, than the oven's heat, or the tray I'd just pulled out of it.

We didn't push for more, not because we didn't *want* it, but because there was confidence now in our longevity. Confidence that there would be more opportunities for this. Which meant…for now, both of us were content to wait. *This* meant we were sustainable. That we wouldn't fizzle out, brightly exploding like a supernova only to fade away into nothing.

No.

We would simmer, we would boil, evaporate, condense, then simmer again.

Forever, and ever, and ever.

Steady as the stars.

Unless Felix decided to kill me, of course—but I was seriously beginning to doubt he was going to do it. Not that I *minded*. I had found, as of late, that I rather *liked* being alive. I liked it a lot. I liked *him* a lot. Loved him, actually. (I know, I know, what was wrong with me, right?) Loved him more than pencil holders, sweater vests, chocolate chip cookies, and rhubarb pie.

Loved him more than I loved my car, *his car*, or the chihuahua I'd had growing up.

Loved him brighter, warmer, more brilliantly than the stars that hung fat and golden when we peered at them through his telescope.

Loved him more than my rituals. Loved him more than blood. Loved him more than the thrill I got from killing.

I was as happy to share silence with Felix as I was to share his bed.

I had ten identical glass containers lined up on the counter, a spatula in my hand, my bare feet chilly where Felix's—even chillier—feet snuggled up atop them. Like he was trying to leech my warmth away like an overgrown koala.

Felix cuddled against my arm. His fingers bunched in the fabric of my frilly apron. I didn't try to dislodge him, even though he was making it admittedly difficult to work. Perhaps that was love. Craving someone's presence even though it should've been annoying. Even though realistically things would be easier alone. Never wanting to be alone again.

I'd never been much of a romantic.

But I decided, then and there, that I wanted Felix to annoy me for the rest of my life. Logic be damned.

Buzzing with happiness, I fed Vlad a few scraps of chicken fat, and then finished divvying my food into Tupperware containers. As the sweet crooning of our song danced through the air, Felix hummed along, his voice vibrating my arm.

I'd thought we were on the same page.

That we'd both just wanted a break that night.

But apparently…I'd been wrong.

Because the day of the party, shit hit the motherfucking fan.

Felix was *not* sated.

I just…hadn't known that.

Hadn't known that I wasn't giving him everything he needed.

Hadn't had the conversation with him about what exactly we were—at least…not yet. About the "rules" Winnie had said we needed if we were going to be happy. About *expectations*. I hated that she was right, but she was.

I should've communicated better.

Another box arrived for Felix the morning of the Summer Bash. I spotted it through my kitchen window, sitting on his doorstep, ready to spoil. And like a good soon-to-be-official boyfriend, I decided to store it in my fridge for him—confident that this time I would not forget.

I would've brought it into his house, but I worried about disturbing him. I'd woken him up once before, and I didn't want to do it again. Besides, I'd been keeping him up rather late, for him, anyway, and he needed his beauty sleep before our social debut later that day.

I was…*excited.*

Yes, I could admit that.

I may have told the *entire* office.

I may have shown them all pictures of our matching suits, and the rings I'd bought us online.

I may have called both of my sisters individually to brag that I was no longer single. I maybe—*might have*—told them to start shopping for Felix for Christmas.

I also may have printed off a notice to put on my office door so that everyone would know I was leaving early and not to disturb me until the following work week. (Looking at you, Harold.)

I'd ask Felix to be mine officially tonight, and I was prepared to be the *best* boyfriend in the history of all boyfriends. Narcissistic? Maybe. But that was one of the more forgivable of my flaws, if you considered murder a flaw.

Which I didn't.

I figured if I brought the box inside, then returned it, I'd redeem myself. Never mind the fact that Felix never needed to know what happened to the last one. I was already heading over there for the block party later that day, and I figured I could bring the new box with me and deposit it safely in his fridge when he was awake.

Only…

It never even occurred to me that Felix had *needed* that package.

That perhaps there was a *reason* he'd had it delivered today of all days.

And that while I was applying aftershave and singing—rather awfully— to Ella Fitzgerald—getting ready for our date after work—Felix was across the street, during *daylight* hours, with the curtains drawn, *panicking.*

The moment I stepped onto my front lawn, blond hair primped to perfection, my skin buttery soft, the lemon-sage scent of my aftershave wafting through the air, I knew…something had happened.

I knew, because there was a car parked in Felix's driveway.

It wasn't Barry's red minivan.

And it wasn't my Mercedes.

It wasn't recognizable at all.

He has someone over.

"Fuck, fuck, fuck." Rage, devastation, frustration—unlike anything I'd ever felt before filled my body. White-hot. Wicked. *Angry.* When I'd killed in the past, I planned it out. I scouted bars, I found bullies—the same cookie-cutter kind of men that had caused Alberta's death. For *weeks*, I stalked them to make sure that they fit my criteria.

When I lured them outside—under false pretenses—when I swiveled around, not the nerdy, defenseless man they'd expected—but a predator— it was all meticulously planned.

Every last, careful detail.

Down to the way I killed them, twisting their necks till they snapped and their eyes rolled back. Satisfying. Easy to clean up. *Practiced.*

I was a *planner.*

But there was no plan in my mind. Not at all. As I tore across the street, used the key Felix had given me, and entered his front door. I could hear voices, but my mind was scarily blank.

I knew…I *knew* this was my fault. I knew that Felix had his "needs", and I hadn't thought to ask for boundaries. The dust on his bed had given me hope—though it had made me wonder where exactly he slept, if his bed was so abandoned.

My vision was red, red, *red*.

My eyes burned as I stalked through the house, quiet as a mouse.

If I'd been in my right mind, I would've noticed that I had left the front door open. But I wasn't. And I didn't. All I could think about was the fact that I hadn't told Felix I wanted to be exclusive, even though Winnie had warned me that I needed to.

Why didn't I tell him I want to be his boyfriend?

I told everyone else.

Hell, I've been calling myself his boyfriend since the first time we went out together.

And yet…I had never told *him*. I had never *asked* him if exclusivity was something he wanted.

I had given him my heart but I had taken the coward's way out.

I hated regrets.

They ached, and they hurt. And they made me feel tiny and helpless. All of sixteen, standing in an alley behind a bar where I'd found my sister's body. I'd known she was having a tough time at school. But I'd been powerless to help. I hadn't expected her to get cornered like this—on her way home. Perhaps she'd stopped inside for a glass of water? Her friend's father owned the bar after all.

I'd never know.

I'd never know because she was dead—and gone—and I couldn't ask her.

I had always been a man of action.

It comforted me when the ground turned to quicksand and my stomach filled with acid.

This wasn't like before. I wasn't helpless. I wasn't young.

I knew exactly what to do.

And I did that now, falling into my usual pattern as I slipped quietly toward the archway that led to the living room. I could hear the voices behind it. They were quiet, soft. Not…amorous? But that didn't mean anything. Felix had said he had "friends" and I…was realizing just how little I wanted him to interact with anyone aside from me.

Possessive, yes.

Toxic, yes.

But, I had never claimed to be a good person. I never claimed to be anything other than what I was. I was a no good, selfish, very bad man.

And I needed to tell Felix what he meant to me. What I wanted from him. That he was special, that he was my forever—for however long that lasted. Because he felt *right* inside my arms. Because he smelled like lemons. Because his pointy, slightly crooked teeth and his crinkly little scrunched-up freckle-covered nose had made me fall in love. Because he made me happy.

Because my monster ached for him.

Because he needed me.

Because *I* needed *him*.

I never wanted to let him go again.

But first…

First, I was going to kill the man who had taken his attention. I was going to stop this cycle from continuing. I was going to snap his neck and end this game, once and for all. With my secret laid bare for Felix to see, he'd get the choice to keep me, or kill me.

And I'd let him pick.

Because I loved him more than I loved anything, even myself.

Felix's guest had his back to me when I rounded the corner. He was talking, the guest, not Felix. And it was obvious that Felix wasn't really listening.

"I've always been a big fan of your movies," the stranger said, rambling on. His...*movies?* I glanced at the movie posters that lined the walls, scanning them—my head still fuzzy with rage. "I can't believe I got to actually *meet* you."

They looked as familiar as they had the first few times I'd seen them, only now...I looked at them with a different lens.

Felix nodded along to his guest's words, but his eyes weren't connected to the conversation. I knew this because I was rather intimately acquainted with any and all Felix expressions, and I could proudly say—despite my usual lack of expertise in human emotion—that I could easily deduce his current emotion. And he looked...*huh.*

He looked like he was in a *hurry.*

He did not look excited, or happy, or invested in the conversation at all. Which was good. Because the only person he should be invested in talking to was me, and I stood by that.

He probably felt rushed because he was expecting me to come over soon for our matching-tuxedo-fake-groom social debut.

There was a lump in my throat and a pit in my stomach as I stared at the two of them interacting, even though I could clearly see that Felix was not invested.

"Quiet please," he said softly, voice as melodic and sweet as ever. There was an air of finality to it. Strong despite being buttery smooth. My racing thoughts halted at the same time the asshole-visitor's words did. Simultaneously, something *electric* flowed through the room. Something *heavy*. For a moment it was hard to breathe. The stranger shifted, body still as if he'd been frozen.

As if…by simply commanding it, Felix had turned him off entirely. As easily as pressing a button.

You'd think I'd pay more attention to the man who had so obviously been "altered." But I did not. Because I had, and always would have eyes for one man and one man only. And Felix had finally, *finally* noticed me.

He made a surprised little sound, his lips parting—his…very red, very *stained* lips. A little smile spread across them as soon as our eyes connected, the flicker of his peculiar, slightly crooked teeth sending butterflies erupting in my stomach where the pit had sat only moments prior.

This was not the look of a man who didn't care for me.

His eyes said, *you're here.*

They said, I missed you.

They said, I'm lonely, lonely, lonely.

And then guilt scoured his expression, dashing away the light as quickly as it had come. Something wavered then, trembling in the air between us. The weight that had filled the room only growing heavier as we stared at each other, at an impasse.

Felix was about to give me his secrets. I could see it on his face.

They trembled, brittle and ready to topple.

All it would take was a single push.

Chapter Twenty

"YOU'RE HERE EARLY," he said, surprised. Normally, I'd be at the office for another hour at least. I hadn't realized that I had forgotten to tell him that I would be arriving to take him to the party as soon as the sun went down. I supposed it didn't matter now.

"Felix," I said, voice dangerously low. One step, two steps, three steps closer. The man didn't move. Felix didn't either. He looked…caught, like he didn't know what to do.

His eyes swam with emotion.

"I realize—because I have been informed by Winnifred, the sister that you met, with the freckles—" I added, because I wasn't certain he'd remember her. "That I have never formally asked you for exclusivity."

Felix balked, eyes widening significantly. "Exclusivity?" he blinked, obviously confused. "Marshall, what—"

"I want the guests to stop." My hands were shaking. God, I hated telling people my boundaries. "I don't want to share you anymore."

Felix's expression softened, the odd bloody-looking mess on his lips distracting me. "You're not sharing me."

"I want to be your boyfriend," I said, my heart racing.

Still, the stranger didn't move. It was like he wasn't there at all. Merely a mannequin. Distantly, I recognized that this was odd. That *all of this* was odd. That it hadn't looked like Felix was engaged with him in anything intimate at all, and therefore I had no idea why he was over in the first place.

Still, I felt that sense of helplessness I had when I'd seen the car in the driveway and thought I hadn't satisfied him.

"I understand that you have certain needs."

"Do you?" Felix's voice wavered. His lips were red, red, red. "Marshall, I don't think you do."

"I will fuck you eighty times a day if it means I will satisfy you."

"You already satisfy me."

"Then why is there a man in your house?" I didn't mean to yell. I didn't. But it just kind of…happened anyway? "Why, Felix? Why is there an endless parade of suitors banging down your door even though I am right here." My eyes were burning, and I couldn't seem to make them stop. Tears spilled down my cheeks and I hurt. *I hurt so much.*

"If I need to tell you to be my boyfriend, I will. If I need to tie you up and hide you away, I will. But I'm tired of *sharing*. You are the only person I've ever wanted and it's not fair that you don't want me the same way."

"But I do," Felix's voice wobbled. I could see his hands shaking. Could see the way he shrank in on himself. "I want you more than anything. I want you more than I…" he sucked in a breath, and a trembly, broken gasp rang out.

Felix put his thoughts together, and I let him. Because I was too busy being a crybaby to do anything but stare and shake and try to piece together the truth.

"I want you…" Felix tried again, steadier this time, "more than I want my old life back. I want you more than I want to be who and *what* I was before I became *this*. I want you more than I want gray hair, or wrinkles, or to be a real person."

"Nothing you're saying makes any sense." My hands felt sweaty and hot, my pulse racing. "And you *are* a real person. I don't…I don't understand." Maybe I was blind. In hindsight, I totally was. I'd missed all the signs. But in my defense, why would a man who was rooted in reality the way I was, ever guess that such a fantastical conclusion was the truth?

"I'm not a real person," Felix countered, and his eyes were wet. "Unless I'm…with you."

When I'm with you, I'm not lonely. I don't feel like a ghost.

"Oh." The aching parts of me settled as easily as they'd been riled. I knew I still was missing something. The secret he'd kept. And as Felix's tongue flickered out to swipe away the remaining blood on his lip, my brain began to whir.

One step, two steps, three steps.

I moved closer to him, because I needed him more than I needed my next breath.

Winnie's words from earlier in the summer came back to haunt me.

"You can't expect him to follow rules when you haven't even told him what they are."

"I want to be your forever," I said for the second time since we'd begun dating. "I want to be your *only* forever. I want all of your attention, all the time. And one day—I plan to marry you."

The cats were nowhere to be found, mysteriously not attempting to trip me as I crossed the distance between me and my target. The man that Felix had somehow paralyzed, still had not moved. He hadn't turned to speak, hadn't interrupted. Still as a statue, but more uncanny, because he was flesh and blood and he should not have been so…frozen.

If he'd had *any* self-preservation at all he would've run.

But he apparently did not, because he continued to stand facing Felix. Continued to stare at him, despite the fact that I was currently hunting him. Two steps more, and suddenly…the side of his neck became visible.

I nearly stumbled with a sickening lurch, my hands clenched into fists.

Was that…?

No.

No.

It couldn't be—

But it…it *was*.

Without pausing my stride, I took in this new reality with a clarity I hadn't felt before. The world spun, but the stranger's neck remained painfully in focus as I stared at it. As I stared at the *bite mark* on it.

It only took me a second to recognize what it was, and *who* it came from—as Felix had left similar bruises all over my own body. I'd recognize the shape of his peculiar teeth anywhere. Only Felix had always been careful with me—only ever accidentally nicking me. And this man's bite *weeped*. Blood slipped coppery red down his throat, drip, drip dripping.

I'd interrupted them.

Felix.

Feeding.

One quick glance to Felix proved my suspicions correct. The red that was smeared across his lovely lips was very obviously blood. I just hadn't… realized. *How hadn't I realized?* For a man who was rather intimate with the substance, I was apparently quite obtuse. And Felix looked… *God*, did he look perfect, especially now that I knew what was decorating his delicious mouth.

Gorgeous and feral.

A wild, wicked thing.

All lean powerful muscles—compact and useful. A predator's build.

His eyes glowed luminous and red.

His fangs glinted.

Fangs.

Because that was what they were.

Because Felix was a vampire.

Because Felix's paramours were apparently not paramours at all but sustenance. And the kills he'd managed were truly accidents. Probably as accidental as overheating packaged food in the microwave, or leaving a pot on the stove long enough it burned.

He'd simply drank too much.

And they…well… They'd paid the price.

My thoughts were ping-pong balls, ricocheting around inside my head as I came to terms with my new reality. A reality that made no sense. None. And yet…made a surprisingly large amount of sense at the same time.

This explained so much.

I wanted to think longer, to mull it over, especially as it seemed Felix had our guest controlled. But…my skin still itched to eliminate the competition, especially now that I knew his blood sat warm inside Felix's belly.

Fuck this.

I decided then that Felix would never feed from anyone other than me. It felt right.

As did the next words that came out of my mouth, reverent, and soft—like I was speaking to a spooked animal—because that's exactly what Felix looked like right then. His red eyes were wide. His lips were parted. And he was shaking.

Shaking like he thought he'd just lost everything.

"You look so beautiful covered in blood," I said softly, my hands clenched into fists. One step, two steps, three steps. I was barely a foot away from the unwanted visitor—Felix's supper. "Were you hungry, darling?" I asked, because I suddenly knew what was sitting pretty in the package in my garage. I had a feeling if I opened the box I'd find bags of blood, neatly packaged up and labeled. So much was beginning to make sense. Like the fact that Felix only ever had guests when it had been a while between his packages—or I'd…stolen them? Accidentally.

Why he'd been so reluctant to go on a date with me when I'd first asked. Because he'd been hungry. And he'd needed time to feed before he could be alone with me.

Because he…oh.

Because he wanted *me*.

That's what he'd meant that night at the drive-in.

And before—when he'd mentioned needing to prepare before spending time with me.

My cheeks flushed, my heart fluttering like crazy as my cock perked up immediately.

Felix wants to eat me.

I wanted to let him.

I hadn't given him nearly enough credit. Look how *innovative* he'd been! Look how desperate he'd been to spend time with me, desperate enough he'd do anything. Including inviting his "supper" over only a few hours after his box hadn't "arrived" on schedule, so he wouldn't have to cancel our date.

Felix had often said he had a hard time controlling himself around me, and now I knew why.

I'd taken his food away—and my clever, wonderful love had been forced to improvise.

Felix looked frightened.

Maybe because he didn't know what to say.

He didn't know how to explain *this*.

I didn't know what to say either—because there was no logical explanation for what I was seeing. And yet…even more things started to make sense. Like dominos falling into place one by one. Memories assaulted me. Memories of things I hadn't understood, and ignored— only now…there was no ignoring the truth.

Felix's fear of the sunlight for one.

His aversion to food.

The fact that he didn't want to be recognized—probably for the same reason the-man-who-was-now-his-supper had complimented his movies. I realized now why the dark haired actor I'd seen on the screen at the drive-in theater had looked so familiar. Why I'd recognized Felix before I'd even known him. Why the movie star's name was Lucky—the very definition of Felix's name.

Why Felix dyed his hair. (He was harder to recognize that way.)

Why Felix hid. (He had been the King of Hollywood.)

Why Felix never ate. (I kept accidentally taking his boxes of blood away.)

Why Felix spoke like he was from another time. (Because he was.)

Why Felix covered his living room in posters. (They were his movies.)

Why his front hallway was full of framed letters. (Fan letters, more than likely.)

Why Felix had never been frightened of me. (He was a predator, himself.)

Why there was a coffin in the storage room, and Felix's bed was dusty. (He slept there, not upstairs.)

Why Felix's family was dead. (Of course they were, it'd been ninety years.)

Why he collected things. Things that reminded him of his life before.

His home was a time capsule and a prison.

Living in the limelight, there was no room for the abnormal. Felix had to have aged out, didn't he? There was only so long a man could remain the same age without people noticing. I imagined, if I Googled Lucky, the movie star from the 30s, I'd find that he had died rather young.

Only he hadn't.

Because he was standing right in front of me, with a stranger's blood smeared across his lips.

He was standing right in front of me, with his heart on his sleeve, vulnerability quaking in his gaze—like he expected to lose me before we'd ever really begun in the first place.

There was no denying the truth.

The dominos had fallen. The results were in.

The love of my life was a vampire.

I should've been horrified, terrified—some combination of adjectives that were negative and awful. But…I wasn't. I wasn't. Because Felix may be a vampire, but he was also the man that I was desperately, terrifyingly in love with.

"*Marshall,*" Felix said my name, and everything that had been wrong inside me since the moment I'd seen that car in his driveway fell away.

His voice was brittle and *quaking.*

His hands shook.

"I'm a *monster.*" Felix's eyes burned a hole into mine, tears spilling down his lovely, pale cheeks.

I wanted to reach for him.

I wanted to *hold* him.

I wanted to comfort him, and not once—ever—did giving him a cheeseburger cross my mind.

But first…

I needed to even the playing field.

I needed to tell him *my* secret too.

So I raised my hands, hovering them on either side of the stranger's head. He didn't move, still frozen. His skin was warm, and his pulse fluttered beneath my fingers as I closed my hands around his head. I should've felt bad for what I was about to do—but I didn't.

He'd *touched* Felix.

The fact that it hadn't been sexual didn't matter.

He'd touched Felix.

And for that he deserved to die.

So I squeezed—and as easily as if I'd done it a thousand times before—I twisted his neck.

The last of our secrets fell away—quite literally—as a sickening, *delicious* snapping sound filled the room. Moments later, his body crumpled, falling to the floor in a broken heap. Uncaring, as my point had been made—and my eyes were reserved for one man, and one man only—I stepped over the corpse. My gaze never left Felix's face. I didn't miss the way his eyes widened, or the way he'd flinched, staring at me the same way I stared at him.

Two predators, recognizing each other for what they were for the first time.

My heart was pounding—I reached for Felix with the same hands I'd used to kill his guest. It was a gamble. I wasn't sure he'd accept me now that he'd seen what I could do. There was no mistaking how practiced the motion had been.

And I was certain…he was having a few revelations of his own.

Probably about why I knew how to dispose of bodies.

Why it had been second nature for me to latch onto his kills and drag them through the woods.

Why I'd crossed the street and offered him help that first night.

"Good evening," I'd said, standing in his jungle of a yard while I watched him struggle with the corpse. *"Would you like a hand with that?"*

My bones creaked as my hand hovered, waiting in empty space—lonely.

Felix had asked me over dinner once if I ever got lonely. Until he'd asked, I hadn't noticed. But since then…every day I was without him was the new loneliest day of my life. He completed me in a way that even killing never had. He smoothed my ragged edges. I didn't feel empty or odd when he was around. I felt…like myself in a way I never had before.

Which was why it was only natural to meet him in the middle, once again.

So I told him the truth, answering his honesty with my own, one last time.

"I'm a monster too." My hand trembled. I waited.

Outside, the sound of footsteps should've registered. People crossing the street and heading toward Barry's, probably. I sucked in a breath, my lips wobbling. Felix stared into my eyes, searching them.

His eyes said, Marshall, Marshall, Marshall.

And then, his hand slipped into mine. I squeezed. Tighter than was probably necessary—but in that moment, all I wanted was to feel him squeeze back. And squeeze back he did, tight—tighter than a human should've been able.

We fell together like we always had, gasoline to flame.

His lips tasted coppery sweet, salty and lovely. I licked into his mouth, chasing the last traces of blood as I yanked him into my arms—uncaring of the body on the floor at our feet. He was as light as ever—and yet, I felt lighter.

I'd never thought acceptance could feel this good.

I'd fought for it over the years, yes. Fought for it when we moved from the farm to the city, and I learned that there were new ways to fit in that I hadn't known about before. I'd fought for it at college, at the same time I fought for my degrees. I fought for it when I moved here—attending Barry's parties because I was terrified of sticking out too much.

Acceptance had never tasted like blood before.

It had never felt like Felix's body against mine, his legs around my hips, his hands in my hair.

It was a beautiful, wonderful thing.

And I realized that all this time, the only person I'd needed was right here. The only person I cared about, was currently clinging to me. And like a princess in a tower, he'd been waiting for me. Growing dusty as the years settled, just waiting for me to be born. For me to move here. For me to love him, to obsess over him, even more than one of his fans.

I pushed him to the couch, crowding him against the leather. It squeaked beneath us and I moaned against his mouth, grunting when his hands raked down my back, rucking up my tuxedo suit jacket. I whined when he spread his legs wider and I was able to line up our pelvises. Our dicks were hard. And god—the friction.

I grunted, rolling into him with a happy, content little sound as I licked into his mouth over and over again.

He knew exactly what to do with his tongue to make my eyes roll back, and he did so over and over and over again. The little hussy was trying to break my focus. Trying to *dominate* me, even when I was the one on top of him. But no. *No.*

It was my turn, dammit.

The beast inside me reared to the surface, closer than he'd ever been before. I pinned Felix down, growling at him. His eyes grew wide, his gaze snapping to my gritted teeth and the tension that flickered in the corner of my jaw. He licked his lips and did the one thing he'd never truly done.

He submitted.

Fully, completely, beautifully.

His body spread wide, his eyes softening—the trust there, the distance obliviated.

This was what we'd been missing.

This.

The truth had separated us and now that it was out, our monsters could finally meet. Tongue to tongue, cock to cock, heart to heart. I unbuttoned Felix's tuxedo pants, groaning softly when my fingers grazed the swell of his lovely, long cock. It pushed insistently against my hand as I dove down, sucking greedy, needy little kisses along his neck.

Hickeys blossomed beneath my tongue, only to disappear moments later. It felt like a game, bringing them to the surface as I fumbled with getting both of our pants open and our cocks out. Felix gasped—head tossing back, his pale hair spreading across the cushions the moment I wrapped my fist around the both of us and began to tug.

"Oh fuck—hnnn," he sobbed, the long line of his throat tensing, tendons dancing. Setting a brutal pace, I stroked us together, my own hips fucking tightly into my fist as Felix's fingers dug into my arms. "Fuck, yes. I—ah—" he couldn't seem to manage a full sentence, and I felt victorious.

"Take it," I hissed out, hips pumping as our cocks pressed together, wetter every time I rubbed the leaking precum from the tips down to slick the way. It was a little too dry—a little painful—but we both liked the pain. Felix grinned at me, and it was the prettiest damn thing I'd ever seen.

He peered at me through his lashes as his broad chest trembled. I could see his nipples pushing against the white fabric—white to match the black of my own suit—and I leaned down, sucking on them with greed as our hips fucked together.

"Fuck, fuck, fuck," Felix's hands tangled in my hair, a desperate sob escaping him as I bit one of his nipples, hard. My spit made the fabric nearly transparent, and I whined against him, moving to the other side to repeat the motion so I could see the perky pink nipples strain against his shirt.

"You're so beautiful," I somehow managed, worrying his chest with my teeth. "Even more now that I know you're mine."

"Yours," Felix promised, saying it like it was easy. Like it was second nature. Like it took no thought at all.

"You won't feed on anyone else," I told him, his cock pushing into my grip.

"I won't," he agreed, breathless and needy. His hips flexed, his dick growing warmer by the second as I rubbed and teased it. My cock was darker than his—closer to purple than his was when it was aroused. His dick was a little over half the size of mine, and it was more than a little delicious to see them pushing together.

"You can't go out without me," I begged, biting a line across his chest, then up his lovely throat.

"I won't."

"You can't look at anyone but me."

"I wouldn't."

"Because you're mine—" My voice wobbled, my shoulders shaking as I grew closer and closer with each promise that rang between us. Sweet as wedding bells. "You're mine."

"I'm yours."

"And I need you—" I kissed his ear, blocking him from view—protecting him from the world, as I wanted to do for the rest of our lives. "I need you to need me like I need you."

"I do."

"I need you to love me like I love you."

"Oh, Marshall." Felix's voice wavered, breathless and rough, one of his lovely hands cupping the side of my face, jerking my head away from his ear so he could look at me. His eyes were warm. So *very* warm. Warmer than summer days. Warmer than rhubarb pie fresh out of the oven. Warmer than Vladmir when he curled up in my lap while I made collages.

"Because looking at you hurts—" my voice broke. "You're so beautiful." My heart thrashed. "Because I don't deserve good things, and that's what you are—" Felix made a wounded sound, gripping my face tighter as my eyes burned, and hot tears spilled free. Hotter even, than the cocks I still held clutched tightly, possessively in my hand. "Because no one has ever loved me the way I need."

"Oh, darling," Felix's voice was warm, warm, warm. So full of love it floored me.

"Felix," I managed, voice cracking.

"You know…I thought—" he shivered, hips pushing into my grasp. "I became…this—" A vampire, "Because I worried that without my beauty and youth I'd have…nothing." His voice shuddered, the truth echoing between us, shivery warm. "Now I realize, what an honor growing old would have been." Tears burned in his eyes. "Especially if I had been able to do that with you."

I smiled, a wobbly, awful smile that I was sure was pathetic, and not at all sexy. But Felix didn't seem to mind.

"Nothing good lasts forever," Felix said softly, stroking his thumb along my cheek, catching a stray tear that had slipped free. "I know that firsthand." He sucked in a breath—a breath he didn't need. "But you will."

"Steady as the stars," I promised, heart fluttering.

"Two eyes, two hands, and a grin," Felix echoed, the words I'd spoken to him all those weeks ago.

"Not special," I countered, leaning down till our noses brushed.

"Not at all," he hummed, fluttering a kiss against my lips.

"Forever?" I offered, now that I knew that for him…forever was infinite.

"Soon," Felix promised.

And then we were kissing again. Warm, wet, delicious. He slid inside my mouth, his fingers tangling in my hair and I lost myself in him. My hand moved more quickly, my orgasm fast approaching as the rollercoaster of emotions we'd shared over the last few minutes coalesced.

When we came, we came together.

Because that was what we were supposed to do.

Felix gasped against my lips, a broken, needy whine. His hot cum spilled against my fingers. I followed after, feeling victorious that I'd managed to make him come first. I caught what I could of the mess, feeling quite proud when that ended up being all of it.

That was…of course, when the fact that I'd left the front door open came to bite me in the ass.

In the form of my worst fucking nightmare.

Barry (the busybody.)

Standing in the doorway, eyes wide, his ridiculous hair primped for the party. I only had a moment to judge him for the amount of gel he used before I realized what exactly he was seeing. Me and Felix, fucking on the couch. Aaaaand the body on the floor. The very dead, very still body, staring vacantly at him—eyes still open.

Fuck.

My.

Life.

Chapter Twenty-One

BARRY RAN—because apparently he had some sense. Dolly and Tiffany blocked his escape—because they were good, loyal beasts—and Barry fucking kicked at them. He missed, but still. Anger burned liquid hot beneath my skin as he bolted down the hallway and out of sight.

"Fucking asshole," I grunted, rage simmering.

He was going to pay for that.

The absolute fucking pig.

Who does that?

Who kicks a fucking cat?

Asshole, asshole, asshole.

If I hadn't hated Barry before, I certainly did now.

Felix and I shared a glance before we were both on our feet. We checked on the cats—but both seemed fine, if not a bit spooked. They steered clear of the corpse, scurrying away and up the stairs like nothing had happened at all.

I licked the cum from my hand, and Felix groaned, watching me as he buttoned up his pants as quickly and efficiently as he could, before moving on to mine.

"I'm going to have to kill him," I said simply, my mind already whirring through how exactly I'd catch up before he could tell anyone what he'd seen.

"I can fix it—" Felix promised. And for once…I believed him. I cocked my head at him, and he grinned, wide and wolfish. We made our way to the front door, but Felix stepped back, away from the peep of light that spanned the hallway. Barry had left it open—because of course he had. Inconsiderate, nosy-ass bitch.

Never mind the fact that I had done the exact same thing, and been equally nosy only a few minutes prior.

"Take my phone," I said, pulling it from my pocket and passing it to him. "The sun is setting and you should be able to come outside soon." He took my phone, pinching it between his fingers like he didn't know how to hold it. I snorted, then leaned over and typed my passcode in. "The password is F-E-L-I-X." He blinked, then laughed, eyeing me with obvious affection. "Call Allen, tell him what happened. He'll bring *The Club* over and they'll take care of the body."

"Okay," Felix echoed.

"When the sun is down, come find me."

He nodded, eyes wide.

I kissed him.

I kissed him hard, giving his mouth one last ravenous flick of my tongue before I retreated, and marched out the front door, a man on a mission. A murdery, delicious mission. I didn't know exactly what Felix meant by

"I can fix it." But I was determined to stall until he came to save the day.

Of course, because Barry was a bitch—with self-preservation—he was running down the block toward his own party. I could only hope that I could catch him before he said something to the wrong person, or god forbid, called the cops.

His hair was flopping all over the place as he bolted down the street, wearing what looked like a suit from a dollar store. I marched after him, offering a few smiles and waves toward the other people that headed toward his house for the party. The whole block would be there—which did not make incapacitating Barry easy.

Still, I'd manage.

The sun was sinking below the tree line. I probably had ten minutes or so until Felix was safe to leave his home. It was a wonder I hadn't gotten any blood on my suit—not that you'd be able to easily see it on the black fabric if I had.

Stalking down the street, I had never felt more elated in all my life.

I had the man of my dreams—a movie star!

I'd made Felix come before I had!

I was wearing an impeccable tuxedo.

I had already killed one man, and here I was, about to kill another!

All in all, it was a rather good day, wasn't it? For the first time since I'd met him, Barry was about to bring me immense joy.

I caught up to him five minutes later. He was hiding behind the giant wedding cake that sat smack dab in the center of his backyard. There were at least thirty people present. It seemed that his guests had invited guests of their own.

I imagined, in any other circumstance, he'd be elated.

As it was, there was no time to be elated.

Because his hunter had found him.

"Hi, Barry," I said cheerfully from behind him. He hadn't seen me—I was light on my feet, kind of a necessity with a hobby like mine.

"Hi, Marshall." He squeaked out, twisting around to look at me, his eyes wide.

"Why were you at Felix's house?" I asked, because it wasn't like I could just twist his neck in front of all of these people.

"He was supposed to bring a casserole—" he managed, stupidly answering my question instead of running.

If I stalled long enough…Felix would arrive.

Would I get to see him kill?

The thought made me giddy.

Barry glanced around, like he wanted to bolt away, so I reached out, closing my hand tight around his wrist.

"The door was open—" Barry continued to ramble, quaking in my grip. "I didn't see anything. I swear—" He had totally seen something. He glanced around for help, but…people were accustomed to seeing us fight, so no one came to his rescue. I grinned wider, leaning in close.

"You kicked our cats," I told him—and because it would probably be my last time to say it, "And I *hate* you."

"Marshall—" Barry's eyes widened, like he knew this was my version of goodbye.

"And I know you changed the theme last year specifically to try to make a fool out of me."

"I'm sorry—I'm sorry."

"I wore *flamingos* because of you."

"Marshall, I'm sorry—" Barry tried to jerk out of my grip, but I wouldn't let him. The table with the cake wobbled, and he panicked, trying to catch the cake.

"I've hated you since the day I saw your smarmy little face," I told him. "You made Felix dunk himself in cold water."

"It was for charity—" he continued to try to wiggle free. Why he wasn't calling for help, I didn't understand. Oh—yep. There we go. He opened his mouth, sucked in a breath—and I reached out to close my other hand over his mouth to stifle it.

"You smell like garlic," I told him, grinning evilly, my glasses glinting. *That* was for Tiffany. "And your hair is stupid." And *that* was for Dolly.

The sun had officially sunk below the horizon.

Yes.

Yes.

I jerked Barry away from the table, intent to bring him out of the crowd where we could take care of him in private. I was bigger than him. By quite a bit. I was bigger than everyone, if we're being honest. It was easy to manhandle him without it looking like it took any effort at all—and I only had to do it for a minute longer and—yep.

There he was.

Like gay-vampire-Moses, Felix parted the crowd with a single look. He stood at the other end of the yard, dressed immaculately in his white tuxedo. Like an avenging angel, gorgeous, ethereal, delicious. He had not been as lucky as I had—as there were a few flecks of blood splattered across his lapel.

He looked so damn pretty standing there—the stars creeping into view in the purpling sky. His pale hair was wild—wilder than normal, and his red eyes shined.

"Quiet," he said, his own voice barely loud enough to be heard.

Somehow, like magic—maybe because that's what it was—the crowd silenced. Everyone. All at once. The peep of crickets was suddenly impossibly loud as Felix scanned the crowd for me. Glowing, glowing, glowing. There was something ethereal and terrifying about the way his red eyes burned bright in the dark.

Fairy lights danced across the yard—the immaculately dressed crowd, parting for him in tandem, like he was somehow…controlling them. Empty-headed puppets. Their eyes were as vacant as the corpse we'd left on his living room floor.

So this…was how he'd been getting away with murder.

As Felix strode confidently toward us—no hat, no glasses—all his brutal, supernatural strength on full display, I fell even *more* in love with him. I hadn't even known that was possible.

He was a walking (literally) contradiction.

Pastel-loving-murderous-gremlin baby.

My sweet, bumbling fool.

God, I was obsessed with him.

Barry wriggled in my grip. And I knew then, that Felix had not enthralled him like he had the others. *Why* he'd chosen to leave him alone quickly became clear. Because when I released him, Barry bolted toward the back door of his home, halfway between me and my murderous, gorgeous lover. A slow, wicked smile spread across Felix's face, his eyes flickering with the first twinges of bloodlust I'd ever seen on his face.

And it was…glorious.

It seemed my little fool had a bit of the devil in him, after all—even when my cock was not inside him. (Ha!)

Felix had let Barry go free, not because he couldn't control him, but because he wanted to hunt him.

Oh fuck.

My dick was *so hard* right now.

I watched, enraptured as Barry scrambled at the back door, trying to get it open with his sweaty sausage fingers. Only for Felix to appear behind him—liquid quick. So damn fast I'd hardly seen him move at all.

Barry twisted away, and Felix let him, still grinning as Barry burst back down the porch steps, running toward the other side of the yard. He dodged through the very still bodies of the people Felix still controlled, and a few of them crossed their arms—reminiscent of soldiers—blocking his escape.

More frantic, more sweaty, more abhorrent—Barry turned back around and ran the other way again.

Over and over, back and forth. Felix chased him. Playing with his food like a cat plays with a mouse. And it was…magnificent. Truly the most fun I'd ever had. Delighted by the show, I served myself up a slice of wedding cake, munching on it happily as I watched Felix play.

Barry was a red-faced, sweaty mess by the time he stumbled to a stop in front of me. It almost seemed as though he'd given up entirely, the light in his eyes slowly dimming.

Any sympathy I had for him died, however, when in a last ditch effort to escape he knocked into the food table, his weight toppling it over. I tried to jump out of the way, but there was nothing that could stop the next set of events. The way the white wedding cake toppled, all ten layers of it teetering and sliding, slamming right into me.

I hit the ground with a little grunt—shocked—and covered in icing.

And that was…apparently it for Felix.

"This is Armani," I gasped out, rightfully offended—the wind knocked right out of me.

Felix was there half a second later, helping me to my feet as Barry attempted to make a run for it again. I was on my feet in seconds—hello superhuman speed—wow. That was more than a little sexy. And then Felix was in front of Barry, blocking his way, his eyes dark.

The murderous intent was heavy in the air.

Thick, cloying, delicious.

The lovely wedding waltz still played from the speakers set in the corners of Barry's backyard as Felix made his last, wonderful move. In slow motion almost, I watched as Felix's lovely red gaze focused on Barry's throat. There was a brutal ferocity to his movements—a grace, much like a dancer—as he closed the distance between his razor sharp mouth of fangs and Barry's neck.

A slick sound emitted as Felix bit into him, then just as quick, pulled back—bringing a piece of Barry's throat with him. Immediately, Barry gurgled, his airways cut off, blood spurting from the open wound. It was…immensely satisfying that for once he'd finally shut up. He coughed, stumbled, one, two, three steps—then fell to his knees.

Felix kicked him over, boot connecting with his shoulder, Barry's body flopping to the ground in a puddle of his own cake and blood. Riveted, I stared at the mess Felix had made of him—for only a moment—then turned my attention back to the artist himself.

Felix's other kills had been accidental, yes.

I could see that now.

Perhaps he had gotten too zealous when feeding.

He'd felt guilty. At war with himself. Upset.

But this…no. There was no guilt on his face now. There was only righteous fury. Anger that was so beautiful I wanted to taste it. Satisfaction so sweet, it made my taste buds tingle. This was no accident. My bumbling, worried little accidental murderer had become a full-fledged killer.

And he…*loved* it.

Enraptured, I watched in real time as Felix came to that conclusion too. He stared at Barry, his eyes wide, a slow, curling smile stretching across his lips. His gaze snapped to me, and I…well… I shuddered, unable to help myself.

Then, just as quickly as he'd become a predator, my little love melted. The bloodlust faded, his eyes warm, his broad shoulders relaxed.

"You're filthy," Felix said softly, clucking in concern as he crossed the distance between us, reaching out to smooth his hands over my tux. He got icing on them, and I smiled—unable to help myself.

"You've got a little—" I grabbed a handkerchief from my pocket, reaching out to gently dab at the blood on Felix's face. Normally, I'd want to taste it. To taste his depravity. But apparently, even I had my limits.

And tasting anything that had been inside Barry (the soon-to-be bloated) was one of them.

"Thank you," Felix smiled at me. He looked…a little nervous. But I quickly soothed his fears, pulling him in tight, my lips at his ear.

"I have never been harder in all my life," I murmured, just to feel him shiver.

"Fuck," he responded, fingers finding my hips, digging in.

"Soon," I countered—teasing him, like he liked to tease me.

The crowd continued to stand around the edges of the lawn, expressions vacant. As though they hadn't witnessed the bloodbath we'd caused at all. Barry's corpse, lying in the wedding cake, felt like a symbol if I'd ever seen one.

"Felix…" I said softly, kissing the shell of his lovely, almost pointy ear.

"Marshall," he murmured, tipping into the touch.

"I know I'm covered in cake—"

"You are."

"I know you're probably disappointed that tonight did not go as planned." I knew I was. A bit—maybe not a lot, as this had ended far more entertaining than I'd been expecting. There were a few beats we hadn't met, however, that I was missing.

"I am," he tipped his head up, and I moved back to look down at him. To look down at the monster I loved, as the beast inside me roared with pride. He was mine, mine, mine. Sharp teeth, murderous tendencies, and all.

"How long can you maintain control of the crowd?" I asked softly, grabbing his face, smearing icing with my fingers. Felix grinned, his eyes crinkling. The lovely swoop and dive of the waltz that played over the speakers filled the air. Crickets chirped. The stars were high above.

"A while."

I reached into my back pocket, removing the item—the gift—I'd bought him weeks ago from it.

I offered it to him, and his dark brow furrowed as he opened the tiny velvet box. A startled sound escaped him, his eyes widening as the two matching rings glinted up at him. "Marshall…" he said softly, voice hoarse.

"It's not a wedding ring," I said softly. "At least…not yet."

"I see." I grabbed one of the rings from the box, bringing his hand up—

his blood-streaked hand—and slid the ring onto his ring finger.

"But it could be. When you're ready."

"When I'm ready," he said softly, staring down at it, eyes flickering with emotion.

"See?" I slid the other one on, allowing him to pocket the box himself, as I pressed our hands together, fingers tangling. The rings tapped, and Felix stared at them—stared at our mismatched hands, his small, mine large. He sucked in an overwhelmed little breath. "We match."

"We do," he murmured, and I knew he wasn't just talking about the rings.

But something deeper, something more central.

It wasn't often a monster found his mate.

He knew that as well as I did.

"Now that *that's* over with," I hummed, catching his gaze, my heart pounding. "We're here. We're dressed—the music is still playing."

"It is."

"It seems…silly not to take advantage."

"It does," Felix grinned, and it made my heart hurt.

"Felix Finley," I said softly, releasing him so I could step back, feet smooshing into more cake. I offered him my hand, half bowing.

"Marshall Warden," he replied, staring at me like I was the single most beautiful thing on this earth. No one had ever looked at me like that. It seemed fitting that he would. My love, my heart, my star. My sweet monster, still smeared in blood—his white suit as stained as mine was.

"May I have this dance?"

His eyes sparkled as he placed his hand in mine, giving it a tight squeeze. "I thought you'd never ask."

We danced.

We danced.

We danced.

Chapter Twenty-Two

FELIX AND I danced till the moon rose high in the sky, the blood on Felix's face dried, and the other members of *The Club* found us, all seemingly unsurprised by the mess we'd made. Allen shook his head at me, though his eyes were warm.

He pulled Barry's body away—effectively cleaning up our mess, as the rest of *The Club* members grumbled and swore. Felix commanded the guests home, and they emptied out of the yard in a frog march, still unaware of how bloody the night had ended. Felix said they'd wake up the next morning with no recollection of what they'd missed.

And still—

We danced.

Eventually Felix and I left Barry's backyard. We traveled across town and parked off the road where we normally did. We'd decided it would be best if we checked up on *The Club* and our corpses, but that didn't mean we weren't going to take our sweet time arriving. I had an idea as I shut the car door and held my hand out to Felix.

He tangled our fingers together. And as we stepped beneath the foliage, an evil, wicked, *wonderful* plan was born inside my head.

We'd done this once before—under very similar circumstances. But then I'd still been my prickly, irritable self. I hadn't paid attention to him the way I should've. Hadn't loved him the way he deserved to be loved.

He deserved a do-over.

And that was exactly what I was going to give him.

I only hoped that he'd remember—because if he didn't, my words would not make any sense.

I've often wondered if I would've made some of the choices that I did—if I'd had someone who stood beside me. Perhaps I never needed the world to love me, but just one…single person. Maybe that would have been enough.

"So…we're boyfriends," I started, as we began the trek through the woods to the crematory where our kills were currently being disposed of. Nerves fluttered around inside my stomach as I waited to see if he'd understand.

He didn't at first.

He just looked confused as he nodded, and then…after staring at the look on my face, it finally seemed to click. Felix blinked, processing my words for a few more seconds before a sunny, *bloody* smile spread across his lips. I could literally see the moment he recognized the parallels between this moment and our first night together in these very woods. Which had been my intention, so I was more than a little glad it had worked.

"Yes," Felix answered, still grinning.

The tables had turned, and I couldn't even be mad about it.

Licking my lips, I held a tree branch up for him to cross beneath, and continued speaking, "We've been boyfriends for a while."

"All summer."

"We've never really talked about it."

"We don't talk about our feelings if we can help it," Felix countered. My belly fluttered. This was fun. This was so fun. *Was this flirting?* I loved it. I loved him. I love-love-loved him.

"That's fair," I replied, beaming back at him. I should've been angry, seeing as I was covered in icing and our romantic night had been ruined by Barry, but I wasn't. Because this was…well… This was romantic, wasn't it? Special.

A mirror of the first night we'd actually spoken to one another.

A redo.

"I like your suit," I countered, lifting another branch. Felix noticed this time every time I did it, hopping beneath them with a pep in his step that had rarely been there.

"I like your face," he flirted back, awfully. "Thank you."

I laughed.

Giddy, I continued, faster this time. "Having a lover is fun." My heart fluttered like crazy. Crickets chirped. The stars hung in the sky above, dancing above us. I felt lighter than a feather.

"It can be," Felix hummed, his eyes twinkling with mirth. "It can also be bloody."

"Yes," I agreed, biting my lip to stop from laughing. I knew he knew what I was doing. And he didn't stop me. In fact, he looked even more delighted than I felt as he waited, eyes wide, ready for me to continue the game I'd started. "You are quite small."

"I am." Felix agreed, snorting out a happy little laugh. "I am vertically challenged."

"My perfect little fangy hobbit."

"Rude!" Felix smacked my chest, and I stumbled back a little, gasping out a laugh when I realized he'd forgotten to hold back. The fact he'd been stronger than me all this time hit me like a freight train and my dick became suddenly, painfully hard.

Chuckling, I stalked after him, ducking between the tree trunks, my cock stirring as I watched him flit through the woods in a merry blood-splattered chase. I didn't worry about getting caught. Didn't worry about unkind eyes, or nosy townspeople. Because now I knew Felix could fix whatever mess we found ourselves in.

It was freeing.

I felt like I could breathe.

"You have very nice biceps!" I called after him as he ducked behind a tree. Only, seconds later, I felt him at my back—so quickly I hadn't even seen him move—and his arms were wrapping tight around me.

He squeezed, and I sighed, tipping my head toward the stars, my fingers curling around his wrists. They were so dainty, such fragile bones for a man that could snap me in two.

"I was so in love with you," Felix admitted, face hidden against my back. The mirth in his words was gone, replaced instead with the fragile truth. "I still am."

I swallowed the lump in my throat, staring up at the stars as my heart fluttered unsteadily.

"How long?" I wasn't sure I was ready for the answer, but I wanted it anyway. Needed to know he loved me as much as I loved him. Needed to know he needed me as much as I needed him.

That we were steady as the stars.

"Since the day you moved across the street." Felix's voice quivered, and his arms shook. He rarely admitted things like this. Things so close to the heart. "I saw you and I thought…my god, he's beautiful."

He could hear my pulse racing, and that should've felt invasive, but it was comforting instead. Like he could read my body when my words were clogged and my mouth grew stuck.

"Looking up at the stars was the closest to seeing the sun as I'd gotten, till I saw you."

"Oh, Felix." I twisted around, grabbing onto him and pulling him up into my arms. He went willingly, wrapping his legs around me like a goth koala as his head buried inside my neck.

"I was so nervous—that day you saw me with the body."

"You were?"

"I wanted you to help."

That was a shocking revelation. I blinked, hands stuttering to a stop for only a moment before I resumed petting him, leading him through the woods toward our destination now that the chase had ended—my prey caught.

"I did help."

"I know…" Felix sounded guilty again. "You wanted all my secrets… right?"

"Yes." That was a no-brainer.

"This is embarrassing. Maybe a little…creepy?"

"Tell me." His spine was silky soft when I crept my hand beneath his shirt and began to rub it.

"I killed him…because I got distracted."

"Distracted…" I waited, well aware that there was more to this.

"Thinking about you?" Felix shivered. "About what you'd do if I were to drink from you—" I shivered, the thought of feeding him making my skin buzz. "About what you'd do if you saw us. Maybe you'd get jealous, or angry—maybe you'd toss him aside and offer me your throat."

I never would've done any of that. "That's not like me at all."

"I know," Felix laughed.

"Or…I mean…" My own cheeks felt hot now. "It wasn't like me. Then."

"Oh?" There was a lot laced in that one simple word.

"Oh," I murmured, burying my face in his soft lemony hair. "So, you were distracted…"

"You were home." Felix squeezed me tighter, his heels digging into the back of my thighs. "And you smelled so good. And I…couldn't control myself."

Oh fuck.

God.

That was the sexiest thing I'd ever heard.

"You killed him because you wanted me." My dick was so hard I was half-tempted to push Felix into the nearest tree and shove it inside him. I wasn't going to. Because that was rude. Or at least, I thought I wasn't going to.

Until he made this soft, devastating, needy little sound and I thought, fuck it.

Boyfriends fuck in the woods, don't they?

Bugs and dirt be damned.

The stars watched on as I fought my way through Felix's rather lovely suit. They dangled above, full of promise as I turned him into the tree, slicked myself up with the packet of lube I always kept on my person, and shoved inside him.

Steady, steady, steady.

I fucked him.

Fucked him till he whined and scratched at the bark, tearing into it as though it was brittle as paper, his body squeezing me as I rutted like a beast in heat.

It wasn't until the sky began to streak through with peachy pinks, that Felix and I finally returned home.

Home to the cul-de-sac where two predators had unknowingly purchased houses right across the street from each other.

Across the street from the small but clean house with the picket fence, up the broken sidewalk that was once littered with weeds.

Up the rickety porch steps, and into a house that was more befitting of Dracula than a man who unironically wore pastels. A man who wore his heart on his sleeve etched in unpracticed, loopy embroidery. A man who was magic, even before I knew what kind of creature he was.

When we fell into our bed beside each other—after showering, obviously—I counted my lucky stars.

Counted Felix's freckles too.

Finally kissed the little mole beneath his eye.

And together, tangled beneath the covers, we decided what I was going to say when my coworkers asked me what I'd done for the weekend. Which ended up being that despite its hiccups, tonight could not have been a more perfect night.

Felix and I may not have deserved to rest after what we'd done, but we rested anyway. Content to be selfish. Content to slumber. Content to live happily ever after.

Four eyes, four hands, two grins.

Two monsters.

Forever.

Soon.

Was it cowardice, that I dared not kill him?
Was it perversity, that I longed to talk to him?
Was it humility, to feel so honoured?
I felt so honoured.

8. D. H. Lawrence, "Snake".

Chapter Twenty-Three

SOON ENDED UP being farther away than I anticipated. Not because I wasn't ready to join Felix in our shared, bloody forever—but because he had informed me, quite seriously, that he loved the gray in my hair. That he wanted to see more of it. That we should wait till the front had entirely shifted—and then…then—I'd take the change.

You know what really blows my stack?

The fact that I found out halfway through my fucking life that there is apparently a secret supernatural government. And said government *apparently* operates—on occasion—delivery vans that bring sustenance to frightened little ex-movie stars. Ex-movie stars, who, even after nearly ninety years in hiding, were still terrified of being found out.

I told Felix that it would be easy enough to just tell people he was Lucky's grandson, should they question him, and the look he leveled me with was so *flabbergasted* I almost felt bad. Like it had never even occurred to him to claim to be related to himself.

He'd told me he'd had no children, and I'd told him that people didn't know that.

Not for certain.

And that uncertainty would be what would lead them to believe him.

Bit by bit—little by little, I helped coax Felix out of his shell.

The sun was a no go. Garlic was fine—though he didn't eat anything other than blood. We didn't know if holy water was an issue, and though I was curious, I wasn't curious enough to try on the off chance it did hurt him. He couldn't enter homes without permission—a fact that became quite annoying because the first time we visited Winnie in her apartment in the city, I'd had to all but force her to do it.

"Let him in," I'd demanded, hands on my hips.

Winnie had stared at me, her dark eyes dancing with the mischief they were always full of. She stood in the doorway, gesturing down the hall as if to say "after you."

"No." I huffed out, annoyed. "Invite him in."

She cocked her head at me, then laughed—luckily not catching on.

"Felix…" she said, addressing my tiny, hat-shrouded lover. "Would you like to come in?"

Felix perked right up, his metaphorical tail wagging, and I had to bite my tongue so I wouldn't reach out and squeeze the absolute shit out of him, he was so damn cute.

"Why Winnie, I thought you'd never ask."

They'd become fast friends…to my horror.

Especially when I discovered that Felix did not, in fact, own a cell phone— but a dusty old antique that hung from the wall. Which…explained why he had never answered my text messages. And also meant that he needed a phone. As soon as possible.

When I'd bought him one, we'd spent an entire weekend texting back and forth while sitting together on his couch while I tried to teach him how to use it. Felix texted like an old man. His tongue poking out, with one finger hitting each key very slowly.

It was…the cutest fucking thing I'd ever seen.

When he discovered the camera, I ascended to a higher plane. Because randomly, throughout the work week, he would send me pictures of things. I was starting to suspect that he set alarms to wake himself up so he could do so throughout the day. His sleep suffered, but our relationship did not. How could it? When I got selfies of Felix snuggled up in his coffin—yes, an actual coffin, my little goth gremlin—with all three of our cats. He sent me blurry pictures of the things he'd seen in his telescope the night before—though I couldn't see what the hell he was trying to show me. I always replied with emojis, because he got a kick out of them. Though… it did take me quite some time to select the correct one. Sometimes, I consulted Winnie. Which she found great delight in. Apparently she thought it was very entertaining helping me flirt with my boyfriend.

When Winnie and Felix had exchanged phone numbers, however, all hell broke loose.

She sent him pictures of me as a child.

As a child.

And Felix—because he was Felix—asked me a thousand and one questions about them. Like…why was I wearing a cowboy hat? (I lived on a farm, where we dealt with cattle, those things often went hand in hand.) Is this why you're so good at lawn work? (I didn't really think those skill sets crossed over, but okay.) Why was I frowning while wearing Christmas pajamas? (Because they are awful, and I refused to ever do it again.)

Unless he asked.

Obviously.

But yes. Felix. Winnie. Friendship. Ugh.

I was happy to see him coming out of his shell, but that didn't mean I wanted my sister to be the person he talked to. What if she told him about that time I'd tripped face-first into a pile of cow shit? I didn't want him to know that about me. What if she told him about how when I was little I'd suck my thumb so often my mother had started painting my nails to dissuade me? Because chipping the polish—and its acrid taste—were far more unpalatable to me than letting go of my oral fixation.

When Felix stared at the photos of me, a wistful expression crossed his face every time. He stared at the sunny spread of the farm I'd lived on for most of my childhood, and my heart would ache for him, and all that he'd lost. Felix had no photos. When he'd left his old identity behind—all his belongings had ended up at estate sales.

Now, they were auctioned off online for exorbitant amounts of money. Collectible items for his fans—who were still very much around, despite it having been over seventy years since the last time he'd appeared on a big screen. Part of him, I think, delighted in the knowledge that all these years later he was still loved.

But I think…it made him sad too.

It was a life he could never return to.

I asked him once, why he'd taken the change. Why he'd chosen the darkness the way he had.

"I thought…" Felix had answered, his voice hushed, head leaning against my shoulder. We were tucked up on his couch, our cats staring at us from their perch on the cat tree. I had a glass of wine in one hand, and Felix was so soft as he nuzzled against me. "I could make it last." The quiet tremble to his voice nearly broke me. "Like…time would slow, and I could keep it forever."

"The fame?"

"The adoration," he corrected gently. "My childhood was not…what one would call happy. I think…I just…"

"You just?"

"I just wanted to be loved," his voice trembled and I set my wine glass down, reaching for his face and giving it a squeeze as I tipped it upward. The look on his face shattered me. My heart ached.

"I love you," I said simply, and Felix laughed—even though I could tell the simple statement meant the world to him.

"You have my face on a t-shirt," he countered, eyes dancing. "You have an album on your phone titled 'Felix' with over three-thousand photos in it." I nodded, because both of those things were true. "You had my name tattooed over your heart." It was better than getting his face tattooed on my ass. "You doodle our names together on your work notes." I hadn't known he knew that. My cheeks flushed a bit but I nodded. "You love me…more wholly than any of my fans ever have."

I blinked, eyes narrowed. "I am your number one fan."

"You're much more than that," Felix kissed me, steady and soft. He tasted like forever. My heart fluttered.

Felix told me the sun was one of the things he missed the most about being alive.

So I, because I was the best partner-boyfriend-lover ever, made a plan to give him whatever sunlight I could—in whatever capacity I could.

And three years later—when my gray had grown in, and we'd outgrown our tiny town—we moved to an apartment in the city together. I will admit…a lot of the reason we decided to abandon the suburbs was because now that the both of us had shared…*hobbies*—it was much easier to partake in said *hobbies* when there was a larger population to whittle at.

There was anonymity in the city that we'd never got in the countryside.

And more resources for a person like Felix.

If he had still relied on the shipments of blood from SAC (the Supernatural Alliance Committee) the city would've been an ideal place to live. They had more access there than they had to our small town. Not that that mattered—because by the time we moved there, I was Felix's full-time blood donor.

And I fucking *loved* it.

There was something incredibly satisfying about the fact that I could be not only his lover, his partner, his number one fan—but also his sustenance too. My blood ran through his veins. It fueled him. We were connected in a way I'd never thought was possible.

Once, I'd joked about him eating me. And that thought hadn't bothered me one bit. In fact, it excited me. I wanted to be inside him, in whatever capacity, as many times and in as many ways as possible.

Call me possessive, I don't care.

I'd always miss Allen and his crematory, but I figured—it wasn't like Beach Town was too far off the beaten path to visit.

And that was *another* thing.

Another bomb that had dropped right after we'd killed Barry. *Apparently, The Club* I'd been a member of hadn't been a murder club at all. Go figure. Instead, it was a hunting club. Of the supernatural variety. And all this time, when I'd spoken about stalking my prey—about eradicating them—about rituals and biding my time, the members of *The Club* had thought that I was hunting creatures like they did. Not humans. Oops.

Except, of course, *Allen*.

Bless his heart.

He'd told me to be more open-minded once, when it came to Felix— and I understood now he'd said that because he'd been one of the only people in town that actually knew *what* Felix was. Don't ask me how he knew. Honestly, I didn't care.

If it had been anyone else, I would have. I would've questioned everything. Perhaps I wanted to eradicate them for having dared know something about Felix before I did.

But Allen had won my trust, and my friendship—and thus, I was content to let him keep his secrets.

Felix, however…was another case. For three blissful, *bloody* years, I learned every secret he'd ever had. I learned about his first crush—a boy in grade school. He'd gotten spanked with a paddle one time, for trying to slip notes into the other boy's lunch box during class. The teacher had thought he was stealing from his bag—of all things.

Stealing.

My Felix.

My lovely, soft-hearted, (sometimes murderous) but always kind, Felix.

Ridiculous.

The only thing Felix had ever stolen in all his life, was my heart.

And that wasn't much of a robbery. Not when I was content to let him keep it.

I admit, I'd hunted down the first man Felix had ever slept with. Through the wonderful, wide web. It wasn't that hard, honestly. All I'd needed was his full name, and the town Felix had grown up in. Apparently, the little bitch, was ninety-five. Lived in a retirement home in Maine. I half debated going on a road trip to visit him—so I could stomp out the competition immediately—but when I told Felix about my genius, masterful plan, he quickly put a stop to it.

My little killer had morals, after all.

Our kills had to have "deserved" it.

I thought the fact that his first crush had been the reason he'd received corporal punishment made him deserving enough. But Felix informed me that we had to have new *rules*. And…as a person who *liked* rules, I couldn't deny him that.

Our new murder code became:

• They needed to deserve what was coming to them. (Felix)

• They needed to be bullies. (Me)

• The "offense" that they were "punished" for needed to have occurred within the last fifty years. (Felix)

• Killing everyone Felix had ever slept with was not an option.

• "Food" was the exception.

The last rule I didn't like, as it meant I couldn't hunt down anyone from his past, but Felix insisted it was necessary. Especially, when we were talking about forever. A very real forever. A forever that wasn't metaphorical but infinite. Infinite happily ever afters, infinite kills, infinite kisses. I supposed, in light of that kind of future—I could handle a little compromise.

When I inquired about the actual turning process itself, Felix was very upfront with information. His turning had been traumatic. He hadn't known what he was getting into. He'd been blind-sided. Abused. Mine would be far different. It involved paperwork, getting approval from SAC, and I had two options. I could choose to have a public turning, enacted by the local Council. Or…when the paperwork was filed—and we received approval—I could be turned by Felix himself.

There was a long waitlist—because apparently even supernatural governments were annoying that way.

But…Felix said he *knew* "a guy".

A guy who could get us on the list—

The list that would mean eventually—when I was gray enough—I could become just as fang-y as Felix was. Until then, I spent what free time I wasn't with Felix soaking up as much sunshine as I could.

We'd been approved for over a year now.

We were waiting for the right time.

Moving had gotten in the way, as had Winnie's wedding—you can bet your ass I teased the hell out of her when I found out she was dating someone. A lovely woman who was half her size, and twice as smart as she was.

Our apartment in the city was located inside a building that housed strictly supernatural beings. Not that the general population knew that, because they didn't. Felix—after much cajoling on my end—had finally worked past his personal hang ups about being seen out in public. He was still a bit skittish, but three years of praise, of reassurances—and finally, wonderfully, he was comfortable going out without his damn hat on.

I knew this would be good for him. That the city would be good for him. There was a certain anonymity here that would positively affect our "date nights" and the murder we enjoyed immensely on them. But it would also allow him the shield he so desperately craved. He was coming back to society after so long away, that many things often startled him.

Felix had been isolated for far too long.

I knew this.

And even though the idea of him talking to *anyone* but me rankled, I…was willing to—grudgingly—put his needs ahead of my own wishes. Which meant, I did my damndest after we moved into our new penthouse apartment, to try to matchmake him with the other supernaturals that lived inside the building.

All of the people I approved ended up not clicking.

Felix ultimately did not need my help—because he was precious and perfect and sunshine incarnate, obviously. Anyone would be lucky to be his friend.

A month into living in the city, Felix finally made a friend.

Nancy was a female vampire who lived on the floor below ours. She had a cat—that got along swimmingly with all five of ours. Don't judge me. Five cats is a perfectly respectable number. We'd started off with the three—and then…Allen had found one rooting around in the trash outside the crematory.

And after that…what was one more?

We already had four.

Anyway—cat tangent over.

Felix's friend…*Nancy*—was…alright, I supposed. Her hair was massive and full of secrets. She liked pop culture, way too much, but Felix enjoyed their movie nights, so I didn't say a word. She crocheted with him. Which was something I had tried to do—and failed miserably. And at night, she jogged with him around the city—getting him out of the house, and gossiping with him about trends, and apps, and blah blah blah.

Nancy won major points with me when she didn't comment on the nights (which was most of them) that I trailed behind the two of them in my car to make sure they stayed safe. Realistically, I knew that they were both vampires and probably did not need my protection. One handed, they could probably even bench press my Mercedes if they found it necessary.

Nancy was like Felix.

When she'd been turned, she'd discovered it came with its own set of challenges. According to the both of them—because I'd asked—all people were different. Being turned didn't necessarily mean you'd get the perks that Felix had, super strength, speed, and his rather handy "thrall." Some people turned and nothing much changed at all.

Aside from insatiable bloodlust, and never-ending life.

Apparently with the "perks" came equally frustrating "downsides." Like the fact that Felix could not go out in the sun at all—whereas some vampires who had not received as many "gifts" as he had, could.

Which was why—when he was off jogging with Nancy one day—six months after our move—I enlisted help from all three of my sisters to surprise him with the plan I'd cooked up back when we'd still lived in the suburbs. Felix had told me his birthday was in June. June twenty-eighth, to be exact. And though it'd been many years since he'd seen sunlight, and he should've been used to its lack by now, he still sat by the heavily curtained window some days when he woke up early and soaked up its warmth.

"There's no way we're going to finish before he's back," Winnie complained, because she was a complain-y complainer who complained. I was not taking any of her shit today. I was a man on an important mission. I had a Felix to impress. Winnie and the "No Glove, No Love" bumper sticker I'd gotten her for Christmas, could kiss my ass.

Not literally.

Oh god.

Fuck.

Ew.

"Shut up and paint, Winston."

"Okay, Marsha."

Melissa laughed—and Winnie…well.

She shut up and painted.

When Felix came home—after I'd quite literally herded my sisters out the door with a broom, all it took was one sniff of our home for him to know what I'd been up to. He scanned the industrial style apartment, looking for the paint, I no doubt bet he smelled.

"Marshall Warden," he laughed, eyes crinkling with affection as he cocked his head to the side. "What have you been up to?"

Grinning broadly, I gestured for him to lead the way—and together, we entered the guest bedroom I'd just redone in record time. The paint was still drying, the scent thick and uncomfortable in the air. I was half-tempted to plug my nose, but I didn't. I was far too excited for that. Clenching my hands into fists so I wouldn't reach out and grab Felix—because I wanted him to focus on his gift, dammit—I waited with bated breath.

"You…" Felix stared at the room in wonder. I didn't need to see his face to know what expression he was making. It was the same one he'd made when I asked him to marry me—legitimately—the day we'd shared our first kill in the city. The same face he'd made when I told him I wanted to turn with him. The same face he'd made when I explained to him how vast the fortune I'd accumulated was. Not that we needed it, as Felix apparently, had a rather cushiony bank account of his own.

"You did this for me?" He asked, his voice wobbly. He twisted to look at me, and the second I saw the look on his face, I reached for him. I curled around him, soaking up his sunshine. He clutched at the back of my sweater vest with a wet little sob.

Proud of myself, I nuzzled into his shoulder, trying to see the room through his eyes. To understand what he was feeling.

The bright yellow paint was still tacky on the walls. Little white paw prints spanned the room in random loops along the walls. I'd hand-picked every last detail of the space. From the giant sun accenting the back wall—and the brilliantly bright lights that flooded the space with gold—to the cat trees, litter boxes, and toys that lay neatly in their places throughout the room. There was a cabinet beside the sun mural that housed the other necessary supplies, of which I'd done extensive research. Clorox, Lysol, Rescue wipes and Rescue spray, diluted bleach.

"Forever is a long time," I said softly as Felix clutched me close. "I wanted to give you a little sunshine—and perhaps…"

"Perhaps?" Felix's voice wobbled where it was buried against my chest.

"Something to work toward."

I filed the paperwork for our cat rescue the next week, bright and early, Monday morning.

Lucky's Ward received its first honored guest only a few days after opening. We contacted the local animal control to make sure he had no owner, took him to the local vet for a check-up, and a week later…he was officially ours.

I didn't think I'd ever seen Felix happier than he was, sitting in that room, surrounded by the furry children he was raising.

Every day I fell more in love with him.

Five years after Barry's Bloody Bash, the front of my hair was entirely gray.

Logically, Felix and I had a small wedding ceremony. Felix had laughed when Winnie had jokingly told me she thought I'd be a bridezilla, but I'd known she was right. If we tried for a large wedding, I was sure to nitpick every last detail.

I'd obsess over it.

Which was why…small and *personal* was better.

More romantic, anyway.

Especially as it would be my last day as a human.

Felix and I wore white and black respectively. We hired an officiant and dressed all our cats in matching formal wear. They were incredibly well-behaved, crowded around our living room. My father sat in his wheelchair, Melissa behind him, and Winnie to his left. He'd given me a single grunt and a head nod—and I'd nearly burst into tears, I'd been so moved.

The view of the city at night through the giant glass panels on the wall made Felix *glitter* as we said our vows. Winnie ugly-cried the entire ceremony, and I was…*giddy*.

Giddy.

Because Felix was mine now in every possible way I could claim him.

Except…one.

When everyone left, we peeled the cats out of their clothing—after taking several hundred pictures for our shelter's Instagram, and rounded them upstairs.

Our song played soothing and sweet, notes lilting through the air as Felix and I danced around our living room, just like we had all those years ago.

Felix sipped from my neck as we swayed, sucking and gnawing, the sharp bite of his fangs lulling me into a sense of fuzzy calm with his venom. He lapped at my throat, cleaning up his mess as I moaned softly against him, my cock poking insistently against his belly.

Every time I was reminded of how dangerous he was, my body reacted.

"Are you sure about this?" he murmured, lips glistening red, his lovely tongue flickering out to catch the last taste of my blood.

I nodded, my heart stuttering, pleasure coursing through my veins.

"I've never been more sure of anything in all my life."

I'd been wearing my ring for five years now, but its weight felt somehow… *different*—now that we were as official as we could be, considering the fact that Felix did not have an active identity. That was something we could remedy, but we hadn't found the need. At least…not yet. One day, I'd have to get a new identity too, as Marshall Warden-Finley could not live forever at age forty-three without attracting notice.

"I'm glad we waited," Felix said softly, stroking a hand through the white and gray strands that filled the front of my hair. He traced over my cheekbone, eyes dancing with heat. It simmered between us. My belly flipped, and my already hard cock jerked.

"Me too," I managed, voice deep.

"I have…one last gift for you—" Felix murmured. "A wedding gift."

I perked up. For a person that hated gifts, I sure loved his. "You do?"

"Yes." Felix's fangs flashed when he smiled, and I tipped down low so that I could taste it. He was so soft. So wonderful, I couldn't help but push into his mouth, my tongue sliding along his fangs to taste the remnants of my own blood.

"We're going to go hunting, my love," Felix promised, pulling away enough that he could speak. "I'm going to turn you, and we're going to go hunting. Together."

"Please—"

I gripped his hips tight, fingers biting into the soft flesh as Felix dragged his mouth, slow and hot across the corner of my jaw, down my neck, to the base of my throat. His teeth worried the skin there, pressing into it in a sharp, delicious tease that had my hips pumping, chasing friction.

"Would you like me to turn you like this?" he asked softly as I tipped my head to the side, bending my knees to give him more room. "Or…" his lips dragged back up to my ear, his breath fluttering along the shell of it and making me twitch.

"Or?"

"Would you like to be turned…when this big—" One of his hands found my cock and gave it a firm squeeze. "Delicious cock…" Another squeeze. I whined, rough and needy, rutting into his hand like a senseless beast. "Is inside me?"

"Inside, inside, inside," I chanted—uncaring that I sounded like an absolute idiot as I did. My voice was throaty and vibrating with need as Felix pulled back. His grin was infectious. Delicious. Intimidating in a way that made me hard enough to pound nails.

"You would like that, wouldn't you?" He softened his grip on my very hard, very needy cock and I sobbed. "Pretty, capable Marshall," Felix clucked his tongue. "Reduced to a dog in heat the moment he catches my scent."

"Fuck."

"It'll be different," Felix warned, leading me by my cock, gently pushing on it and backing me toward the couch. "When you're turned."

"It…will?"

"Your senses will be heightened." His palm pushed more firmly against my aching dick.

Following his prompting, I backed up another step, already panting for him. My gaze snapped from his face, to his throat, imagining what it would feel like to actually be able to break skin. Then it traveled across his shoulders—so fucking pretty in his white tuxedo—down his tiny waist. I licked my lips, imagining those legs spread around me, my cock pistoning inside him. Our hips slapping. The sound was obscene enough that picturing it alone was enough to make me blush.

"You'll feel…*everything*." Felix loosened his grip and I sobbed, burying my head in his lemony hair. Electricity zapped down my spine when he moved again, his hand shifting till one of his nails scraped teasingly over my slit through the tight fabric of my dress pants.

"E-Everything," I echoed, trying to pretend like I was listening when all I could think about was yanking his pants down, throwing him against the wall, and shoving myself in dry.

Felix gently tapped at my balls at the same time my calves hit the base of the couch. "Look at you," Felix purred, kicking my legs open wider so his fingers could creep back farther. He squeezed my balls and my eyes rolled back. "Always led by your dick when I'm around."

My chest heaved, and Felix laughed—a low musical sound.

It wasn't mean.

But it was delicious.

I liked it when he got rough like this. Liked it when he bit, when he grabbed, when he forced me to do exactly what he wanted, whenever he wanted it. I may be the one that fucked him, but there was no denying who exactly was in charge here.

"Even on our wedding night," Felix added, and he sounded amused. His other hand rose up, curling over my jaw, tipping my head to the side so he could stare at my throat. He'd always used to do that—stare—before I even knew what he was. I just hadn't known why.

Now that I did, the movement grew even more tantalizing.

A predator, sizing up his prey.

My beautiful little monster.

"Your heart is racing," Felix murmured, thumb skimming down the length of my throat so he could trace the veins. "Are you scared?"

"No," I gasped out.

He grinned. "I didn't think so."

And then he was tightening his grip on my cock and urging me back. Like a puppet, I fell backward onto the couch, legs spread, my cock still clutched in his grip. Held captive by the only man I'd ever loved more than myself.

"Oh…Marshall." Felix groaned, sliding into my lap—his rightful place. He looked…god, he looked like sin, dressed in white—like his hands weren't as blood-stained as mine. He peered at me through his lashes, red eyes luminescent because he was freshly fed. "I own you," Felix murmured, lips dragging over the corner of my jaw, over to my ear. "Don't I?"

"You do," I gasped out, my cock weeping, ruining my suit pants. But I couldn't bring myself to care.

"My husband," Felix purred and I whined, hips jerking into his grip. "My big, loyal guard dog." I grit my teeth, trying not to openly sob even though I wanted to. "The love of my life."

"Forever," I promised.

"Forever," he agreed, and then—his hands were deftly flicking the button on my pants open, sliding my zip down—and oh. Oh fuck. Yes. Yes. I jolted into his touch, cock angry and red where it peeped out of my clothing. Felix fanned his fingers along it, sliding them down to wrap around the root, before dragging up, up, up. My head tossed back, the scratchy glide of his cool palm sending me spinning.

"Where's the lube, darling?" Felix asked, lips at my ear, tongue slicking along inside it as my hips began to twitch. Like the dog he accused me of being, I chased his tightness, head full of visions of taking him.

I'd had him hundreds, if not thousands of times.

But each time was somehow better than the last.

He was intoxicating.

"I—uh—" I tried to speak, to answer his question—but nothing would come out. All I could think about was fucking him, my hips thrusting eagerly into his grip, over, and over, and over.

"Stay here." Felix gave my ear one last, parting lick, before he was gone.

I sobbed, fucking into the open air, my lonely cock standing proud. The weeping head leaked some more, my foreskin peeled back as my fingers bit into the leather couch cushions. But as quickly as he'd disappeared, Felix reappeared.

Naked.

The long, pale line of his body taunted me as he slid gracefully down the last few steps on the stairs that led to the upper floor of our loft. My dick jerked, and I groaned, reaching down to give my balls a little tug so I wouldn't spill right then.

Felix had nice feet. Shapely, neat.

Sexy as hell ankles too—ankles that taunted me every time he decided to tease.

Up my gaze went, tracing the supple, muscular length of his legs. *God, those legs.* Long and pale, hairless, because he'd shaved. (I'd greatly enjoyed watching him do it—and helping when he let me).

Felix was sex incarnate.

Especially when he slid across the carpet as smoothly as if he'd been floating. Effortlessly confident. As the years had passed, Felix only grew more gorgeous. Confident in a way he hadn't been before. We had grown together, stronger than ever before, both of us becoming the monsters we were always meant to be.

Felix's cock mocked me, peeping at me where it lay in a nest of dark, gorgeous curls. Dark waves that matched the curls on the top of his head. He'd stopped dying his hair in preparation for the wedding—and fuck.

Dark-haired Felix was my kryptonite.

Mouth watering, I tipped my head back, meeting the glowing molten red of his gaze as he crossed the distance between us. The ring I'd given him glinted on his hand as he held out the bottle of lube, brow arched.

"Hand off my property," he said softly in greeting, his voice crackly soft. I released my cock immediately as if burned, a fresh drop of slick slipping down my crown as I groaned. "Thank you."

"Mmm," I bit my lip, staring at his tight little tummy. Staring at his ribcage—god, it was fun to nip at. Staring at his perky pink nipples—my favorite place on his body to abuse. The way his thick pecs bounced a little when he shifted, just to tease.

"Do you know…" Felix purred, finally crossing the last of the distance between us before climbing onto my lap again. "How fucking gorgeous you look right now?" Felix passed me the lube, and greedily, I squirted some onto my fingers, getting them warm as he spoke—though my eyes never left his face.

My cheeks flushed.

"With that big fucking chest," Felix flicked one of my nipples and I groaned, reaching back with my clean hand to skim up the outside of his thigh. I expected to be chided for my impatience, but he was in a giving mood, apparently, so he didn't. "Those shoulders—" Felix traced down my trapezius muscles, to the swell of my shoulders, fingers digging into the muscle there appreciatively. "You're going to be so frightening when you're changed. My gorgeous fucking beast."

I panted after him, pushing my luck, my hand skimming up a little higher, fingers digging into the meat at the crease of his groin and upper thigh. His hips jolted, his cock poking out at me, calling my name. I wanted to sink it into my mouth—to suck and slurp while I pushed my fingers up inside him.

But we were both aching.

And as much fun as playing and teasing like this was—I could see the need on Felix's face, just as ragged and brittle as the need I was sure echoed on my own.

I could imagine our future so clearly.

I'd had five years to visualize, after all.

Felix kissed me, swallowing my groan as I slid my fingers back behind his balls, rubbing his perineum. Back I slipped, further and further, my other hand holding him still while my slick fingers finally found their home. His hole fluttered against them, sucking at them greedily. I'd fucked him twice today already so he was already loose and a little wet.

Probably still leaking my cum.

Groaning, I leaned forward, biting at his shoulder as I slid my finger inside. He squeezed around me and sighed, head tossed back—like all this time he'd been waiting for this like I was. I slid a second finger in, eager to watch his brow furrow.

My cock jerked, and all I could think about was sinking into him.

Of fucking him.

Of making him whine and bounce on my lap.

Impatient, I pulled my fingers out. Felix grunted, shifting his hips wider when I tapped his thighs. As if he'd done it a thousand times—because he had—he arched his back. His lovely ass shifted, cheeks parting to give me room to work. Meanwhile, his fingers dug into my shoulders, and—oh fuck, yes. Yes, yes. Sweet, slick, delicious, Felix's hole glided down with a practiced swivel of his hips to kiss the aching head of my cock.

I grunted, flexing into him immediately—my natural reaction to feeling something slick, tight, wet. Felix gasped out, my crown popping in.

"You have such a nice, fat cock," he shuddered, fingers digging in hard enough to bruise.

I grunted, still biting into his shoulder, worrying the flesh there as my eyes pinched shut. I grabbed his hips with both hands, then in one swift movement, plunged him down onto my aching prick.

"Fuck," Felix gasped out, his tight grip growing slack as he ground down into me. My perfect little, fangy cock slut. His lovely, peculiar teeth flashed as his head tossed back and he groaned. And then I was…just… fuck yes.

In, in, in.

I slapped him down onto my pelvis, grinding, fucking, chasing oblivion in the tightness of his body. Our skin was sweaty, slick, sticky as I pounded up into him hard enough his eyes rolled back. He liked it rough as much as I did—and we'd both been wanting this all day.

Husbands.

Together.

For the first time.

"Marshall—" Felix gasped out, my name music on his lips. He dropped his head back down, his eyes black with lust, lips flushed and kissable. I released his shoulder, more than a little pleased that it took a couple seconds for the bite I'd left to disappear.

"I want it," I promised him, watching his fangs glint, my pulse racing. I couldn't stop fucking him. I couldn't. My hips had a mind of their own, slapping into him with a rabid, feral rhythm that made him choke and stutter. "Give it to me."

Forever was so close.

"Marshall—" Felix sobbed, dropping down, his lips dragging over my neck, a slow tantalizing glide.

"I'll give you everything," I promised through gritted teeth. "Just— please."

This was it.

This was the end.

I was about to die.

To be reborn.

I'd waited, waited, waited for this.

I'd ached for this.

I'd needed this.

And here…we were.

At the precipice of something new, something beautiful, something intimidating and evil—but wonderful. The concept of living forever would've been intimidating if I had not known I'd be spending eternity with the lovely man currently squeezing my dick.

But I did know that.

I knew that forever with him was better than anything alone.

When Felix's teeth sliced into my neck, it felt different than before. Sure, he'd fed from me so many times I'd lost count. (608 times—I lied.) There was an air of warmth in the air, flickering, electric. Excitement thrummed through my veins, making me jittery and needy, and my stuttering hips even greedier.

The sucking, gluttonous slurps as Felix took me inside him—in every way he knew how—filled my head. I buzzed from the inside out, fireworks bursting behind my lids as his venom flooded my body. More and more, over and over. Icy hot. It burned-burned-burned.

It burned—it.

It.

It.

It—

Oh.

The last thought I had as my head fell back against the couch, my hands falling limp at my sides, slipped through numb lips. "You look like an angel."

"Oh, Marshall." Felix made a greedy, hungry sound, his eyes dark with heat.

Through a fog, I watched as Felix pulled back, then sliced his own wrist open with his teeth, slippery red blood staining our suits as he pressed it to my mouth. Hot, coppery wet, his blood filled my mouth—but all I could think—

All I could think was that I love, love, love, loved him.

And I was honored to have the opportunity to do it *forever*.

Forever.

Forever.

Forever.

Floppy hats or not.

Felix was right, by the way.

Everything was better when I was turned. The burning clutch of his body—suddenly warm now that we were both temperature-challenged. The sound of his breath—shuddery and soft when I fucked into him, glancing off his prostate till his eyes rolled back. The way he moaned, the way he clutched at me, hot-tight-hot.

I buzzed-buzzed-buzzed.

My stomach growled, aching, aching—

Still buried inside Felix's body, my own teeth found his neck—sinking inside him as a vicious, needy hunger burned through my body. Hungry, hungry, hungry. Empty, empty, empty.

"That's it," Felix moaned, voice low. His fingers found my hair, twisting tight into it as he swiveled his hips. For once, mine had stilled—even my need to fuck stalled as the hunger overtook my body. "Take what you need, sweetheart. I'm here."

Felix had told me when he had been turned it was a scary, lonely experience.

I felt nothing of the sort.

The world shifted—the floor moving—and suddenly, I realized I'd been the one to move us. Felix was on his back, his legs around my waist, his throat parting beneath my teeth. I tried to be gentle. I tried—but I—

Oh fuck.

Yes.

Please, please, please.

Hot, slippery, delicious blood filled my mouth. I gasped and sobbed, taking more—taking as much as I could, slurping, insatiable. Felix swiveled his hips again, and I realized—belatedly—that I'd started fucking him again.

Inside his tight, wet, delicious heat.

Then out—only to push back in with a snap of my hips.

Humping him as my cock leaked, and I—Oh. Oh. Oh.

Heaven.

Bliss.

My skin was buzzing, the couch creaking as my fingers tore through the fabric.

"That's it—" Felix gasped out as I fucked him brutally, taking more blood from him than he'd ever taken from me. Distantly, I realized I hadn't asked him if it would affect him if I drank from him. But I could only assume the answer was no—because the way Felix was grinding into me, clutching my head closer, closer, closer made it obvious that he liked this.

He liked this so fucking much.

I could understand.

Because I liked it too.

Loved it.

Love, love, loved it.

When I finally came, it was with a garbled, broken gasp. My teeth tore from his neck, and I watched bleary eyed as the skin began to immediately knit itself back together.

Felix's eyes were glowing—and mine were too—I could tell because I could see the red light reflected back in his gaze as he grinned.

He grabbed my face, fingers digging into it the same way I always did to him.

"Look at you," he purred. "My beautiful, wonderful husband."

"Felix," I gasped out, surprised I could find words at all.

His name seemed to be the only thing I remembered.

I could feel my cum slippery and hot where it wetted the way for my cock to continue to rub up inside him. His brow scrunched as my hips started moving again—probably sore now that I could actually match his strength.

Grinning, I reached down for his cock, only to find that it was as spent as mine was.

"You are beautiful," Felix told me, his voice quivering. His eyes were a little wet, and I could see why. Until this moment we'd talked and talked and talked—but now…now our forever—the forever we'd promised was reality.

I licked his blood from my lips, finding myself somehow even more insatiable than before.

Still, the aching, gnawing hunger in my gut remained.

"Felix," I said softly, a quiet, needy croon.

"I know, darling," he echoed back, leaning up to kiss me—bloody lips and all. "I know."

And he did.

He'd warned me of this. Of the hunger. I'd been prepared. Or at least…I had thought I was.

Now I wasn't so sure.

"Please," I gasped out.

Felix nodded, scrubbing his fingers over my cheeks, probably enjoying how pathetic I looked right now, begging for him, my cock still hard and wet. "You need more," he murmured softly, fingers slipping down to pull my bottom lip open so he could see my fangs.

My fangs.

What a weird, strange thought.

Fangs.

Fangs that I would use to drink blood.

"Whatever you need, darling."

And then…like the good sport he was, he let me pull out, flip him over, and feast on his ass. Quite literally. By the time I was done, there were weeping bite marks all over it, and all the cum I'd filled him with had mixed on my tongue with his blood.

When I mounted him again, it felt like the beast inside me was right at the surface. Slap, slap, slap, I fucked into him, forcing him flat onto the couch as I gasped and growled, nails digging into his flesh.

I could see why he bit so much now. It was almost impossible to control the need to eat.

To take him inside me, in whatever way possible.

"Take it, take it, take it," I chanted, the slick, sweaty rutting lighting me up from the inside out. "Take it, take it—" I growled, dropping down to sink my teeth into his neck again, this time from the other side.

I fucked him four times.

In a row.

By the time we finished, Felix was covered in bite marks. Bite marks that were slow and sluggish to heal, as I'd exhausted his blood supply apparently. He was sleepy soft, cuddled up in my arms as I lowered the blackout blinds so that the first dregs of sunlight wouldn't touch our skin.

We retired to bed.

Bloody.

Blissful.

At peace.

And as Felix and I curled up beneath the covers, our limbs tangled, our still hearts pressed together, the monster inside me finally slept.

"Goodnight, Marshall," Felix murmured, sleepy soft.

"Goodnight, Felix," I countered, voice just as slow.

Tonight we'd wake when the sun sunk low.

We'd take what we needed. Stalk the streets for prey. Delight in the game, the chase, the pleasure of the kill

We'd raise the kittens we'd saved.

We'd spend Christmases together.

Felix would crochet more wisteria.

I'd detail my car.

Husbands.

Monsters.

Lovers.

Then we'd rest.

And do it all over again.

Forever, forever, *forever*.

Spooky BOYS will return soon with...

Revive Me!

OFFICIAL RELEASE DATE TBD

Acknowledgments

THANK YOU SO much for reading *King of Hollywood*! I hope you enjoyed it! This book caused such an epiphany for me and it will always be special in my heart because of that.

I realized, through writing Marshall and Felix's love story, how important it is to me that my books are always fun. I hope you could feel that reflected in my writing, and that it made you smile as much as it made me smile.

Some years are harder than others, and I hope this book brought you comfort, made you laugh, and made you fall in love.

Special thanks to my amazing alpha readers and all the incredible work they put into reading this book. Thank you to Molly, for her incredible formatting skills. Thank you to my writing group, DL, Kat, Kit, and Mozzie for helping me think when my brain did not want to work. For sprinting with me as I raced toward the finish line, and for being all around, incredible humans. Thank you to Amanda Meuwissen, for being the reason this book came into existence by creating the Tales From The Tarot collab that it was originally featured in, you are a true gem. And thank you to you, my readers, because you are the ones that give my writing meaning. You make my world a better, brighter place.

Love,

Fae

About Fae

FAE IS OBSESSED with anything romance. From a young age she realized she had a passion for falling in love over and over again. She loves to tell stories through both her art and writing. With a passion for classical monsters, meet-cutes, and contemporary romance, you can often find her with her nose stuck in a book and her pet corgi, Champa, on her lap.

She currently resides in Utah with her amazing husband and her collection of squishmallows. When you read one of her books you can expect to find love stories between humans, monsters, and loveable assholes that will make you laugh (and cry) as you get lost in their worlds for just a little. Every story comes with a happy ever after guarantee.

Find her online at:
WWW.FAELOVESART.COM